THE TIES
THAT BIND

THE TIES THAT BIND

A FIONA FITZGERALD MYSTERY

WARREN ADLER

DONALD I. FINE, INC.
NEW YORK

For our family, our fortress

Copyright © 1994 by Warren Adler

All rights reserved, including the right of reproduction in whole or in part in
any form. Published in the United States of America by Donald I. Fine, Inc. and
in Canada by General Publishing Company Limited.

Library of Congress Catalogue Card Number: 93-74479
ISBN: 1-55611-395-1

Manufactured in the United States of America

10 9 8 7 6 5 4 3 2 1

Designed by Irving Perkins Associates, Inc.

This novel is a work of fiction. Names, characters, places, and incidents are
either the product of the author's imagination or
are used fictitiously. Any resemblance to actual events, locales, organizations or
persons, living or dead, is entirely coincidental and beyond the intent of either
the author or publisher.

—1—

"That's it," Fiona Fitzgerald said aloud. She rose on an elbow and looked at the red digital numbers on the bedtable clock, a reflex, as if the moment of revelation needed a marker.

"What's 'it'?" Harrison mumbled, stirring. She felt the warmth of his naked flank where it touched hers. She had duly noted, dating from their third or fourth all-night coupling, that the man slept on his back.

Her occasional bed partners usually slept in a semi-fetal position, fitted against her back like a spoon or vise versa where she was the outside spoon. These were the cuddlers, her special preference. But, there were also the non-touchers who needed their space to effect an untroubled slumber. Whatever their choice, Fiona respected their preference.

Her own view was that if you were making such an intimate trusting commitment as an all-night sexual encounter, you owed it to your partner to maximize fleshly contact throughout all the cycles of activity from arousal to satiation. Harrison Greenwald faltered only at the cycle's end when he slipped into slumber on his back. Thankfully, his breathing passages were not constricted and he did not snore.

"He is beleaguered by females."

"Who is?" Harrison said, lifting his head to view the red digital numbers. Like her, he was programmed to the tyranny of time. "At three in the morning."

He made way for her in the crook of his arm, where she lay her head, and she slipped her arm around his far rib cage. In her normal single state, which was most of the time, this was the part she missed the most, the nocturnal tête-à-tête.

"My boss."

"The Eggplant?"

"A term of affection used only by his underlings."

1

"So how is he beleaguered?"

"His mother is a black matriarch, a boss more exacting than Simon Legree in any incarnation. His wife is a demanding, dissatisfied, pushy, ambitious bitch who daily laments the Eggplant's lack of upward mobility in the most class-ridden black society in America."

"These traits in women are not exclusive to blacks," Harrison said. "May I remind you that I am Jewish."

"Not necessary. I have observed close-up the result of that ancient barbaric Hebrew ritual to maim the male child."

"Merely an identification process, like branding. I'm told it does not affect performance."

He grew silent, awaiting a response.

"If you're waiting for a comparative opinion, forget it."

"We were on the subject of the Eggplant's being beleaguered," Harrison said. "It apparently had a gender context."

"Harassment," she said. "He is being harassed by females. Reaches to the core of the psychology of male domination. The new legal reality of sexual harassment is driving the poor bastard up the wall. He's got two sticky cases in his bailiwick. Two women cops claiming that they have been verbally abused and sexually intimidated and threatened."

"Which is illegal . . . and wrong," Harrison said. A negligence lawyer, he was a bleeding-heart kneejerk liberal in the old mode, a man whose compassion, real or contrived, was a weapon in his cause, which was to help empty the coffers of insurance companies.

"In principle, I agree. On the other hand . . ."

"There is no other hand. The victimization of women is unacceptable."

"In general victimization is unacceptable. But sometimes what passes for victimization is a double-edged sword. In my world, the macho male cups his crotch for reassurance, to be sure it's still there. The perception that he is somehow oppressing women is sometimes like a nervous giggle. His whole life is centered around receiving applause from women. 'Man, did that earth move,' she mimicked. 'You are the best.' That's both the act and the metaphor. If a man says to me: 'I'd love you to suck my Johnson.' Is it victimization? Of me? Or of him? I can castrate his career, destroy him with the stigma of sexual harassment. The stigma is the castrating knife. Or should I give it back to him in kind, say something like: 'Not today, Jack, I left my magnifying glass home.' He'd laugh. I'd laugh. End of story. We've harassed each other. Only he won't even think of taking me to court."

"Not bad," Harrison said.

"They changed the rules in midstream. Especially for the guys. Hell, they may have taken the fun out of the flirt, the double entendre byplay. I can understand that and I feel sorry as hell for them. They've got wives, mothers and daughters and we've got fathers, brothers and, speaking for myself . . . lovers."

"What is that plural 's' doing there?"

The sexual harassment discussion surrendered to the sudden detour. Harrison had a sensitive, possessive streak and was a highly alert listener.

"I was being generic."

Of course, loving partners all wanted to feel that she'd given them exclusive rights to her body. In fact, she had. Aside from the health considerations that were a given, she considered it a breach of faith to be unfaithful. Trust was the highest priority in her life. And she expected it to be returned in kind.

Unfortunately, trust had not been given the same priority by some of those who peopled her past. Betrayal had made her wary, defensive. Protecting her vulnerability was an obsession. Sometimes, like now, when she was in the full flush of trust, she gave herself permission to believe that she had, at last, found fealty, knowing it could be a false premise, but wanting it badly enough to let her guard down.

"I'd rather you used the singular," Harrison said, turning his body to face her frontally, pressing her close to him.

"There are no plurals, Harrison. Not in the present."

"My fantasy is that you had no past, no baggage, no previous . . . experiences. That I'm the first."

"The first was awful."

"Until you, all were awful."

Like a good Jewish boy, Harrison Greenwald had confessed not only his many sins, but the many sins, real or imagined, that were perpetrated against him. His fear of involvement, despite his longing for it, was a mirror image of her own, which did not make for a very permanent arrangement. Under these conditions, love or attraction, even their rutting, frenetic couplings could not, they both were certain, be sustained.

Like a good Catholic girl, she was hopelessly indocrinated despite years of denial and severance and lived in perpetual fear of being chosen for the pit of hell, which did not necessarily mean the hell depicted by the great Michelangelo on the ceiling of the Sistine Chapel. Mostly, she worried about the hell of her vulnerability, the hell of being betrayed, the hell of broken trust. It was an idea that lay in her subconscious with the tenacity of a maggot in the flesh of a corpse.

"Tell me, counselor, what is the defense against sexual harassment, however defined?" she asked, the detour ended.

"That again?"

"Indulge me."

"The defense?" he sighed. "His word against hers. Whatever gender makes the accusation."

"Doesn't the victim's word have more credence to a jury in those circumstances?"

"In most circumstances there is a bias toward the powerless," Harrison admitted. "That's how I make my living." His arms insinuated themselves under her until he held her in a reclining bear hug.

Finally, she was ready to get at the heart of her motive in raising the subject.

"Which is why the Eggplant assigned a woman to be my partner, thereby lowering the risk of more sexual harassment problems. It is not uncommon in the cops for a male senior partner to harass a woman junior and vise versa. It's more like a rite of passage than a vicious power game. Under the guise of being a born-again feminist, the Eggplant is playing the evasion game."

"And that bothers you?"

"Yes, it does. Especially since I understand his real motive. This way, he avoids the hassle."

"It's a perfectly logical strategy."

"For him. Not for me. I don't like being pigeonholed."

"Have you confronted him with your theory?"

"No."

"Why not?"

"From his perspective he's got a point. As a representative of my gender, I don't want to create a full-blown misogynist. In my opinion he's already halfway there. Besides, I like to leave people with their illusions."

"And what are his?"

"He has many. But the one I want to leave him with is that he's capable of manipulating people. He's a fabulous interrogator. I wouldn't want him to lose confidence in his ability to do that."

"But you're always telling me that a badge has no gender."

"It hasn't. But the person who wears it has a gender."

"And you'd prefer a male partner?"

"In my heart of hearts?"

"Where else?"

"Yes. I'll miss the byplay, the innuendo, the flirting, the double entendre, the fun of confrontation. And yes, the dirty talk. I love casting joking aspersions on their dick power. It's all part of the culture."

"You also like the feeling of superiority. You're better educated, better—sorry about the snobbery—bred, and a lot prettier. You're also financially secure and, of course, you've had all the advantages. You're a white princess lost in a blue-collar world."

"You are a snob. And I'm not lost. Besides, some of them are a hell of a lot smarter than you nose-in-the-air lawyer types. And most of them are prettier."

"And what happens when they hit on you?"

"In their mind, it's obligatory. Actually, it's only theater. I usually threaten dire physical consequences, mostly in the crotch area. That, too, is obligatory for the girl cops"

"You're confusing me," Harrison said, kissing her neck, caressing the back of her head, then moving downward until both hands were squeezing her buttocks.

"He's assigned this black amazon to be my partner and has indicated that he's putting us into investigating female homicides."

"Exclusively."

"That's his implication. It's also his cover story. He has concocted this crackpot theory that women must know more about their gender than males and therefore would be more effective in busting cases where the female is the victim."

"What does your new partner say about that?"

"Oh, we haven't met yet. I've been told about her. Her name is Gail Prentiss. She worked LA homicide and is transferring over, no small achievement. She's from DC, her father's a prominent surgeon, she's highly educated and is supposed to be a knockout."

"One would think that a woman detective would be more effective if the woman was the perpetrator. You know, they'd-be-able-to-get-into-her-mind sort of thing."

"Not enough female perps to go around, I'm afraid. Murder is primarily a male avocation."

"And this just occurred to you"—he turned slightly to see the digital clock again—"at three-thirty A.M."

"Moment-of-truth time," she said. "That's when you have it out with yourself and/or your partner."

"Here's one," Harrison said. "Why the cops?"

"For me or for them?"

"Both."

"You try first."

"I say it's for people who like enforcing. A sense of control for people who do not ordinarily control anything."

"Now explain me?" she asked, feeling suddenly younger, girlish, asking Daddy a question. In the FitzGerald home Daddy, the senator, the man, was everything, her mother merely a saintly supporter, bearing silent witness to his many betrayals.

"Being in the cops?" he asked, obviously stretching the time to find an appropriate answer, letting it cook in his mind.

"Go on, let's hear it," she said, reaching down, caressing. He did not need the special attention, she noted. His breathing grew deeper, the intakes shortening. "From my smartass Jewish lover."

"Shiksa whore," he said, reaching down in a mutual caress.

"Tell me then, before I forget the subject matter," she said, reveling in the exquisite softness of his touch.

"You are deep into guilt," he whispered. "You love guilt. Catholics and Jews love guilt. It is their reason for being. You like to be around guilt, playing with guilt, exposing guilt. How's that?"

"Do you feel guilty, Harrison?" she said, feeling the accelerating moisture of desire begin to work its way into her cells.

"Always," he whispered. "Especially now."

"About what?"

"Betraying my forefathers. Eating treif."

"Treif?"

"That which is not kosher."

"Me, too," she said, moving on top, feeling him inside of her as she leaned backward, her hands supporting her on either side of his thighs as she rotated her body. Their eyes, accustomed to the darkness now, locked together in an ecstatic mutuality. "Fucking Christ killer."

"Treif."

"Christ killer."

She felt it begin, at first the distant rumble, then the approaching waves, moving with the accelerating tide, a mysterious pounding force of nature.

"Wait for me," she heard him say.

"I won't," she cried.

"Oh yes, you will."

He thrust upward, meeting her movements, his hands grasping the corners of the mattress.

"Jew bastard."

"Shiksa cunt."

The waves crested, engulfing her, releasing long spasms of pleasure.

Spent, she folded over him, her lips close to his ear.

"Man, that earth sure moved," she whispered.

"Let's hear it for my earth-moving equipment," he replied.

"Seems to do the job, but I'm still testing for durability."

Harrison groaned a fake response of frustration and kissed her hair.

Later, she held him, watching his face and feeling the steady rise and fall of his chest as he slept.

—2—

All eyes turned her way as she entered Sherry's, the DC cops' coffee shop of choice, a battered and bruised relic of the fifties, just two blocks from headquarters. Even Sherry, used to all conceivable sights and foibles, paused in mid-sentence to take her in.

Fiona eyeballed her at six-three or six-four. She seemed to have been sculpted from dark Tennessee stone by an artist with a sensualist's eye for the monumental. Her ample breasts, which seemed in proportion for her, would have been considered gross on a smaller woman.

Yet, she moved as gracefully as a cattail with a curl in its upper stem lightly bent by a soft breeze. Her hair, cut short, fit like an old-fashioned swimming cap. Small pendant earrings swung from well-shaped ears. Her face was all bones and angles with yellow-flecked brown eyes peering out over milk-chocolate skin.

Her legs, moving on shoes with moderate-length heels that probably gave her an extra inch, were well turned with muscular calves. This was a woman whose appearance alone demanded both attention and respect. Nobody, but nobody messes with me, her persona seemed to shout to anyone within hearing distance.

Fiona could not help but notice the closely observing eyes that followed this formidable woman as she moved toward the booth in the back where Fiona was seated. She speculated what the males might be thinking or feeling, perhaps an erotic tug or some nervous joking reference to her proportions. Beware, Fiona thought, all those who dared to express such observations within hearing distance of woman.

There were some facts about her that Fiona already knew from the Eggplant. She had worked in homicide in Los Angeles for three years, where she had an impeccable record, which meant an excellent closing percentage. She had reluctantly sought this transfer to Washington because she needed to be near her ailing father. And she had a B.A. and M.A. from UCLA in Criminology.

"I'm Gail Prentiss," the woman said, ignoring the gauntlet of eyes as she reached the booth where Fiona was waiting. "You're Fiona FitzGerald, I suspect." She offered an incredible, white-toothed, girlish smile.

"Your suspicions are well founded, Prentiss," Fiona said, trying for her own version of a girlish smile. She was, in fact, stunned by the woman's effect on her. She had expected, she admitted to herself, something lesser, much lesser. Prentiss commanded the room like an extraordinary work of art.

There was also no question in Fiona's mind that the woman knew her effect on others and had probably developed her own method of using it to her advantage. Fiona found herself resisting intimidation, attempts at which rarely made the slightest dent in her confidence. Who would be the junior in this relationship, Fiona wondered, already seeing her expected place usurped by Prentiss's sense of physical authority.

Prentiss had barely sat down when Sherry arrived with a coffee mug that she set in front of Prentiss and, without asking preference, poured strong, steaming, no-nonsense black coffee into it. Then she waddled away, dispensing coffee as she went down the line.

"Breakfast?" Fiona asked.

"I'm fine," Prentiss said, fixing her inspecting glance on Fiona.

"Seems like the Eggplant has put us in the soup together."

"Eggplant?"

"Our good Captain Luther Greene's moniker," Fiona explained pleasantly. "He knows we call him that. Probably hates it."

"We all have our cross to bear," Prentiss said, flashing her girlish smile. Fiona noted that her breasts formed a protruding ledge over the table's edge. Prentiss's sharply inspecting eyes seemed to take in the astonishment of Fiona's gaze. "I've lived with a lot worse appellations."

"I'll bet you have."

It occurred to Fiona that her very awesomeness might have suggested to the Eggplant his idea of female pairing to investigate female homicides. Perhaps, too, it was a private joke. Pair the white queen with the black queen and see how the cards fell. She rebuked herself for the racial reference, but then race was the dominating motif in this environment, with gender a close second, especially among the black men and especially in the Eggplant's gender-and-race-tortured mind.

As to what she believed was the Eggplant's truer motive, the elimination of the possibility of sexual harassment, this amazon carried immunity from such activities in her genes. No male would dare risk even the tiniest castrating look from this female, no less make an attempt to bed her.

"You like the idea of a woman partner?" Fiona asked, noting the uncommon humility displayed by her question.

"I like the idea of an intelligent partner," Prentiss said. "I can tell by their resentment that you must be one helluva detective."

"As you said, we all have our cross to bear," Fiona said, regretting the natural sarcasm that the remark implied. She'd have to stop that with this woman, she cautioned herself. It was the side of her that she showed most around the department, a kind of shield against revealing any soft edges. Soft edges had to be carefully disguised, even if it was only to ward off the pain of the vocation, that steady drumbeat of horror that permeated the life of a homicide cop.

"I don't see it as a cross," Prentiss said. "Our gender belongs in this business."

"So you think the captain has a point?"

"It's an interesting experiment," Prentiss said, noncommitally. Of course, Fiona reasoned, she was new. It would be self-defeating to be less than a diplomat at this stage. This woman, so startlingly noticeable, must have long ago devised a coping system to react to any new situation.

"Experiment?" Fiona said. "Yes. I guess that's what it is. Although the chances are, we'll be getting mostly domestics, where the perpetrator is hardly a mystery."

"Maybe he thinks we'll be more tenacious," Prentiss said. "More zealous in closing cases where the perp is a male."

"The castrating female syndrome. That's one way of looking at it," Fiona agreed. The woman had insight, which was a superb trait to have in a partner. Oddly, even the Eggplant had not expressed his goals in that way. His version was that women better understood women, who invariably were the victims, not the perpetrators. Prentiss had quickly seen the other side, the push to discovery and judgment, an idea that reflected the Eggplant's fear and, perhaps, ultimate belief in the idea that women hated men.

Fiona felt the power of Prentiss's probing glance as the woman studied her over the lip of the coffee mug as she sipped. Not to be outdone, Fiona picked up her mug and stared her down, neither woman giving way. A man, Fiona knew, would have flinched. Not this baby.

"So what do you see?" Prentiss asked pleasantly. This, Fiona speculated, was her most congenial side.

"Intelligence. Someone in full control of herself. A lady who knows where she's going."

Prentiss smiled again and shook her head from side to side.

"I'm glad you feel that way," Prentiss said. "However inaccurate."

"Not for one moment do I believe your self-effacement," Fiona laughed.

"Fair enough. I won't believe yours either. I've done my research. Fact is, we're both damned good."

"Not much humility at this table," Fiona said.

"Why should there be?" Prentiss chuckled.

"When you got it, flaunt it."

"There's truth in those words, woman," Prentiss said, with just a touch of black street intonation, as if to signal that she could be at home in whatever coloring her space consisted of.

"You must have been insufferable in LA," Fiona said without sarcasm or insult.

"I was. I was racing up the ladder until my daddy got sick. I had to be with him."

"Does he know that it took a career sacrifice?" Fiona asked.

Prentiss laughed.

"Is that funny?"

"You don't know my daddy. The whole underpinning of his life is that his daughter is infallible, a perfect specimen, without flaws. He informed me early on that I would never have trouble making it on my own, however or wherever. The fact is, he disapproves of my calling. He considers it beneath me."

"Well, we have something half in common then. I was my father's sun, moon and solar system. Mother thought my immortal soul had bought it."

"Of course, Dad would have preferred that I had become a doctor or a lawyer," Prentiss sighed. For the first time, she let her eyes look elsewhere

than into Fiona's. Her eyelids fluttered as if she were about to break down
in tears. But when her eyes lifted again, they were clear.

"Only you couldn't resist the lure of the cops. My current significant
other believes that people who become cops control nothing in their lives
and are therefore eager to practice enforcement on others."

"Maybe," Prentiss shrugged, and seemed to look inward for a long
moment. "I guess we all have our special reasons." Fiona wondered what
hers were. "I wanted to be a homicide detective." Her eyes glazed and she
looked beyond Fiona, into some private void. "I suppose it satisfies some
deep-seated thirst for vengeance." She sucked in a deep breath, then offered
a smile. "I have self-actualized myself."

Vengeance? Fiona wondered.

It was obvious to Fiona that Gail Prentiss was taking little risk when it
came to her private self. Except that, despite the heavy guard the woman
had erected around herself, there was just enough passive revelation and
hint of vulnerability to suggest an understanding between them.

Sensing this, Fiona realized that there was something remarkable about
the Eggplant's plan. Had this happened when Fiona was paired with
partners of the other gender? There had been a closeness, certainly a
loyalty, but this struck her as different. She wondered if that meant deeper,
more intimate. Was this a fact or merely a wish? She wasn't sure.

"One thing is certain," Fiona said. "It's the motivation of the bad guys
that we have to be concerned with. Not ours."

"I'll buy that."

"I say we take the leap of faith on the Eggplant's idea . . . Gail." She
savored the used of the woman's first name, watching Prentiss's face for
any sign that the first name appellation was unwelcome. Gail Prentiss
smiled.

"I've leaped . . . Fiona."

Fiona felt her throat constrict as the blood rushed to heat her face.

"My father was the first senator to protest the killing and horror of
Vietnam. It flushed his career down the toilet."

It had suddenly seemed necessary for Fiona to offer her new partner the
defining issue of her life.

"Yes," Gail nodded. She would, of course, have been extra thorough in
checking Fiona out, far more thorough than Fiona had been in researching
Gail's past.

"Although very young at the time, the aftermath created in me a profound hatred of murderers," Fiona said, wondering, as always when she gave this explanation, if it made any sense at all. She had heard every argument to the contrary about her being "misplaced" or in an occupation "beneath her" in this blue-collar and often thankless occupation that brought her an income but could not begin to pay for her lifestyle. Thankfully, she had the subsidy of her inheritance.

"I suppose a number of your colleagues think of you as a hobbyist, slumming in the slime."

"It does require an extra effort on my part to overcome the bias," Fiona said, studying Gail for a reaction.

Gail performed her girlish laugh and put a bouquet of graceful, tapered fingers on Fiona's arm.

"I've got the advantage of skin pigment. But I know the drill, although in LA, few knew my real background."

"Which is?"

"My father is a second-generation surgeon who was the head of the National Chirulogical Society, which is an organization of economically comfortable black surgeons. Mother, who died a number of years ago, was a Ph.D. from Howard, very class conscious. She insisted I come out as a debutante in our annual ball that makes its white counterpart look like a bash at Sloppy Joe's. Contrary to accepted stereotypes, I am the daughter of privilege, a bookend image of yourself."

It was obvious to Fiona that Gail had an elitist view of herself, typical of Washington's Gold Coast blacks, who saw themselves as victors in their epic struggle to rise above their humble origins and, therefore, as inherently superior to their white counterparts. Fiona's insight told her that it was important for Gail to "equalize" the relationship before embarking on the commonality of sisterhood.

"Unfortunately, my daddy is dying, Fiona. He is and will always be the most important man in my life."

For the first time, Fiona caught the emotion in the brief, very brief crack in Gail's voice. But it explained why she had had to come home.

It seemed a big enough slice of bonding for a first occasion and Fiona, as the "old hand," diverted from the personal stuff to outline how the squad and department worked. She filled Prentiss in on the politics of the job, the various competing ambitions, including the Eggplant's desire to be the police chief someday, a job that was as prestigious as it was politically dangerous in the current climate.

Mostly, she offered as much insight as possible into the machinations of Captain Luther Greene, his frailties and strengths, his hot-dog tendencies, his fears and his professional brilliance and courage in the clutch. She also reiterated what she had learned about the various female harassments that he was currently enduring and her theory about the resultant reaction, which was this pairing process. Except for any mention of race and its implications, Fiona felt she had given Gail a balanced picture, which to any new staff person seemed necessary, perhaps crucial to their future in the homicide squad.

She also gave her a rundown of all her colleagues, cataloguing their foibles, eccentricities and, most of all, their hot buttons and vulnerabilities. There was no need to dwell again on matters of class distinction. They both knew what that meant and how those waters were navigated.

Even as Fiona spoke she felt that her information was overkill to a woman like Gail Prentiss, whose formidable intelligence easily accommodated facts and quickly absorbed understanding.

Gail had listened closely to her explanation while Sherry waddled by again to fill their coffee cups.

"Got it," Gail said, when Fiona had finished. She looked at her watch.

"Morning call," Fiona said. "He needs to berate us on Monday mornings. We all consider it his therapy. The weekend for him has been horrendous. The corpses have rolled in at their usual accelerated weekend pace. Mostly gang and drug-related killings with the usual innocents that got caught in the crossfire. There's not enough personnel to do the job. But his nerves are jangling from his home life as well, his bitch of a wife singing her song about the man's failure."

Gail shook her head in sympathy.

"Both of us come in fresh," Fiona muttered. "I was off duty this weekend and this is your first day. So be forewarned about the culture shock."

Gail slid out of the booth and stood up to her full height, her ramrod straight posture emphasizing her bosom. Standing, Fiona, who was a mere five-seven, was able to see the full extent of the woman's size. As they walked past the booths, all heads turned to inspect Gail, this magnificent phenomenon.

Fiona had, at first, expected to feel some sense of sympathetic embarrassment for the woman because she was so conspicuous, but as she followed in her wake and watched the shocked inspection of the gauntlet, she felt, instead, pride, pride in her gender.

Outside, as they moved in tandem toward the headquarters building, Fiona could not contain herself.

"You are something, Gail. I'm going to enjoy seeing the looks on the faces of our colleagues when I introduce you around."

Gail made no comment. Her thoughts seemed elsewhere. Certainly, she had learned years ago how to cope with other people's reactions to her, although, watching her peripherally as they walked, Fiona could sense that there was something else that went with this territory of lofty magnificence.

She wondered if that something else was loneliness.

—3—

As expected, the various members of the homicide division could not take their eyes off of her, men and women alike. Fiona knew, of course, that those that affected the personas of insatiable studs, the crotch grabbers, would fantasize challenges. Others might be contemptuous, perhaps even jealous of her commanding physicality.

The Eggplant managed to conceal his Monday morning irritation for a brief polite moment in which he made his general introduction of welcome to the new officer.

"We welcome you to the fold, Officer Prentiss, and wish you luck. You'll need it here in the murder capital of America. We are the hired hands of an indifferent society, modern civilization's human garbage collectors. We are the avengers of those who dare to violate the sixth commandment, 'Thou Shalt Not Kill.'"

He took a deep breath, impressed with this little homily to the newly arrived. His nostrils quivered and he patted the side pocket of his pants in a reflexive search for matches to light his once ever-present panatelas, now outlawed in the building. He chewed them unlit now.

"Ladies and gentlemen, we have had ten murders this weekend, our usual fare." The statistic had already been posted in the squad room. It was no mystery to most of those present, some of whom had worked on them over the weekend. A number, the obvious ones, had already been closed, the killers apprehended. Others, they all knew, would never be closed.

The Eggplant droned on, cataloguing the most difficult cases, describing the circumstances. Two children had been killed by drive-bys and the leads had already evaporated in the melting fear of the eyewitnesses. After about a half-hour of this recital, his message became a harangue and he worked himself into a sweating stew of frustration and anger. He was obviously tired and overworked, overwrought and besieged.

One of the children was a nine-year-old female and it fell to them, under the Eggplant's new dictum, to take the case, following up the scene work done by colleagues during the weekend mop-up. The child had been playing in an alley beside her house in southeast Washington. Suddenly there was a spray of bullets from a semi-automatic and another innocent child was caught in the crossfire, a common by-product of the city's gang wars.

Both Fiona and Gail knew the drill. There would be no credible witnesses. The parent, usually a single mother, would be paralyzed with shock, the grandparent, invariably a single woman not quite out of her thirties, would be livid with uncontrolled rage and a great-grandmother, church-going, law-abiding, self-sacrificing, would view the spectacle with resignation and despair, a family of female victims.

Heading southeast, Fiona used the car phone to call Dr. Benson, the medical examiner, and her closest friend in the department. He always took her call, whether at the forensic lab or in his office.

In this case, the call had added significance. Dr. Benson always personally performed the autopsies on child homicides, hoping that the secrets he meticulously uncovered in the dead tissue would whip up enough anger in the squad to speed the apprehension of the killers. It invariably accomplished the former but rarely the latter.

Performing them always left him deeply depressed. At times, it fell to Fiona to nudge him back to, if not tranquility, at least normality. He knew that he could avoid the whole process by delegating the duty to others, but for his own inexplicable reasons, he insisted on doing them.

"Yes, Fiona," he said, his deep bass pervading the car. She had the phone on mike.

"I'm here with my new partner, Gail Prentiss, Dr. Benson."

"Please to meet you, Doctor," Gail said.

"I am very fond of your father, dear," he said. Dr. Benson was always well tuned in on what was happening in the homicide squad and invariably knew the buzz before Fiona.

"Thank you, Doctor," Gail said. "You know, of course, that Dad is not very well."

Dr. Benson sighed.

"Yes, I do."

"We're on this Thompson girl," Fiona said softly.

"Beyond belief. Her face was gone."

"Poor thing," Fiona said.

There was a long pause.

"Why the innocent children?" he sighed.

Fiona and Gail exchanged glances of understanding. It was a question that could never be answered.

"No leads?" Dr. Benson asked.

"Not so far," Fiona said. It was rare to find any in this type of crime, unless one of the witnesses eyeballed the perps. Most, unless they were very close relatives, were too frightened to come forward.

"Are you alright, Doctor?" Fiona asked gently.

"In despair, ladies. In despair."

His feelings were genuine.

Fiona wanted to tell Gail more about Dr. Benson, how his compassion and wisdom sustained her, how much she loved him and worried about him, but she was forestalled by another call.

"FitzGerald and Prentiss." It was the Eggplant's voice.

"You're off the Thompson case. Bigelow and Phipps will take it. We've got something else for you. Female Caucasian, early twenties, Mayflower Hotel, Room 737."

"Nothing more?"

"Messy sex crime. The assistant manager just hung up. He was hysterical."

"Be there in ten," Fiona said, swinging the car around and heading back to Connecticut Avenue.

"Make it five," the Eggplant said, signing off.

Fiona made it in eight, sirens blazing. They got to the hotel's entrance just as the uniforms arrived in three squad cars. Rushing through the lobby, they made it to an elevator bank and crowded into an elevator keyed in by the ashen assistant manager to circumvent the computers.

"You won't believe this," he cried. "You just won't believe this. There's a woman in there . . . Christ . . . I never saw anything like it. You won't believe it. Checked in Thursday night."

"Calm down," Gail said. "Just the woman in there? No one else, dead or alive."

"Isn't that enough? Oh, my God. You'll see in a minute."

Six uniforms, the two female detectives and the assistant manager stormed out of the elevator into the corridor. In front of the door, Fiona turned and raised both hands as the assistant manager, with nervous fluttering fingers, attempted to open the door with a key.

"Just myself and my partner, people," Fiona said, turning to the others, taking instant command. "Keep everyone out until we tell you," she barked to the senior uniform. "And secure the corridor." She took the key out of the hands of the assistant manager, who had continued to be unable to get his fingers to master the door-opening process.

"Sorry," the assistant manager said. He was a thin, balding man with round glasses, impeccably dressed and giving off the scent of heavy, sweetish after-shave lotion. His facial skin was dead-white. He stepped aside and leaned against the corridor wall. "I'll wait, if you don't mind."

After putting on plastic gloves, Fiona and Gail opened the door, pushing it aside slowly and not passing over the threshold until it was fully opened. Alert to any surprises, they unsnapped their holsters as a precaution, although they did not draw their weapons, each taking a swift single step inside the room.

"No wonder the man is freaking out," Gail said.

Dominating the room was a queen-sized bed. Beside it, a bedside lamp suffused the room in an eerie yellowish light. In the center of the bed, spread-eagled, was a woman, yellowed flesh floating on a pool of blood, sunken, unseeing, terrified eyes fixed in a frozen stare. The woman's last life image was obviously one that triggered a sense of mortal fear.

Her arms and legs were tied to the bedposts with a kind of silky rope and a wad of washcloth was stuffed into her mouth as a gag. Stab wounds covered her torso from her neck to her pubic hair and seeping blood had dripped over the vertical edges of the sheets, leaving specks of blood on the flowered carpet that suggested the beginnings of a Jackson Pollack painting.

It was one of the worst murder scenes Fiona had ever covered and for a moment her detective's eye seemed clouded over, her alertness blunted. She felt physically and mentally immobilized by the sight.

"You okay, Fiona?"

It was the soft, assured voice of Gail Prentiss, who, towering beside her, was surveying the scene with a far more controlled and analytical eye than

Fiona was able to muster. Unable to function, Fiona turned away and went into the bathroom, noting instinctively through her numbness that the room seemed overly clean, a sure sign that the perpetrator had expended a great deal of energy concealing his tracks.

She turned on the cold tap and splashed her face, letting the drying process cool her further. The shock was mildly reviving, returning her somewhat to alertness. She forced her concentration.

There was not a spot in the bathroom to suggest to the naked eye that a bloody mess was lying on the bed just a few feet away. A number of wrung-out towels lay in a corner of the room, suggesting that the effort to eliminate evidence was thorough and meticulous.

A cloth case stood on the Formica counter. Fiona unzipped it. At first glance, it contained the usual articles used by any traveling woman. She made a mental note to go through it thoroughly after bagging it as evidence.

Carefully picking up the bathroom telephone, Fiona punched in the Eggplant's private number. She cleared her throat and fought for calm.

"A bloody pig sticker," Fiona said. "The work of a real sex weirdo."

"The tech boys are on their way," the Eggplant sighed.

"You want to be a spokesman?" Fiona asked. Of course, he did, she knew, but the pause that followed indicated that he was more reticent than usual.

"Really ugly, is it?"

"The worst," Fiona said.

"White lady?"

"As the driven snow," Fiona said. "It's an uptown case."

"Any theories?" the Eggplant asked.

"Too early to tell. Could be a serial killer. The perp seems to have done a thorough cleanup. The only filthy piece of work is the deceased and her immediate surroundings."

She felt herself talking more than she normally did upon arriving at a murder scene. Her reactions since entering the room were, for her, professionally uncommon. She knew exactly why.

"Bare bones to the press, FitzGerald. But only if necessary. Keep the lid tight, and see me when you get back here. If I were there, I'd be drowning in shit."

To Fiona, it seemed a rare example of his total trust. Of course, he knew that she was fully aware of all the public ramifications. A murder in a prime hotel meant sending ugly signals for the tourist business, which was suffering enough with the murder-capital moniker. Aside from the pure business aspect, it was the kind of murder that wasn't good for the image of the country. It sent bad messages about crime and violence and the safety of people, especially to young women visitors coming to the capital of the only superpower left in the world.

There also seemed another ploy at work. The Eggplant was putting her out front on this one. There would be no place to hide. She supposed there was a gender twist to it as well.

Hanging up the phone, she gave her face a passing glance in the mirror. Her skin looked pallid and a nerve was twitching in her cheek. This was the face of a distressed woman.

Back in the bedroom, she noted that Gail had placed a small footstool next to the bed to minimize any disturbance to the floor. She had also put plastic booties over her shoes, which emphasized the preparation and attention to detail she invested in her work. She was kneeling on the footstool and writing in her notebook. When she saw Fiona returning, she looked up and began to read from her notes.

"A Caucasian woman, twenties, hard bod. Name is Phyla Herbert, from Chicago. Two suits, one skirt, three blouses, all hung up like soldiers in the closet. Underwear in top drawer of chest. Small empty suitcase in closet as well. Beside it, a briefcase. Lots of resumes and other paraphernalia of a job seeker. Should be easy to trace her movements using the hotel telephone log."

Fiona listened carefully to Gail's recitation, but kept her eyes averted from the body, hoping her action or lack of it would go unnoticed. She was bluffing and knew it. This was not like her. She would have to force herself to look.

"I told you, my dad was a surgeon," Gail said. Nothing escaped her. "I've watched him operate."

Fiona ignored the comment. Squeamishness seemed her only logical cover. Gail appeared to relish the inspection. Fiona noted her intensity, her large yellow-flecked brown eyes studying the body and surroundings with laser-like thoroughness.

She felt an odd resentment, as if her authority was being usurped, although she knew that Gail would be deferential, respectful. Nevertheless, the feeling was there. Yet, there was no escaping that she had to deal with the body and its implications, including the personal aspect. She was, after all, a homicide detective, the senior officer in charge of the crime scene.

"Suck," Gail muttered.

"What?"

"Suck," she repeated. "Here, printed under her bangs. And over here on both thighs, 'scum' on one thigh and 'cunt' on the other."

She must force herself to look, Fiona cried inside herself, her head turning, eyes focusing. There it was, the body dead-white under its blanket of speckled, browning blood. And the words Gail had spoken were clearly printed in cherry red lipstick in block letters on the dead woman's forehead, inner thighs and arms. Her areolas, too, were reddened by lipstick, unevenly, like a child's crayoning.

And more. A long red streak led down from her neck to below her navel with the word "whore" printed in a crude semi-circle around her pubic area. For a brief moment Fiona's eyes clouded, then, by force of will, cleared again. Was it possible? Déjà vu, or fate playing an ugly game.

"Graffiti," Fiona said, croaking the word, fighting for her bearings, desperately trying to control her agitation. Another flash of memory exloded in her mind. Oh God, she needed to run from this.

Gail continued to observe the body as Fiona again turned her eyes away and forced her concentration on other details of the scene, hoping to find something that Gail had not yet noted, an unlikely prospect. Soon Flannagan and the tech boys would arrive and the body would be carted off and studied by the medical examiner's office. She was certain that Dr. Benson would do the autopsy.

What Fiona wanted most was to leave this place. The room was oppressive, claustrophobic. She became aware of a growing knot in the pit of her stomach that would not dissolve. Her hands shook and droplets of perspiration were oozing out of her pores.

"You okay?"

It was Gail, towering over her, studying her face. Fiona nodded, wishing that Gail would stop observing her as if she were the victim. She hated this reaction, shamed by her own vulnerability.

Suddenly there was a ruckus in the corridor signaling the arrival of Flannagan and his merry techs.

"Son-of-a-bitch," Flannagan cried as he stood at the foot of the bed observing the body. "Is there no end to man's inhumanity to woman?" Flannagan said. He was an old hand at this and had ghoulishly kept score of how many murdered corpses he had seen in his career.

"Pushing five thousand, Fi. Another ten will do it."

"Spare me," Fiona managed.

Flannagan eyeballed the corpse and shook his head.

"Proves that no one can ever say they've seen everything. Right, Fi?"

He looked toward her, but she had turned away. The knot in her stomach had risen to her throat, making it impossible for her to respond. She thought she was about to throw up.

A police photographer took pictures, bouncing around the room, looking for every possible angle. A uniformed sergeant, who had taken charge in the corridor, opened the door a crack and called for Sergeant FitzGerald.

"We got reporters crowding us," he said.

She was out of it, lost somewhere, unable to respond, her mind groping in some dark hell. For support, she leaned against the bathroom doorjamb, feeling she was about to break apart. An old memory was crashing through the rusty gate of denial. She tried, valiantly tried, to hold it back, but it came rushing out at her like an overwhelming tide.

"What should I tell them?"

The uniformed sergeant's voice was urgent.

"They're crawling all over us."

The words came at her from a distance, but she could find no response in her brain.

"Nobody comes in here," Gail barked, the authority in her voice absolute. Fiona felt the woman's hands on her arm, leading her gently into the bathroom, where she closed the door quietly behind her, pressing the button lock.

There was a glass in a plastic wrapper. Gail tore it off and filled it from the tap, handing it to Fiona to drink. Fiona, hating the show of weakness, needed to cup it in both hands to keep it steady enough to bring to her lips, which she did finally, taking a brief swallow.

"It happens, Fiona," Gail said. "Happened to me twice in LA. Comes like a shock wave, then it passes."

Fiona nodded. Not once had it happened to her. Ever. Until now. Nor could Gail possibly guess the source.

"Take some deep breaths and try to get some more water down."

Fiona obeyed. All personal will had disappeared. The back of her blouse under her suit jacket was soaked through. Letting the tap continue to run, Gail put her long, tapered fingers into the stream, then brought them to Fiona's temples. Fiona felt the healing powers of Gail's cool, soothing touch. Despite her embarrassment, she was grateful.

"Color's coming back, Fiona," Gail said.

Her equilibrium was returning, although she could not clear the knot in her throat. But the clouds were dissipating in her mind.

"Would you like to rest here a moment?" Gail asked, reaching for the lid of the toilet seat.

"No, Gail," Fiona managed to say. "Leave it."

Her alertness seemed to be returning. Toilet seats were often a good source of prints, especially males'. Fiona admitted a secret thrill in finding a detail possibly overlooked by Gail.

"Back in the saddle?" Gail said with a wink.

Fiona smiled, breathed deeply, nodded, then turned the knob of the bathroom door. Flannagan's team had bagged the body and were busy combing the room for latents. The ropes that had held the women had been untied and bagged in plastic, as well as the woman's clothes and other articles.

After a last minute check of the scene, Gail and a somewhat recovered Fiona came out into the noisy bustle of the corridor. The media goons, hoping for a juicy scandal, rushed forward with their cameras, microphones and recorders. This was their meat, a sex murder in a downtown hotel frequented by the power brokers, lobbyists and politicos.

"Understand it was a pretty messy sex crime, FitzGerald?" Sam Firgus said, his voice booming above the others. Be alert, Fiona warned herself, recovered enough to appear credible. The very word "sex" was enough to conjure up lascivious tabloid revelations.

Fiona's immediate instinct was to offer what was expected, the traditional "no comment." But it was obvious that the elements of the scene and its ramifications had already begun to leak like a sieve. She decided, instead, to be guardedly and selectively factual.

"We found the body of a woman in her twenties. Multiple stab wounds."

"Was the woman nude?" a lady radio reporter asked.

"Yes."

"Was she raped?"

"Can't say at this time."

"Do you think it's the work of a sex deviant?"

"Too early to tell," Fiona said. "We will await further lab tests."

"Do you know who the woman is?" someone asked.

"Yes. But we won't be announcing it until next-of-kin are notified."

"We understand she was tied spread-eagled to the bed," Firgus said. There was an image that would warm the heart of the media hounds.

"I'm not prepared to comment on the position of the body."

"Come on, FitzGerald, level with us," Firgus pressed.

Fiona stayed calm.

"Sorry," she said. "Nothing must interfere with the integrity of the investigation." She noted Gail's approving nod as she stood silently beside her.

"Any political connection?" Firgus pressed, obviously seeking some further titillating angle that would send the story soaring into the national and international press.

"We have no leads at this time to connect anyone with the crime."

"Who is that woman with you, FitzGerald?" Firgus asked. There was simply no way for Gail to be unnoticed.

"My partner, Detective Gail Prentiss," Fiona said.

"Interesting," Firgus said. Fiona hoped that he would not raise the gender issue. He didn't.

The questions persisted for ten minutes more, with Fiona offering little information, deliberately trying to make her answers flat and uninteresting. Unfortunately, this one was a standout even in the murder capital of the United States. Worse, it had explosive implications, known only to Fiona. But there was just enough titillation to assure the Eggplant of further harassment, both from the media and his superiors.

In the car heading back to headquarters, Fiona could not ignore the turbulence in her mind. Vivid memories washed over her with hurricane force, memories she could not avoid.

"Any theories, Fiona?" Gail asked.

"Not yet," Fiona lied. "You?"

"Has the feel of a serial killer with an elaborate modus operandi."

Elaborate? Fiona shrugged, determined to appear noncommittal. Could it be him? she asked herself, as the images of that day rushed back at her.

—4—

The vividness of these images were staggering in their similarity, especially after having been wrapped in the thick fog of denial for nearly two decades. Not that it hadn't surfaced in different guises during that time, mostly in unpleasant and painful recall.

On those rare occasions when the memory did surface, it always came disguised in dreams, mostly nightmares, sometimes remembered on awakening, the faces blank, the bodies distorted. Only the pain was chillingly real. Yet she had learned to quickly eradicate even these fleeting remembrances from her mind. Until now.

Farley Lipscomb was her father's lawyer then, a man of awesome dignity, tall, confident, self-assured, the kind of man who could read the label of a candy bar and make it seem like he was dispensing the wisdom of the ages. Fiona's parents seemed to be in the company of the Lipscombs often.

Letitia Lipscomb was, even then, in the mainstream of Washington's social life. Wealthy in her own right, she had the wherewithal to entertain lavishly in her lovely home off Massachusetts Avenue in the heart of Embassy Row. She had her sights set on becoming one of Washington's most important hostesses and was obsessive in her zeal to collect Washington's big-fish celebrities. Fiona's father, the senior senator from New York was, of course, an excellent trophy for her capital aquarium.

Her social goals coincided with her husband's ambitions and, in a company town like Washington, she was able to produce an accessibility that worked well for Farley Lipscomb's burgeoning practice.

To Fiona at the time, the social trappings of Washington were the ultimate in ostentatious phoniness and Letitia was characterized in her mind as an authentic stiff-necked Wasp aristocrat. The idea was embellished by her manner of speaking, an obviously contrived British accent delivered with a nasal twang that made, to Fiona's ear, even the most sincere compliment seem like a sneer.

26

As for Farley Lipscomb, Fiona had characterized him as a man imprisoned by his wife's social ambitions.

Even in retrospect, she supposed she had a crush on Farley and was sending him disturbingly arousing signals. At that moment in time, she rationalized, she was in deep rebellion, performing a kind of obligatory rite of passage she supposed, for a carefully mothered and strictly indoctrinated eighteen-year-old Catholic girl.

She had, by then, discovered the hormonal rhythms of her strong sexuality. Two years before, she had lost her virginity, courtesy of her high school boyfriend on the eve of their parting for different colleges. She to Amherst. He to the University of Virginia. It had been a rather messy business, she remembered. Actually she had been the aggressor, manipulating the frightened young man to penetrate her. It turned out to be more of a feat of mechanical engineering than an act of passion. The episode ended their romance.

In time, the event had become one of those memories of happy embarrassment, a shared secret that triggered an eruption of blushes and giggles whenever she bumped into her old swain, who had become a popular weatherman for a local television station. Every time she saw him on the TV she would roar with laughter, remembering the ridiculousness of what had been meant to be a profound moment.

By the time she had declared her interest in Farley Lipscomb, she had acquired additional sexual experience and an exploratory attitude that did not rule out married men. She did not consider herself promiscuous and her choice of partners was very selective.

She thought of the activity as a kind of research into her strong libido and sensuality and, in those days, as a way to get her karma in balance with her nature. It was, of course, before the onslaught of AIDS, although well into the era of advanced birth control technology. It was a time when abstinence was still ridiculed and to be a virgin past eighteen was a sign of galloping frigidity.

In an odd way, she decided that she had inherited a strong sex drive from her father, who, was notoriously vulnerable to the blandishments of other women. She was also aware that her mother considered sexual activity as a kind of penance that had to be endured for the greater good of hearth and family.

By then, Fiona had developed healthy, uninhibited fondness for men and, despite the occasional disappointments, she managed to enjoy deeply pleasurable orgasms more often than not. Her fantasy life was rich and varied. She owned a vibrator and frequently indulged in masturbation. She conceded to herself, there might have been some guilt and shame in such bawdy self-indulgence, considering her upbringing and her mother's inhibited view of sex as a necessary evil. But that attitude soon dissipated with need, pleasure and a general feeling that being in charge of herself, body included, was also a woman's right.

At eighteen, she militantly thought of herself as an emerging modern woman who had arrived victoriously on the threshold of maturity without any of the sexual hangups of her gender. At the time, she hadn't realized that every victory had its costs.

She had begun interning in Farley's office that summer, mostly to satisfy her father's ambition for her, which was to become a lawyer, a profession she had little desire to pursue. She had no specific job, a little typing, a little filing, doing research, but mostly observing the legal profession at work.

Farley Lipscomb was enormously accommodating. He let her sit in on important conferences, where she scribbled furiously on yellow pads as if she were a bona fide member of the legal team. Nor did she have any illusions about her effect on Farley. Often, she caught him eyeballing her in a manner that was hardly platonic. That judgment led her to exacerbate the situation by choosing revealing clothes, shorter skirts and poses that were suggestive and seductive.

After all, she was eighteen. She felt then that she was the center of the universe and that the world circulated around her. Effecting an obvious reaction in men was especially exciting. To see a man like Farley Lipscomb titillated by her charms greatly enhanced her own sexual interest in him.

At that point it was merely a game, a kind of exciting taunt. She fantasized about him and masturbated while imagining him making love to her.

An explosion of lust was, of course, inevitable. He had asked her to work late one evening, allegedly to help him with a case he was preparing. It didn't take long for them to shed the sham of work.

Farley, it turned out, was a man of wide experience and practiced technique in sexual matters and, although she was an open and eager pupil, he was an amazingly adept sexual artist. For her, at the time, his blandishments opened a whole new world of pleasure.

There was another component of their relationship that seemed to justify her actions. Because of his socially obsessive wife, she had the impression that Farley was needy, especially in the sexual realm. His response certainly validated her speculation, although he deliberately eschewed any discussion of his home life. It was as if Letitia did not exist. He had, she had observed even then, a great talent for compartmentalization.

For about a month, they had taken their pleasure in clandestine and often hurried couplings on his office couch or in his leather chair and a number of times on the big shiny conference table in the firm's enormous conference room. Once they had made love in the bathroom of her parents' house during a dinner party at which Farley and his wife were guests. The danger of discovery added to the excitement.

Such risks bonded them. Together, they shared this stupendous secret. In effect, he was playing Russian roulette with his high profile life, gambling his future, his continuing and certain climb to success, by a sexual dalliance with an eighteen-year-old girl. Against his losses, if they were found out, hers would be minimal.

He had even admitted to her that she had become an addiction, that every cell in his body demanded her, that there was no getting enough of her. She was certain that the addiction was mutual.

She knew, too, that there was more to it than sex. What had started out as a kind of exciting adventure was becoming, in her mind and heart, a love affair. She was convinced that what she felt was the real thing, that what her body yearned for was psychic as well, that a profound love had entered her life.

She wondered if it was hero worship, infatuation or romantic daydreaming. She hadn't wanted it to go beyond sexual games. After all, she was nearly twenty years his junior and he was locked into marriage by ambition, connections and money. It didn't seem possible that he would throw over his wife for an eighteen-year-old girl, no matter how emotionally involved he was.

But love and inexperience, as she later learned, could conspire to create powerful wish-fulfillment possibilities. The opportunity opened in her mind. Love, she reasoned, could make anything happen. Although she was too frightened to declare herself, afraid that it might put an end to the affair, she held out the hope that the feeling was mutual. To her, at that moment in time, Farley was her life or, as they say, the sun and the stars.

She could not recall exactly when the idea emerged. In retrospect she knew he had put it there, inserted it, as a missive is put in an envelope. She could recall an exchange they had one day as they lay on the leather couch in his office in post-coital bliss.

"Will you do anything for me, Fiona?" he had asked.

"Of course."

"Anything"

"Absolutely," she replied with sincere and total commitment. She considered this consent the opportunity to prove her love and by so doing capture him forever.

"No matter how strange it seems at first?" he pressed.

"If it's important to you, I'll do anything you say," she had replied.

"Yes. It is important," he told her.

Did this mean that the feeling was mutual? Was it possible?

"Is this a game?" she asked.

She remembered that he seemed to be carefully framing an answer.

"More than just a game, Fiona," he told her.

"I'll do anything you ask, Farley," she had replied, with fervent sincerity.

"It's very important to us, Fiona," he said. "It's the way we'll prove how much we care, how much we trust each other."

Her heart jumped to her throat. This was pretty much what she wanted to hear and the idea spurred her excitement. She agreed without reservations. If it was important to him, it was doubly important for her. She loved this man. Her heart sang. Of course, she would do anything he wanted, anything that made him happy.

"I'll arrange everything," he told her. She wasn't certain what that meant, except that it seemed wonderful. He would be thinking of her, arranging things for them. For days before the Saturday he had designated as D-Day, she was in a constant state of excitement.

He instructed her to pick him up in her car on a street corner a few blocks from his office. She was delighted to follow his strict orders on everything. Despite the occasional risks, which he characterized as an irresistible compulsion, their trysts took place mostly in the safety of his office, where his time and whereabouts were controllable. Publicly, he treated her as any other young intern.

She knew that he was, despite the risk-taking, paranoid about Letitia discovering their affair, and Fiona cooperated with alacrity. In public, she addressed him, always, respectfully as Mr. Lipscomb. And in the presence of others he affected a pose of fatherly interest in her.

When Fiona was in Letitia's presence, she was particularly friendly to her and equally as respectful, representing herself as a naive, wide-eyed innocent. But this newly arranged assignation seemed to be an escalation of risk-taking. Perhaps he had it in mind to publicly declare himself. His words tossed repetitively in her mind: I love you, Fiona. I love you, Fiona.

As Fiona's car reached the appointed rendezvous, she didn't see him, that is, until he moved toward her car. He was wearing a peaked baseball hat and khaki workpants and toting a carry-all around one shoulder. Recognizing him finally, she opened the door and he jumped in. Although still puzzled by his action, she accepted the theatrics as part of his general plan. Besides, it seemed like exciting fun.

He directed her to a high-rise motel not far from the airport, explaining that he wanted a well-constructed place that was more soundproof than those old-fashioned one-story motels constructed years ago with paper-thin walls. The comment had aroused her curiosity, but she did not lose confidence in his trust.

As she pulled into the parking lot, he explained that he had reserved a room in the name of M. Worth from Philadelphia. He gave her an address and zip code and instructed her to pay cash for one night in advance, then to come out and give him the room number and he would meet her upstairs.

It was, she remembered, terribly exciting, wonderfully secretive and intriguing. Nor did she question his instructions, following them with obedience and dispatch, a willing conspirator. The mystery surrounding the process was arousing and, by the time they were together in the room, she found herself sexually stimulated and ready for anything he might suggest.

Anything!

She was hardly prepared for what came next. He opened the tote bag and emptied the contents on the bed. There were lengths of rope, a riding crop, a flat racquet of the kind used for paddle tennis, a leather garter belt, black silk stockings, spiked-heel shoes and what looked like a leather jock strap and another strip of leather. She wasn't sure of its purpose.

There were also some items of makeup—cherry red lipstick, black eyeliner and rouge. She was confused by the odd array of equipment and giggled nervously.

"Props," he said in response.

There were, of course, questions in her mind. But she had remained silent.

"I need this, Fiona," he said. "Still game?"

"Of course."

He told her to strip and put on the garter belt, stockings and spike–heeled shoes, which she did. Then he told her to apply the makeup, exaggerating her mouth and cheeks and putting the black eyeliner on as thick as possible. She remembered she had loved the idea. It seemed like a masquerade.

While she put on the costume, he took off his clothes and put on the leather jock strap. When she had applied the makeup to his satisfaction, she stood in the center of the room, affecting a number of what she calculated were naughty poses. He made no move to come toward her.

"Pick up the riding crop," he said.

She did. It felt smooth and light in her hand. This is fun, she remembered telling herself, acknowledging her own arousal.

"Have you any idea what is going to happen?" he asked.

"No."

Although she thought of herself as sexually experienced, she honestly had not an inkling of what he had in mind.

"If you truly care about me, you'll comply with my wishes. With enthusiasm and without reservations. Can you do that?"

She nodded enthusiastically.

"If this is what you want . . ." she began.

"This is what I need," he replied.

"Anything you ask, darling."

"Then let me explain what is expected of you," he told her. "I want you to treat me as your slave. I'll do anything you tell me to do. Treat me like scum, like a worthless pig. I've been bad. You must accept that. Rotten to the core. I've got to be punished and disciplined. Do you understand?"

She wasn't sure she had. Love crossed all boundaries, she remembered telling herself. Of course, she would comply.

"It's a game, right?" she had asked, hiding her astonishment.

"Can you accept such a role?"

"If it is important to you, Farley."

"It is," he assured her.

"I'll do anything you ask."

"Without reservations?"

"Yes."

"It's only a game, isn't it?" she had asked again, wanting to be reassured one more time.

"Our game."

"Then I'll play."

He flashed a smile and put his finger in her mouth. She sucked it. Then he withdrew it.

"Call me names," he told her.

She hesitated and he seemed disappointed.

"Go on," he coaxed. "Dirty names."

"You filthy pig," she said hesitantly.

"Louder. Worse than that. Terrible names. Please, Fiona."

"You . . . lousy fuck."

"More."

"You slimy bastard."

"Thank you. More," he begged.

She continued. Her voice rose.

He dropped to his knees and crawled toward her.

When she recalled these events years later, she could not remember even the slightest level of protest. She was accepting, absolutely compliant to his wishes, determined to show him her understanding of his need, to prove her love and trust. As she was drawn deeper into the action, she felt more and more that it was her duty to be enthusiastic and energetic, to fully satisfy his wish to be punished and humiliated. He is doing it for me, she told herself, searching for the logic of it.

She did not ask why he needed this kind of treatment. In sharing this secret with him, she felt even closer to him, more loving. In an odd way, she was flattered by his confidence and she wanted to fulfill his expectations to the best of her ability.

He kissed her shoes, begged her to blindfold him with the leather strip. Then he asked that she write filthy words on his body with the lipstick, which she did. With his instructive and pleading encouragement she was prodded to accelerate her actions, to swat his body with the whip.

"I deserve more," he cried, urging her on. "Tell me what I am."

She found herself more and more into the game. He began to call her "mistress."

"You are filth, dung. A piece of shit."

"I am worse than that," he cried, begging her to tie him up. She tied his hands to the legs of the bed.

"Tighter," he prodded.

He was bent over, his naked buttocks jutting out. "I need to be paddled."

She took the paddle from the bed. He asked to kiss the paddle, then, as she paddled him, he counted each blow, urging her to swat him harder. Was there a moment when she felt that this was wrong, or silly, or hurtful, or all three? She would never be sure. Did she feel like she was participating in a perversion? She could not recall.

"I'll never do it again," he cried. "Make me do anything, anything."

It seemed, that first time, an exciting theatrical adventure, and she threw herself into it with abandon. Although her blows were heavy, she did not break his skin and she followed his instructions to paddle him until his buttocks were red. Did she love the role she was playing? Probably. It proved to be an afternoon studded with deep orgasms for both of them. Despite the subsequent guilt and self-loathing that came later, the crisis of confidence she had experienced about her "normality," she could never deny the pleasure of those moments. Never that.

Heading the car back to Washington, she noted Farley's odd serenity. He had turned to her and kissed her lips as she drove, caressing her hair. If anything struck her as strange, or even weird, it was her own sense of total acceptance. She had done what he needed and she was happy about that. He expressed his gratitude, explaining that he had shown her his absolute trust.

"This is the way I have proven to you how much I care."

Her heart jumped in her chest. He truly loves me, she told herself.

Next week, he told her, it would be her turn.

She remembered how she had thought about the idea every waking moment of her life in that week. It did not repulse her. Actually, she looked forward to it, wondering how she would react. Nor could she recall the slightest thought at the time that what she had done and what she was looking forward to doing was bizarre or perverted.

It was, she decided, a method to prove her love, to illustrate her trust in him. As he had done. Besides, it felt good. No one had come to any harm. She showed no inclination to analyze the origins, motivation or meaning of such an episode. It filled his needs and gave them bodily pleasure. And, she was certain, it brought them closer together.

On the next Saturday, the same process was repeated. He met her in the same costume that he had worn the week before, carrying the same tote bag. They checked into the motel in the same way, using the name she had used the week before and paying for the room in advance.

"You'll do exactly as I say, won't you, Fiona?" he asked as he emptied the tote bag on the bed.

A surge of excitement pulsed through her as she saw the items laying helter-skelter on the bed.

"Without question," she told him, eagerly. "Anything you ask of me."

"You'll be my absolute slave. Like I was last week."

She nodded.

Their eyes met. Then he barked out a name.

"You filthy bitch."

Had she been shocked, despite her expectations? She would never be certain.

"You've been an extremely bad girl, Fiona. Haven't you?"

"Yes."

"Did I give you permission to talk?" he asked.

She shook her head.

"You talk only when I order you to. And when you do, you call me 'master.' Do you understand, bitch?"

"Yes."

"Yes, what?"

"Yes, master."

"Whatever I say, you will do. No matter what. Your will is mine. Slut."

She nodded.

"And you must never look me in the eye. Do you understand? Speak."

"Yes, master."

He ordered her to undress him, which she did without a word, not looking him in the eye. Then he ordered her to take off all her clothes and stand in the corner facing the wall.

She felt her excitement surge. A spear of adrenaline moved through her, penetrating, giving her obscene, moist pleasure. She had loved it. She heard him moving around behind her, but she felt safe, trusting him. She was exhilarated by this trust. She felt unburdened, totally in his power.

She could not remember how long she had stood there, except that she enjoyed being there, loved being there, loved obeying.

"You've been a filthy whore, Fiona," his voice boomed. "A terrible disgrace. Haven't you?"

She nodded.

"And because of that I have to punish you. Come here."

She turned. He was completely nude with a huge erection. She remembered that she could not take her eyes off of it. She wanted desperately to kiss it.

He ordered her to lie on the bed on a high nest of pillows and he tied her wrists tightly, achoring her to the legs of the harvard frame. Then he did the same thing with the ankles.

She was spread-eagled on the bed. She felt happy, she remembered. Happy!

"This is just the beginning, Fiona. You've been a pig, a slut, a cunt."

He printed words on her arms, then on the inside of her thighs. She could not tell what he was writing, except that the movement of the cold lipstick on her thighs caused her to climax. She shuddered with pleasure.

"Did I tell you to do that?" Farley asked.

She shook her head.

"You don't deserve to have pleasure, bitch," he said. "Do you understand?"

She nodded.

He sat watching her for a long time, still naked, tumescent. He wrapped his hand around his penis and shook it.

"You want this, don't you?"

She nodded, then whispered, "Oh, yes."

"What did I tell you about speaking?"

She remembered how delicious she felt in the face of this implied threat.

"You don't deserve this," he told her, standing up, coming closer to her. He bent down over her and whispered in her ear.

"You are a filthy slut, aren't you? Well, aren't you? Speak."

"Yes, master."

There were other words he used to describe her and she nodded her consent. Then he took the riding crop and made her kiss it. Suddenly, he slid it across her breasts, then struck her with it. It stung and she cried out.

"Did I tell you to cry out?"

"It hurt."

"It hurt, what?"

"It hurt, master."

"You really need to be taught, you cunt."

Again he hit her sharply across the breasts. Again she cried out. He took the leather blindfold and put it around her eyes. Then he stuffed a gag in her mouth. Deprived of light and speech, she felt herself becoming disoriented, confused. It was not what she had expected.

She felt him untie her ankles. Then he drew her legs over her head in a kind of somersault position and anchored the rope at the head end of the bed, where he had fastened her arms. Her legs hung in the air, her hips partially raised, her underside and genitalia exposed. It was impossible to be more physically vulnerable. Still, despite the discomfort, she begged herself to trust him. This was a test. Wasn't it?

"You need this, you filthy whore."

She felt the hollow whack of the paddle on her buttocks and across her vagina. Then another. It seemed to go on forever. At each blow he called her another filthy name. At first, her arousal accelerated and she expected it to increase. But the pain, contrary to her expectations, was actually starting to diminish any arousal. The game was losing its allure.

But she could not tell him this. She could not speak and she struggled against the bonds. When the blows stopped, finally, she listened as he moved behind her. Then she heard a whirring sound. Some sort of electrical device. She heard his voice.

"You've given me no choice, whore."

The sound grew louder. The device was coming closer. When it touched her skin, she realized it was a vibrator.

"If only you had obeyed me to the letter, Fiona," Farley said. She felt the vibrator press against her body, then waves of excruciating pain. He was pushing the device into her anus.

All pleasure had vanished. The pain was ghastly. She felt herself choking as she squirmed helplessly against the bonds that held her. The gag prevented her from crying out, although she tossed her head from side to side in agony.

"You deserve this, you whore," he shouted above the now grating sound of the vibrator.

His words cascaded in her head. The pain permeated her, filled her, tortured her. She heard her own screams in her head, but no sound as she struggled. She wanted to disappear, lose herself. She seemed to have remembered wishing for death.

Stop, her mind screamed, her head swinging wildly from side to side as he pressed the vibrator deeper into her body. He was oblivious to her struggles, her pain, her agony and her desperate but silent entreaties. He spoke, but she could not hear him above the sound of the vibrator as it shuddered inside her body, spreading its excruciating pain.

She might have lost consciousness. She would never be certain. Nor could she ever be sure what had really gone on in her mind at the time, except that she knew she was experiencing the ultimate mortification. This was not trust. This was not love. This was fearsome, a shocking and painful abuse of her body. It crossed her mind that he was trying to kill her with agony.

It had been a long time since she had dipped into that rusty vault of memory, but she was certain that her recall was accurate.

"You were wonderful," she remembered him saying sometime later, his voice silky. Had she lost consciousness? Was it really his voice? Did he have no memory of the pain he had inflicted? Was this suffering supposed to prove something to him? She felt him releasing her bonds.

"You've made me very happy," he said.

Was he really saying that or had her hearing become impaired? He had brutalized her. Hurt her. Hadn't he seen that? He removed the gag. She recalled trying to talk, but, at first, she thought she had lost the power of speech. She felt paralyzed. Her body ached from the aggressive violence he had waged against it.

She saw stains on the sheet. She was bleeding from her rectum. Lying beside her on the bed, she saw the instrument he had used, stained with her blood. She remembered pulling up the sheets to hide herself, more out of deep shame than modesty. He pulled the blanket up to her neck, as if he were tucking in a child, and put his lips to her forehead. His lips felt like ice. She cringed and pulled the blanket over her head.

What she wanted was to hide under the covers for the next millennium. She was too humiliated and horror-struck to meet his gaze.

"Rest, my darling," he said, patting the blanket. "You were wonderful." Wonderful? Was it possible? Was she dreaming?

"I'll leave you to rest," he whispered. "I'll get back by taxi."

She must have grunted some response, remembering that when she heard the door close behind him, she had staggered to it and fastened the chain lock. Then she had dropped to her knees and cried hysterically for what must have been hours. Love? No way. In her mind love was beautiful, full of care and trust and wonder. Not this.

The room was dark when she had finally found the strength to rise. The pain was still excruciating. She managed to make it to the bathroom, flicking on the lights. She looked in the mirror, appalled by the sight of herself.

He had covered her body with filthy words written in cherry lipstick. The word "pig" was written across her forehead and on one thigh the word "suck" and on the other "whore." He had also painted her nipples and had drawn an arrow beginning at the base of her neck and leading down to the edge of her pubic hair where he had written the word "trash."

She stood observing herself with disgust. Her shame and mortification had not yet turned to anger. Had she really been a willing participant in this disgusting exhibition of sadism. What had possessed her to consent to such terrible physical abuse? Was there something flawed in her own psyche? As for him, she could not bear the idea that she had loved such a monster.

The pain would not go away. She turned on the bath taps full blast, then crawled into the tub. The sting of the water made her cry out with pain. Eventually, as she soaked in the hot water, it diminished somewhat. She spent a long time in the tub, trying to assemble her thoughts, wondering if she should see a doctor or call the police.

By sheer will power, she managed to dress and drive herself home, sustained, she later realized, by her anger and hatred for him.

Feigning a flu, she spent the next few days in bed, suffering through the uncertainty and agony of self-treatment. She made her unsuspecting mother call Farley to tell him that she was ill. The next day she wrote him a terse letter of resignation. He made no attempt to respond in any way.

*   *   *

As soon as she was able, she left town on the pretext that she needed to attend summer school, a decision that surprised her parents but did not stir their curiosity. It took every bit of her inner resources to cope with the memory of the incident, especially at the beginning. Was she that naive, that malleable, that weak? Was Farley that sick that he had no insight into his own predilections?

Even in the subsequent research she did into this type of practice, the dictum of the bondage-and-discipline subculture was that no physical harm should be inflicted. He had gone over the edge. Worse, he had enjoyed her pain.

There was no way that she could face Farley Lipscomb ever again. What had been love, certainly infatuation and desire, had turned into raw hatred.

But not only was this hatred generated against Farley but against herself for allowing herself to become a tool for his perverse acts. Only later, after years of self-therapy and reading numerous studies of this aberration, was she finally able to let go and forgive herself, although never in her heart could she ever forgive Farley.

But the idea that, if the act had remained a pleasurable game, she might have accepted it was still troublesome. With Farley the game had turned nasty, beyond the pale. Nor did knowing that totally mitigate the shame, the awfulness of it.

For a long time after that incident her desire for sex had simply disappeared. She dated no one during the remainder of her time in college. Only gradually did the trauma dissipate although psychic scars remained. Eventually she reached a point where the memory itself became a kind of fictional imagining far removed from what had become the reality of her life.

In time she had stopped thinking about it, perhaps even denied that it ever happened. It was never again part of her menu of fantasies. It was as if her psychic immune system had kicked in and flushed out all visible symptoms of the aberration. Nonetheless, she knew that it had had a profound effect on her life. Giving up her free will, the power over her mind and body, became her most frightening nightmare. Any hint of such an event occuring provoked a strong negative reaction. Perhaps this was why she was never able to sustain a long-term relationship with a man.

In learning about herself, Fiona recognized her own powerful sexuality. She did not need to have the envelope pushed that far to find pleasure and she invariably rejected those who did. Indeed, she had developed a sixth sense to screen any potential lovers. The slightest revelation of a similar tendency was enough to abort a relationship without guilt or explanation.

Ten years after the episode, she had actually been in the company of Farley Lipscomb and his wife at a dinner party given by one of Washington's most active hostesses. She had greeted both him and his wife with politeness. Little was exchanged between them. She was suprisingly indifferent to his presence, as if he, too, had become a fictional character in someone else's play. Indeed, she savored the indifference as proof positive of her psychic wellness.

As for him, he gave no hint that the incident even lingered in his memory. He smiled, acknowledged her with sentiment and nostalgia as would be appropriate to the daughter of an old friend. Not a gleam, not a single iota of subtle recognition of what they had shared that afternoon was apparent in any visible expression or body language on his part.

As time went on, she hardly thought of him as being the same man who had abused her that day. Nor did his constant coverage in the media trigger any response that affected her in any emotional way.

Until she saw the body of this woman in the Mayflower Hotel, she had no reason to let the events of that fateful day resurface in her mind.

But the image of that poor unfortunate woman spread-eagled on the hotel bed, with similar block-lettered graffiti on her body, had brought back the memory with hurricane force.

Her detective's mind could not reject the notion that this woman was victimized by a perpetrator with an MO that seriously matched that of her long-ago lover. The effect on her had been profound, setting off shock reactions that took all her inner resources to control.

The details of that afternoon, she had always felt certain, were etched into her memory. But how accurate were they really? The pain, the horror of the experience, her embarrassment, the assault on her self-respect, the roller coaster ride of her emotions . . . had all occurred. Had time rendered them anecdotal? Nevertheless, it felt like a memory match but she couldn't be certain.

Unfortunately, she had no photographs to validate the similarities of the assault. The physical style of the lipstick graffiti, the words themselves, the knots used to harness the woman, the type of injuries, the way the woman was positioned, the specifics of her wounds were all disturbingly familiar. And the most puzzling question of all. What had caused her death? She would have to allow her mind to meander through the maze of memory before giving herself permission to validate the similarities.

In her heart, she wanted, badly wanted, the perpetrator to be Farley Lipscomb. With the onrush of memory had come the desire for revenge. Professionally, she knew, this was a dangerous and highly unethical position to take.

But she did allow herself to hope that it might be Farley Lipscomb and to secretly create a scenario in which his aberration had grown more uncontrollable and dangerous with the years. Perhaps, too, a search of data banks would reveal the occurrence of a regional patch of cases with the same MO. In good faith, she assured herself, she could not eliminate Farley Lipscomb as a prime suspect, at least in theory. Could she?

And if he was the perpetrator? Even the possibility was a double-edged sword. First, she needed to find some physical connection, some compelling evidence that linked him with the crime. Only then could she dare reveal what had occurred to her so many years ago, a detail that might compromise the accusation, whatever the evidence. A personal motive was dangerous baggage for a detective to carry. If revealed it could be raw meat for a defense lawyer.

Such a personal confession had negative career ramifications as well. It would mark her as someone who participated in what the police culture would characterize as bizarre sexual practices. She could become the butt of the kind of ridicule that undermined respect and corroded working relationships.

But there was still another wrinkle that filled her with dread. Suppose there was no hard evidence, no connective tissue? Suppose she felt it necessary to confront him directly. She dared not speculate on how such a confrontation would play.

He was no longer Farley Lipscomb, lawyer, but Farley Lipscomb, associate justice of the Supreme Court.

—5—

"Jeez," the Eggplant exclaimed, looking over the pictures of Phyla Herbert's much abused body that were scattered over the surface of his desk. He shook his head and clucked his tongue in a genuine reaction of resignation and despair. "Sick bastard," he wheezed.

"Very," Fiona said, exchanging glances with Prentiss, who nodded her head in agreement.

They were sitting in the Eggplant's office, the dust-laden window behind his desk darkening. Beyond his closed door she could hear the ceaseless ringing of the telephones, blaring out their cacophony of death.

Prentiss sat beside her in one of the chief's mismatched office chairs, her notebook on her lap. Throughout the day, she had been a whirlwind of activity, scribbling furiously in her notebook, her head cocked to one side, her shoulder bracing the phone against her ear.

"Give him the rundown, Gail," Fiona said, turning to Prentiss.

Gail's eyes met hers, somewhat surprised. She had, of course, expected Fiona, as the senior detective in charge of the scene, to make the first report to the chief. But Fiona felt drained. It had taken all her energy to cope with her recollections.

Worse, she feared that she would not have the strength to keep her secret hidden, that some errant word or phrase would spark their suspicion that she was keeping something from them. Above all, she did not want them to know that she was pursuing a private agenda. She had made calls, worked the computer feverishly looking for similar cases in the area.

She had met with some success in ferreting out some similarities but there was always just enough of a difference in modus operandi to reject the possibility of a match. She wondered if she secretly enjoyed these rejections, as if each elimination brought her closer to what she really wanted . . . that the finger of suspicion be pointed directly at Farley Lipscomb.

As if to professionalize the idea, she actually called his office to determine whether or not her suspicion had any merit at all. There was always the possibility that he was on some extended vacation in some distant land, which would knock any presumption of guilt into a cocked hat.

The Supreme Court was in session and Justice Lipscomb was very much in evidence. It was, in fact, only two weeks past the second Monday in October. She did not give the receptionist her name.

"Phyla Herbert," Gail began with a crisp economy of language and presention. "Caucasian, twenty-four years old. Recent graduate of University of Chicago Law School. Apparently a whiz kid. Magna Cum Laude. Phi Beta Kappa. Law Review. Father with a prestigious law firm. Mother died when she was a teenager. She came to town Thursday night for a series of interviews. Met with people Friday at the Justice Department, Interior, the Energy Department. Also had scheduled appointments on Capitol Hill with two Illinois congressmen. Also had interviews set tomorrow and was scheduled to head home on Wednesday."

Gail paused for a moment and looked up, possibly to reassure herself of the chief's full attention, which was quickly confirmed. "Based upon Flannagan's assessment, the victim probably died late Saturday night. The rooms on either side of hers were not booked through the weekend. None of the other guests we managed to track down who were booked into rooms further down the corridor heard any uncommon sounds worth mentioning. She never used room service."

"Flannagan get anything more?" the Eggplant asked.

"Reports should be coming in shortly," Gail said.

"Did we get a modus operandi match?" the Eggplant asked. Gail turned to look at Fiona.

"Nothing of signifance, Captain. A few open cases in southern Virginia, but they are prostitute kills, a completely different formula."

"Next-of-kin notified?"

"Afraid so," Gail sighed. "Always the worst part. The father is flying in from Chicago. I must warn you. He is very angry."

Ignoring the comment, the Eggplant fired a question at Fiona.

"Autopsy results?"

"Coming," Fiona said.

Earlier she had talked to Dr. Benson, whose caseload on this Monday was extraordinary. As she had known, he was going to do the job himself. The Herbert woman and the crime that had destroyed her fit into the category of a "must do" for him. His forensic detective work was an essential first step in bringing the perpetrator of such a crime to justice.

"There's more," Gail said with a sideward glance at Fiona, who nodded her permission.

"The father will be a problem. Apparently he put lots of muscle into arranging his daughter's foray into town. All of the interviews came down from the top. Thomas Herbert, as I've discovered, cuts a wide swath through Washington, official and nonofficial. He's one of those political power brokers, well connected to both parties."

The Eggplant shook his head with disgust.

"That's exactly what we need," the Eggplant said. "More pressure from the top."

"I'm sorry," Gail said. "But I thought you ought to know."

"I appreciate your concern, Officer Prentiss," the Eggplant said, with more resignation that sarcasm. "What other joyful news do you bring?"

Gail, not quite knowning how to interpret his comment, offered a half-smile.

"I spoke briefly to all the people she interviewed with. Just preliminary interviews. Two of the people were women. Strangers. The one at Justice was a man. A young hotshot, Phelps Barker. Father is a physician friend of Mr. Herbert's. He grew up with the victim."

"What was his reaction?"

"Shook up. We're seeing him tomorrow." She looked toward Fiona, who nodded. She felt an acute sense of irony, wondering if all the shoe-leathering and interviewing would, in the end, be merely red herrings, detours on the road to Farley Lipscomb. But one factor was obvious; their investigation would take them hopscotching along the "golden power grid."

At her father's knee, Fiona had learned what was meant by "the golden power grid." They were the connecting links through which the power flowed, not unlike the way electricity was distributed. People who were connected to people who were connected to people who made things happen.

They would be crisscrossing the circuitry that led through connectors of wealth and privilege, through corporations and law firms, country clubs, pockets of society connections, through interlocking political power links. They were all hooked together seamlessly along the grid. The energy generated along this grid pumped out rewards to those who knew the complex circuitry and how to move through it without being electrocuted.

Her father had once been part of it, and although he had finally been cast out of the net, Fiona had continued to maintain a connection to it through her childhood contacts. She was a well-accepted asset on the "A list" Washington social scene, a position she continued to cultivate. In her social circles, her profession was considered more exotic than déclassé, and her subtle knowledge of the grid structure gave her a special cachet.

She also had the means and the venue, her lovely house in prestigious Spring Valley, which she often threw open for a small dinner party or a larger cocktail bash, a necessary ritual to continue her level of acceptance on the social scene.

The Eggplant had no illusions about what he was up against when an investigation spilled into the power grid. Thomas Herbert, Fiona knew, would arrive like a bull in a china shop. Grief and outrage are powerful stimulants and he would use whatever muscle he could muster to light a fire under the investigation, a process that always resulted in more heat than light.

"Theories?" the Eggplant asked, shooting a glance at Fiona, who diverted her eyes momentarily, then forced herself to stand up to the question.

"So far, only the obvious," Fiona said, clearing her throat, trying to keep her voice from wavering. "The woman was probably consensual at first."

She felt Gail's sudden movement, the body language of disagreement. Earlier, she had not found the courage to broach the subject with her partner.

"The man was obviously experienced in this type of sexual behavior." Fiona pointed to a photograph on the Eggplant's desk. "Note the proficiency of the knots that held her extremities. For this type of execution, the woman had to be docile and consenting."

"You think so?" Gail said cautiously. "I would have thought just the opposite."

"It's only a theory, Gail," Fiona said gently. "My guess is that he got her to allow him to immobolize her."

"You mean she allowed this psychopath to put her in this position. Look at the result."

"I don't believe she knew the full extent of what he was doing, where it was leading. Perhaps she had done this with him before." She felt her voice weaken and she coughed to mask the condition.

"My God," Gail said. "Look at those stab wounds."

"Doing that was probably the way he achieved orgasm."

"You don't think there was penetration?" Gail asked. Fiona avoided her gaze.

"We'll have to wait on that for the results of the autopsy," Fiona said.

She wanted to add more, like being certain that the woman's anus had been violated by some mechanical device that had caused bleeding. In her brief, very brief assessment of the body, she had noted the condition, masked by the blood that had cascaded over the body from the stab wounds.

"Why do you reject coercion, Fiona?" Gail asked diplomatically, obviously careful to show the proper humility of a junior. "Isn't it possible that her assailant had a gun or, most certainly, a knife that he would have used to terrorize her and make her do his bidding?"

"Oh, I didn't rule that out completely," Fiona admitted. "There were no obvious signs of a struggle and the neatness of her discarded clothes indicated that she might have taken them off with some care. She did have interviews scheduled for Monday. And from the way her clothes were arranged in the closet, she seemed rather fastidious."

"You have a point," Gail said, without rancor. Fiona could tell that she was not convinced.

"Also, note that the clothes were not exactly casual for a daytime Saturday. A pair of jeans was hanging in the closet, which indicates that Flannagan's eyeball assessment of late Saturday night or early Sunday morning is on the money. She might have met someone or had a prearranged date with someone she had known." Fiona paused, choosing her words carefully, wondering if her subconscious was guiding her along a single path. "Or was a friend of the family."

"Some friend," the Eggplant muttered, his gaze washing over the picture.

Gail shrugged, as if she were unsure whether to challenge any of the assumptions in Fiona's theory. It was, Fiona knew, a deduction based upon her own experience. She had arranged her clothes neatly on the chair beside her when she had been ordered by Farley to undress.

"Do you really believe that someone as intelligent as Phyla Herbert could be talked into being a willing participant in this . . ." Gail began, then broke off the sentence and shook her head. It was obvious that such behavior was not in the range of Gail's experience. Indeed, Fiona realized, Gail would, no doubt, be astonished at the extent of the practice.

"Surely we can't discount that possibility, Gail," Fiona said patiently.

"I suppose we're too early in the game to discount any possibility," Gail replied, but without conviction.

"Are you theorizing that the perpetrator was someone she knew?" the Eggplant asked, obviously taking Fiona's theory with more seriousness than Gail.

"Maybe." She shot Gail a conciliatory glance. "We haven't accounted for all of her contacts, particularly in the evenings. Thursday, Friday or Saturday. Since her father was well connected, she might have attended a dinner or cocktail party thrown by mutual friends or business associates."

Fiona paused, watching Gail's reaction, pondering an idea that had suddenly jumped into her mind. Considering Gail's background, it would take a leap of faith for her to believe that a brilliant and well brought up woman like Phyla Herbert could associate with someone who got his kicks in this manner.

Gail, too, was the daughter of privilege and power. Having lived in Washington most of her life, Fiona was aware of the mores of the black hierarchy that had dominated black society in Washington for more than a hundred years.

This was a group more class conscious and tightly controlled than any society of privilege anywhere. Dominated by their own inter-connections and well-forged old family links, they were elitist, educated and successful. Fiona was certain that Gail had been a debutante in a "coming out" event that was one of the great seasonal traditions of this proud, prestigious, super-achieving and self-segregated group.

It was also a society known for its religious fervor and strict moralistic traditions. Church was part of its culture. It was only natural that Gail might reject the notion that Phyla Herbert knew her assailant. In an odd way Phyla might be, despite the racial difference, one of Gail's crowd.

"I'm not saying it's not possible," Gail said. "Anything is possible." She shook her head. "What you're also saying is that she was predisposed to participate in this disgusting perversion."

"It happens," Fiona said. "We all have our vulnerabilities." Had she gone too far? Was she actually trying to create the impression that there was a kind of normality in such a practice? Perhaps even justify her own past participation?

"I wonder," Gail said, with a smile to take the sting out of her rejection of Fiona's theory.

"When it comes to sex," Fiona said boldly, returning the smile, "people have their dirty little secrets."

Gail shrugged, leaving Fiona with the impression that Gail probably did not have any dirty little sex secrets.

Fiona sensed the Eggplant watching this byplay, his head swiveling from one to the other as if he were watching a tennis match. He was surprisingly quiet and intent.

"We've certainly seen enough of it in this business," he said. "Hard to figure how people get their jollies."

Gail frowned and shrugged and made no comment. But Fiona was not yet willing to let go of the subject.

"On the other hand, if she had just met this person, hadn't known him before, he might have sensed in her such a predisposition," Fiona said.

"You think that's possible?"

"Birds of a feather," Fiona said.

"Out of my realm of experience," Gail admitted. It seemed to signal a kind of retreat.

"There's still other scenarios," Fiona said cautiously, aware of her deliberate manipulation. "Take this one. Phyla is out with some silver-tongued, awesomely important man, who can truly help her career. She's bright, ambitious, perhaps 'All About Eve' ambitious. She consents to go to bed with the man. Maybe is even more aggressive than that. She invites the man to go to bed with her. She consents to go along with his . . . with his brand of kink. It gets out of hand. Voilà."

"I don't know," Gail said, shaking her head. "It seems . . . well . . . considering her education and class . . . culturally out of sync."

There it was, Fiona decided. The heart of Gail's reticence. It was still too early in their relationship to have any real insight about Gail Prentiss. But Fiona felt she had come a long way in only one day. She realized, too, that she would have to be extremely guarded in providing any sisterly revelations, especially of the kind that had been filling her mind all day.

Fiona noted that the Eggplant had nodded his head after Gail had made her point. It was clear that he was deeply impressed by her and Fiona was certain that the racial kinship was a source of pride to him in a father-daughter sort of way. It struck her then that, despite the physical awesomeness of Gail Prentiss, she seemed to radiate a tenderness and warmth that was often absent in upwardly mobile career cops, black or white. It was a surprise to her that the Eggplant's attitude toward her also seemed warmer, as if he felt more comfortable with her than with most women, including Fiona.

Yet despite her own kindly feelings about Gail, Fiona did sense in herself a twinge of jealousy. And regret. What Gail had was inborn and uncontrived, a soothing force embedded in her own nature. Fiona generated heat wherever she alighted. Gail had the gift of relating.

"Perhaps the Herbert woman let ambition rule her better judgment," Fiona speculated further, but without conviction.

"That's a tough one, Fiona," Gail said.

"That's why I'm inclined to stand by consensual," Fiona said, coming back to that again, wondering if she was, in her desire to plant the idea in their minds, overstating.

"I'm not there yet, Fiona," Gail said. In her own way she was as relentless as Fiona.

Fiona tried to appear laid back, as if she had merely voiced casual speculations.

"Sexual perversion is a very complex subject," Fiona said, pushing ahead, like a bulldozer preparing the road before the asphalt was poured. She hoped she had assumed a pedagogic air. "I'm inclined to believe that people who practice specific perversions, in this case, bondage, sadism, masochism or whatever, know enough of the code words to find and communicate with each other."

"Her father may not appreciate that kind of analysis," the Eggplant said. "I would appreciate it, FitzGerald, if you didn't make my life more difficult for me than it is."

"Believe me, Chief," Fiona sighed, "we'll walk on eggshells with the man." She glanced toward Gail, who nodded.

"I'm glad you understand that, Sergeant," the Eggplant said.

"But I'm not ready to deny the theory. Not yet."

Enough, Fiona rebuked herself.

"Just bring me the killer and an airtight case," the Eggplant said, standing up. It was his way of announcing that the meeting was over. "And keep me apprised."

He was remarkably taciturn for a man beset by problems at every turn. Fiona wondered if the pressure of the job was making him lose his edge.

"I still feel she was coerced," Gail said, when they left the Eggplant's office, revealing the obsessive durability of her logic. Fiona decided that it was not the time to totally challenge her thesis. Not yet.

There was a subtext here, Fiona knew. The Eggplant had to be pleased with his decision to pair two women to investigate crimes against women. In this pairing, Fiona suspected that the Eggplant had been more lucky than prescient.

He might have expected bickering, backbiting, hysterics and emotion to surface quickly in such a relationship, maybe even a down-and-dirty cat fight. Perhaps he wanted an example that might offer a vital comment that mirrored his opinion about women in a police setting, especially in the homicide environment.

The fact was that he was getting something exactly opposite to his expectations and he seemed, inexplicably, to be reveling in it, a condition that meant he was on the verge of taking credit for introducing what others might think was a brilliant idea.

Despite their different vantage points, both she and Gail were viewing the crime through the eyes of the victim, which was the object of the exercise. On that score Fiona seemed to have the advantage. After all, she'd been there.

As Fiona expected, Flannagan's tech boys found a plethora of potential "clues" and a sparse collection of latent prints. A place of transiency, like a hotel room, was a difficult place to pinpoint a perpetrator through circumstantial evidence. Remnants of human hair, as well as other signs of successive human occupation, were everywhere.

Then there was the time-and-motion pressure on the tech boys. In the murder capital of the world, they were vastly overworked and it was impossible for anyone in the chain-of-evidence identification process to be as thorough as homicide detectives would have liked.

"I'm afraid there won't be much to go on here," Fiona said, handing the report to Gail. Fiona expressed her disappointment, although it provided yet another addition to her theory. Farley Lipscomb, a former prosecutor in his early days, would have the know-how to be quite scrupulous in removing evidence, wiping down the room carefully to eliminate everything but the most microscopic clues.

"There still might be some latents," Gail said hopefully.

"Long shot," Fiona murmured.

Gail frowned.

"You're giving this man lots of credit," she said, concentrating on studying the photographs of Phyla Herbert's body that she had gathered from the Eggplant's desk. Lost in thought for a long time, she finally raised her eyes from the pictures.

"No way," she sighed.

"No way what?" Fiona asked.

"With respect, Sergeant," Gail began, her yellow-flecked eyes meeting Fiona's.

"I'm a big girl, Gail."

"Your entire theory is based on the idea that the victim was mostly to blame for her own murder."

Fiona did not lower her eyes, perhaps plumbing the depths of Gail Prentiss for whatever vulnerabilities lay inside of her. Finally, she turned away and shrugged.

"It's only a theory," Fiona said again. She could tell that, barring proof positive, Gail would never buy it.

—6—

The following morning Fiona sat in Dr. Benson's office drinking hot black coffee and hoping it would help chase the effects of a sleepless night. Gail Prentiss had gone to the Justice Department to see the person that had interviewed Phyla Herbert. In light of the heavy load of investigative work on the case, they had agreed on dividing up the tasks.

Fiona looked at her watch. It was nine. In less than an hour she would be confronted by Thomas Herbert, who would have to go through the horrifying process of identifying his daughter's body. It would be awful. Gail had promised to return by then and meet her in Dr. Benson's office.

Dr. Benson studied Fiona with his Cajun blue eyes, his long fingers constructing a graceful cathedral, the pinnacle of which was placed just under his chin. He was a handsome man, still on the better side of sixty, with steel gray hair and skin the color of soft beige leather.

She had long ago appointed him her surrogate father and he had led her through the darkness of many an emotional valley. For her part, she was always there for him as well, especially when the numbing and often depressing nature of his job would coincide with recurring bouts of deep grieving for his beloved wife, who had died five years before. In Dr. Benson's case, time was not the vaunted healer it was supposed to be.

Throughout the previous night, she had debated whether or not to tell him about her experience with Farley Lipscomb and her theory that he could be the killer of Phyla Herbert. But every time her imagination reached the brink of revelation, she faltered.

She had no doubt about his reaction. He would be enormously sympathetic, fully understanding of her agony and guilt, totally supportive and reassuring. But she feared that he might not agree with her theory, on the grounds that she was letting personal trauma interfere with her better judgment.

Between them was a deep and enduring father-daughter type of relation-ship, full of love and sharing. She had heard most of his confessions and he had heard most of hers. But there was a point where few humans, however loving, were willing or even capable of transcending.

She could not bring herself to reveal the deep complexities of her sexual nature. It was a subject deliberately evaded between them, which was probably the norm in most relationships between people of different genera-tions and genders. She hadn't even summoned the courage, if that's what it took, to reveal deeply personal sexual secrets to a shrink.

Earlier, she had considered herself cured of any residual bad side effects of her experience with Farley Lipscomb, like the two-year attack of frigidity that had afflicted her during her last two years of college. Last night, however, she had sensed the beginning of a reoccurrence.

As he always did since the beginning of their relationship, Harrison Greenwald had called late in the evening. She had soaked for a long time in a hot bath, normally an excellent stress chaser. It had little effect last night.

For the past six months, they had arranged their time together around Fiona's days off. Harrison's time was more flexible, although his practice was exceedingly busy. Their relationship was both intellectually and sexu-ally satisfying and they derived from each other strong stimulation in both departments. She looked forward to their time together and it was not uncommon for them to spend many hours in bed, as they say, exercising the venery. In fact, talk and sex was their principal and joyful recreation. Nor had the effects worn off even after six months of such a routine.

But last night in their conversation, she sensed a kind of blockage, a pyschological barrier that made her fearful and insecure about their physi-cal relationship. It was exactly the feeling she had endured for those two years after the Farley experience.

"You okay, Fi?" Harrison had asked after their conversation trailed off into long pauses and dead ends.

"Tired," she had sighed.

"Bad day?"

"Awful."

"I can come over and cheer you up."

"Nothing would help."

"Tomorrow then?"

The thought of sexual congress induced an uncommon sense of disgust. The old symptoms were recognizable. Years ago it had begun in just that way, a vague sense of disgust, like imagining rancid food, which took away the appetite.

"I need my space this week, Harrison," Fiona said. Harrison was a sensitive man and she knew he would react.

"I thought I was part of your space, Fi."

"You are, darling," she replied, but even she could hear the tentative note in her voice. "I'm just discombobulated." She deliberately used the odd slang, hoping to lighten the atmosphere between them.

"I surrender." He hesitated. "Then when?"

"I'll call you."

For him it would be another sour note. As she expected, there was a long pause between them.

"Fi, you sound ominous."

"I'm just in a foul mood, darling. It has nothing to do with you. Really it doesn't."

"Are you sure?"

"Of course I'm sure," she said firmly. It was the kind of repetitive dead-end conversations that they both detested.

Another long pause.

"You just sound so . . . so cold," Harrison said.

"Oddly enough, I feel cold," she said, shivering lightly as she did so. "I need . . . I need . . . a little patience, darling. It will pass. I promise."

Hadn't it passed before? she asked herself.

The conversation ended, certainly for Harrison, on a note of confusion. For her it was frightening. Remembering her two-year ice age experience, she recalled the agony of isolation. She had tried combating the frigidity, but she froze at the mere touch of male flesh. Desire had simply disappeared. There were none of the usual symptoms of arousal. Her genitalia seemed irrelevant, burdensome. She could not dare to look at herself naked. Her fantasy life, once rich, varied and sexually exciting, disappeared. The curtain had come down on sensuality.

Nor were there any compensating feelings. Even her taste buds seemed to lose power. A kind of indifference invaded all of her senses. Sights and sounds lost contrast, became dull and uninteresting.

Her body's lack of normal reactions deeply affected her attitude toward others. She withdrew from social contact, became morose and perpetually depressed. She endured, coped, but did not seek professional help. Perhaps it was a legacy from her father, the determination to go it alone, faith in the power of the mind to work out personal solutions. Or pure Irish stubbornness.

In the end, she was able to tell herself that she had risen above the trauma. She had begun to feel herself heal, slowly at first, then rapidly. Fantasy began again just below the surface of consciousness. She began to rationalize her actions, blaming herself less. She had simply stumbled into harm's way. Her limits had been tested. Out of this tunnel of despair, she had emerged, certainly wiser and with a lot better understanding of the sexual minefields.

How could she possibly discuss this with Dr. Benson? All night, tossing in her bed, she had concocted scenarios of confession. They did not survive the light of day.

"Are you happy with your new partner?" Dr. Benson asked.

"I like her a lot," Fiona replied. "Very bright. A wonderful specimen of a black woman, bigger than life." Fiona paused. Interspersed between her agonizing last night she had thought a great deal about Gail Prentiss. All her life she had searched for a true female friend.

"And very traditional," she said, which seemed to weaken the case to make Gail that kind of a friend.

Dr. Benson nodded.

"She adores her father, a man of awesome dignity, tall and straight as an oak. He hasn't got long, poor fellow. Aside from his skill as a surgeon he is a man who worships traditional values. He is very wise, impeccable in his moral stance, the kind of person who commands respect and is sought after for advice."

"Gail too has that kind of a persona," Fiona agreed.

Like you as well, Fiona wanted to say. But Dr. Benson abhorred flattery.

Fiona looked at her watch.

"I think we better get on with it. Mr. Herbert will be here soon."

"Awful," Dr. Benson said, shaking his head, but continuing to keep his finger cathedral intact.

"Her anus was violated with a large blunt instrument. There are signs of trauma everywhere in that organ."

Bingo, Fiona told herself. Not that she needed confirmation.

"I'd put her death at sometime Saturday afternoon."

"Afternoon?"

"You look surprised."

"Flannagan figured later in the evening or early Sunday morning."

"Flannagan is wrong."

It flashed through her mind that her "episode" with Farley Lipscomb also occurred in the afternoon.

"Any evidence of semen?"

"Oddly enough, no. And there is no sign of intercourse."

"Any evidence of struggle?"

"Yes. Some."

Dr. Benson became thoughtful for a moment, then destroyed his finger cathedral, put on his half-glasses and looked at a paper on his desk.

"There were thirty-one stab wounds on the front portion of her body." He shook his head and took off his glasses. "They were messy but they weren't deep. I'd say a Swiss Army knife, a size larger than a pen knife. Actually there were two neat slices on the carotid artery, slices, not stab wounds. Very strange."

"Strange?"

"They were made after the woman was dead," Dr. Benson said.

"Really."

She was shocked and for a moment wondered if this discovery would shake her theory.

"Not very long after death," Dr. Benson said. "A kind of after-thought."

She pondered the idea silently for a long moment.

"What was the immediate cause of death?"

"Oh. How could I have neglected the most important fact? I'd say the cause of death was asphyxiation."

"The gag in her mouth?"

"More than that. I'm speculating now, but I believe that the gag contributed to blocking her air passages, when she needed them most. I'd have to check her medical history, but I'd say if you're looking for a cause of death, the principal culprit could well have been an asthma attack."

"Are you positive?"

It was, Fiona knew, a kneejerk reaction. Dr. Benson was rarely wrong.

"About seventy-five percent of the way. It was obvious that the pain must have been excruciating. But I think she went fast, perhaps just as she was intensifying her struggle to be released."

"You think the attack was brought on by the . . . the situation?"

"Sometimes these things can't be pinpointed. Certainly the placement of the gag in her mouth contributed. But we can't be sure. An air passage was blocked. Asthma is an affliction that results in blocked air passages. Ergo . . ."

"A chicken-and-egg situation. Which came first, the gag or the attack? It does rule out first-degree murder."

"Afraid so, Fiona," Dr. Benson sighed. "Too bad. This person committed a most beastly act." He paused, remade his finger cathedral and leaned back on his chair.

"Then, seeing that she was dead, he stabbed her a number of times, which created the mess we saw in the pictures."

"At least the poor child did not suffer the pain of the stabbings."

"Do you think he believed that you would not be able to tell the difference between bloodletting before and after death?"

"Maybe. Sometimes in the press of business, you can't vouch for the thoroughness of your colleagues. We are understaffed and this is the worst murder epidemic in the history of Washington."

Fiona's mind turned over possibilities. Faced with this sudden unplanned death, a man like Farley would have to think things through. Aside from removing all clues, he would have to create a situation that might indicate an unhinged mind, a serial killing, something bizarre and brutal enough to indicate a psychopath, a condition he surely rejected in himself. He would, therefore, want the crime to look like a slaughter perpetrated by someone with a deranged mind.

"One thing is certain," Dr. Benson said. "The man was apparently not a classic necrophiliac. The woman's anus was damaged when she was alive. And the absence of semen indicates that he did not ejaculate in the woman's vagina, which someone of this abnormality might do. My own view is that he was quite clever and wanted the situation to look as if it was perpetrated by a madman."

"I agree," Fiona said, not willing to reveal that she was far ahead of him on that point.

These new facts seemed to validate her consensual theory, but they were hardly compelling enough to accuse Farley Lipscomb. Other men could also be clever. The woman had, in fact, died by what could be characterized as an accident. He was gambling on forensic inefficiency, hoping that his attempt at cover-up would go unnoticed.

"Gail thinks the woman was coerced into participating in his little charade," Fiona said, fishing for further support for her theory.

"Could be," Dr. Benson said thoughtfully.

"You said there was little evidence of struggle."

"I said some evidence, but not enough to show a battle to the end. Which means the woman could have died when the pain reached an unbearable level. An oversized instrument was put into an organ that could not properly expand to receive it without inflicting terrible pain." He shrugged. "I seriously doubt there are people who look forward to that happening." She caught the contempt in his tone. "This woman was deliberately brutalized. She could not have consented to that."

"I'm afraid we're in a business, Doctor, where normality is not the norm."

"Well put, Fiona," Dr. Benson said. "But sex crimes, as we both know, are a real anomaly. The pursuit of pleasure is always a secondary consideration."

"In the case of this kind of act," Fiona said cautiously, "it's about power."

"Probably so," Dr. Benson said. "I'm not an expert in this type of . . ." His voice droned off.

"I've done some research, Doctor," Fiona said after a long pause. "It is mostly theatrics. A game of trust, where inflicting harm is not the object."

"Yes, harm," Dr. Benson said. "But often harm has a different meaning to different people. It apparently was different in this case. The woman, if she hadn't died, would have suffered mightily from injuries inflicted by the perpetrator."

"Yes," Fiona agreed, remembering her own situation. "The person who did this must have enjoyed the spectacle of seeing the woman suffer."

Dr. Benson looked up from his finger cathedral and shook his head.

"I'm afraid I'm from the old school of morality. Sex is a mystery and a wonder, something beautiful. To transform it through these ugly practices, is, for me, beyond the pale." He looked at her curiously and she averted her eyes.

The conversation was getting personal and she felt the need to turn its focus back to the victim.

"In my view, I go all the way on her consenting," Fiona said. What she needed most was an unquestioning ally against Gail's arguments.

"How can you be so sure? Just because there weren't conclusive signs of total resistance."

It wasn't the kind of support she was looking for.

"As you say it may be beyond the pale, but these practices do exist. It does happen. A young impressionable woman could be . . . well . . . might be . . . persuaded by someone experienced in the technique of this kind of seduction." Who was she trying to convince, she asked herself?

"Now there's an area far beyond my expertise," Dr. Benson said. "I can only interpret what the body tells me. In this case the body tells me that it was the recipient of great pain."

"Obviously, she could not have expected things to go that far . . ." Fiona sucked in a deep breath. She decided it was time to retreat. "Anyway it's only a hunch."

"An educated hunch by an experienced detective is no small thing," Dr. Benson said, smiling.

They talked for a while longer, with Dr. Benson's calls becoming increasingly persistent. One of them announced Thomas Herbert's arrival.

"I hate this," Fiona said as she took her leave. He stood up and kissed her cheek.

"Good luck," he said.

Thomas Herbert was a man who looked and breathed success. Even deep grieving could not erase the impression that he was a man used to authority and power. Fiona introduced herself and he took her hand perfunctorily. His flesh felt cold.

"I can't believe this," he said, keeping stride with Fiona as they followed an attendant to the body vaults. "I hope I can handle it, Sergeant."

Before they reached the swinging stainless steel doors, Gail came up to them, slightly out of breath.

"Sorry, Fiona. The traffic."

Fiona introduced Gail to Herbert, who, despite his preoccupation, took the time to inspect her. Gail simply could not be ignored.

Walking into the room, which smelled strongly of the pungent chemicals used to mask the odor of death, they followed the black male attendant to a body drawer along the wall. The attendant, without the slightest hesitation, pulled it open.

"Oh God," Herbert gasped as he saw the sculpted face of his dead daughter. He staggered for a moment, then, with an obvious effort of will, found some semblance of control.

The ivory-smooth face of Phyla Herbert looked composed, almost serene. Dr. Benson had seen to that.

"Beyond belief," Herbert muttered, clearing his throat to stifle a sob. He put out his hand and touched her face.

"My baby," he whispered, tears brimming in his eyes.

Fiona felt a lump begin in her throat. She glanced toward Gail, who shrugged with resignation and turned away. The black attendant was properly somber but indifferent. He had been through the drill countless times before.

Fiona felt the man's pain. It did not take much of a leap of faith to imagine her father in that role if events had taken the wrong turn years ago. The attendant glanced toward Fiona, who nodded, and he closed the drawer.

Herbert wiped his eyes, took a deep breath, then turned away and walked with them out of the room. Fiona led him to a small office set aside specifically for the aftermath of these trying circumstances. There was a battered desk in a corner and some scattered mismatched wooden chairs.

Herbert slumped in a chair, avoiding their eyes, obviously trying to collect his thoughts. His ashen face was now flushed and droplets of perspiration had appeared on his upper lip. Fiona had been through this routine many times before. Unfortunately, repetition did not lessen the effect on her emotions.

"We've got to get this bastard," Herbert said suddenly after a long pause, his lips trembling.

"We will, Mr. Herbert," Fiona said. Herbert slowly lifted his eyes and looked at them both as if for the first time.

"Frankly," he said with evident scorn, "I'm not very optimistic."

"I don't understand," Fiona replied. Of course, she understood. The reputation of the Washington MPD had suffered mightily in the last few years. Judging from closing ratios, the department seemed a model of incompetence, which it wasn't. Actually, the closing ratio on mystery murders, such as this one, was pretty much in line with other cities. But the gang and drug-related killings, unfortunately, were not as easily closed and they pulled down the percentages.

Fiona was determined not to debate this point with Herbert. His mental state made rational argument impossible. Besides, the prevailing mood everywhere was a general cynicism about the police. In this case, the essential point of the moment was to get Herbert to cooperate with their investigation.

"I'm going to see to it that not a stone is unturned to find the sick bastard who did this," he said, staring at both of them with obvious contempt. It was not uncommon, Fiona knew, for a victim's relative to direct his anger and frustration toward the police. At this point any attempt to defend their position would only make things worse.

"First, I'm going back to Chicago tomorrow to bury my little girl," Herbert said. "Then I'm coming back here and I don't intend to leave this town until justice is done."

"Which is exactly our intention, Mr. Herbert," Fiona said.

"Is it really?" Herbert asked.

Fiona ignored the sarcasm. Nothing, she knew, could placate the man while he was in this state.

"Now let's start from the beginning," Herbert said. Fiona and Gail exchanged glances. The man was putting himself in charge of the investigation. Still, Fiona decided, it was not the time to challenge him. Obviously, he was a man used to being the boss and manipulating others.

"The beginning?" Fiona asked. It was more of a reflex than a question. Where, indeed, was the beginning, she wondered, instantly sorry that she uttered the remark. She could see that he had interpreted it as a display of bad attitude.

"Let me say at the onset"—his glance played between Fiona and Gail— "I have been a United States Attorney and have turned down numerous opportunities to be on the federal bench. I have both prosecuted and defended criminals. My firm is one of the most prestigious in the United States. I am the managing partner of my firm, which employs two hundred and seventy-eight lawyers. Moreover, I am intimately acquainted with many of the most powerful figures in this town. I have the clout to make things happen here and, I warn you in advance, I will go to the ends of the earth to find the bastard who did this thing to my daughter. Do you get my drift?"

His drift was inescapable. Fiona was feeling less and less sympathy for the man and more and more for the Eggplant. The Chief would have to react to the man's pressures and there was no doubt in Fiona's mind that Herbert could muster the muscle to make the Eggplant sweat and the department dance.

"Do you understand, girls?" Herbert hissed.

By then, Fiona surmised, he would test her level of tolerance, but she also knew that she would have to tread carefully. The ace card she held, his daughter's possible compliance, could be frittered away by a bungled effort on her part. Worse, she had to continue to hide her suspicions about Justice Lipscomb. If her first theory held, Herbert would be mortified. If her second, a long shot, proved correct, Herbert would be shocked into stupefaction.

Even the revelations of such suspicions without absolute proof would have negative implications. For him, whether proven or not, it would be a no-win situation. Deep conflict lay just ahead.

"We girls do understand, Mr. Herbert," Fiona said, ignoring his deliberate put-down but unable to resist a dollop of vitriol.

"Good. Now." He paused. Her remark seemed to sail harmlessly over his head. "Are there any leads?"

"None yet," Fiona replied, going along.

"Any hard evidence? Latents? Clues? Have the lab boys finished their work?"

"Nearly," Fiona replied. "But they're still plugging along."

"You mean they have nothing?" Herbert demanded.

"Not so far."

"Not so far. Not so far." Herbert slapped his thighs with his fists. "I can foresee what I'll be getting around here. Not so far. That will be the operative phrase. Not so far." He suddenly shot a glance at Fiona.

"I want the best people on this job. Do you understand? The best."

"Is your implication that you're dealing with less than that, Mr. Herbert?" Fiona inquired pointedly.

"I think I'd like a little more experience brought to bear," Herbert said.

"I see," Fiona said nodding her head. It seemed, at this moment, futile to defend themselves. Again she exchanged glances with Gail, who returned a look of unqualified support.

"And please. Don't lay any of that gender bullshit on me. A female detective might do wonders on television, but I'd like to have someone on this case with years of experience in dealing with crimes of this nature."

"You mean an all-male team?" Fiona said.

"I didn't say that," Herbert replied, backpedaling. Fiona was having a progressively difficult time trying to make allowances for his grief.

"I think perhaps I should consult the Chief," Fiona said.

Herbert looked at his watch.

"I'm certain he has been consulted already." So he had lost no time in putting his muscle to work, Fiona suspected. He was already calling in his political chits. Poor Eggplant, Fiona thought. She looked toward Gail and raised her eyes. Prentiss nodded her understanding.

"One thing is certain. We're going to get the man who murdered my daughter."

At that moment, the Eggplant walked in the door. He looked harassed and angry as his eyes roamed the room. Of all the places in the world he would have liked to have been at this moment, this one was, obviously, at the bottom of the list. Fiona knew exactly what had happened. The mayor had been leaned on by members of the Illinois congressional delegation.

"This is Thomas Herbert, Phyla Herbert's father. Mr. Herbert, Captain Luther Greene."

The men shook hands and the Eggplant, in a defensive gesture deliberately assumed the most authoritative seat in the room, behind the battered desk. Neither of the men made any effort to be ingratiating to the other.

"We're pushing every button," the Eggplant began.

"That's not what I've been getting from your girls," Herbert sneered.

Girls? Hold off, Fiona urged the Eggplant silently. In a white man, she would have read the reaction on his skin. With the Eggplant, his eyes told the story. Behind the facade of his official persona, he was fuming. He appeared to have picked up her silent message. Besides, he had learned the hard way all about acceptable feminist nomenclature.

"Have we got the pathologist's report, FitzGerald?" the Eggplant asked.

"I have a verbal report, Captain," Fiona said crisply. She was about to take Mr. Herbert on his first tour of the minefield he insisted on traversing. "And these pictures."

She had carried the set of pictures in a manila envelope in her pocketbook. She slipped them out of the envelope and reverse rolled them to flatten them.

"Would you care to look at them, Mr. Herbert?" the Eggplant asked politely. He shot Fiona a glance of approval.

"Of course," Herbert replied.

"I must warn you," the Eggplant began.

"Warning noted," Herbert shot back arrogantly.

He took a pair of gold folding glasses from his jacket pocket, slipped them from the leather case, opened them and placed them carefully on his nose. With shaking hands, he picked up the pictures. His reaction was instantaneous.

"I'm sorry," the Eggplant said. "They're not pretty."

Swallowing hard, beads of perspiration popping on his forehead, Herbert tried to hold himself together as he forced himself to look at the pictures. The flush on his face disappeared and his pallor indicated that he might be ready to keel over.

"I'll get some water," Gail said, rushing out of the office. Herbert sighed, shook his head and gave the pictures back to Fiona. A nerve had begun to palpitate in his jaw and his nostrils flared as he drew in air. Somehow he managed to pull himself together, and by the time Gail arrived with the water, he was almost under control, although his hands continued to shake as he held his glass and drank the water.

"I want to assure you, Mr. Herbert, that we're moving as fast as we can . . ."

"But you've got nothing. Not so far . . ." His display of vulnerability did not seem to make him less contentious, He cut a contemptuous glance at the Eggplant. "I won't sit still for that, Captain."

"I understand, Mr. Herbert. But you've got to realize . . ."

"That these things take time, right? Well, here are the questions I'm asking and you know I've got the right and the clout to do so . . ."

The Eggplant nodded. He was showing amazing patience.

"The first question is"—he glanced toward Fiona—"are we giving this a full-court press?"

"Of course," the Eggplant replied with exactly the right amount of muted indignation. "These detectives are part of a special team assigned to investigate crimes against women. Our belief is . . ."

"I'm sorry, Captain. I don't buy it. Murder has little to do with gender. I want the best and most experienced. Excellence is the only criteria that works for me. I don't care about race or gender or religion. Are they the best?"

The Eggplant turned toward Fiona and Gail.

"For this case, yes. They are the best."

Fiona felt a shiver of emotion. She was proud of him.

"I don't agree. I would like you to reassess their assignment."

Fighting words, Fiona thought. It was time to throw a handful of salt on the man's open wound. In her judgment, he had gone too far.

"The chief medical examiner, Dr. Benson," Fiona began, turning toward Herbert. "His forensic report shows that the immediate cause of death was an asthma attack."

Herbert flushed.

"An asthma attack!" he shouted.

Gail looked startled. The Eggplant stiffened in his chair. Herbert seemed to fulminate with rage.

"You must need a new medical examiner," Herbert muttered with anger. "I've just seen those pictures. Multiple stab wounds. Do you people think you can get away with that?"

"According to Dr. Benson, the wounds were administered after her death, Mr. Herbert," Fiona said calmly.

"I smell either incompetence or cover-up here," Herbert sneered, raising his voice. "I can assure you, I won't take this. I demand another autopsy. Whoever did this one is obviously incompetent, inexperienced or deliberately malicious. In fact, I will get my own pathologist. You people are amateur night. This is an investigation of my daughter's murder. What is going on here? I demand a reevaluation of this."

He was unhinged and raving and there was no way to calm him. Nevertheless his accusations demanded a response.

"The medical examiner," Fiona began—she was angry now and showed it—"a man of irrefutable competence and experience, did the autopsy himself. He has rarely, if ever, been wrong. If he says that the cause of death was an asthma attack, you can bank on it."

Her firm defense, while not mollifying the man, made him hesitate.

"The stab wounds are obviously the perpetrator's reaction to her sudden death," the Eggplant said, quickly offering his own interpretation. He, too, must have been shocked by the revelation. "His action was, it seems to me, an attempt at cover-up . . . a deliberate action to make the crime look like the work of a . . . an unbalanced pervert."

"A very convenient explanation, Captain," Herbert sneered. He seemed to be winding up for another diatribe against the homicide division. Again Fiona was moved to action.

"Did she suffer from asthma, Mr. Herbert?" Fiona snapped.

Herbert glared at her.

"I don't agree with this conclusion," he said.

"Did she have a history of asthma?" Fiona persisted.

"Why don't you ask your wonderful pathologist?" Herbert sneered. "Besides, if you know the answer, why ask me?"

He was growing exceedingly uncomfortable, fidgeting in his chair, his hands clasping and unclasping.

"I'm going to have my own pathologist examine her. Somebody in Chicago that I can trust . . ." His voice trailed off as if he needed time to compose himself. "Yes. She was an asthmatic. But she had just about outgrown it. She had only one attack in the last three years."

"Two attacks, Mr. Herbert," Fiona reminded him.

"Probably brought on by what she was going through," Gail interjected, breaking her silence, her pity for the man obviously aroused.

"Either way," Herbert said sarcastically, "she was obviously raped and murdered . . ."

Fiona felt moved to reply, but a signal from the Eggplant silenced her.

"You have a point, Mr. Herbert," the Eggplant said. He stood up and looked directly at Fiona. "Would you excuse us for a moment, Mr. Herbert?"

Whatever had been on Herbert's mind seemed to evaporate with the Eggplant's request. Perhaps Herbert was assuming that the Eggplant was acting to relieve Fiona of the case. In any event, he acquiesced without protest.

"Officer Prentiss will stay here with you," the Eggplant said, nodding to Gail.

In the corridor, the Eggplant moved out of earshot to an alcove where there was a soda machine. He fished in his pocket for bills and placed one in the changemaker.

"Coke?"

She shook her head. He watched as the machine rumbled and offered up its can of Coke. It opened with a hiss and he immediately swallowed half its contents.

"Don't do it, FitzGerald," he said, wiping his mouth with the back of his hand.

"Don't do what?" She was genuinely puzzled.

"Tell him your theory."

Which one? she wondered.

"This is not the time to tell him that his daughter was a willing participant."

"I hadn't intended to," she told him. "I was merely going to mention that she had not been penetrated, that no semen was found and that she had been attacked in the anus with an oversized dildo."

"Christ," the Eggplant said, blowing out a deep gust of breath. "It'll make him crazy. He's already stirred up a storm and the *Post* has played it up on the front of the Metro section. I've been fielding media questions all morning." He finished the remainder of the can, crushed it between strong fingers and threw it into the nearby receptacle. "I'm getting too old for this," he muttered.

"Maybe that was her sex thing and he knows it," Fiona speculated.

"I doubt it. In any event, don't expect him to confirm it."

"That's why I kept my big mouth shut."

"I'd rather he read the report," the Eggplant said. "He's already down on Benson's opinion. Let's not stir him up any more than we've done already."

"He had it coming."

"I don't disagree."

"I know. You feel sorry for the bastard."

The Eggplant looked down at his hands.

"There you go showing me that compassionate streak again, Chief. Don't worry, I won't blow your image."

The Eggplant shook his head and smiled. Fiona shrugged away any more sentiment and they started back to the office where Gail and Herbert

were waiting. Before the Eggplant opened the door, he paused and studied
Fiona's face.

"You really believe she was consensual?"

"Yes," she said firmly, convinced by her own experience, instinct and
Benson's findings.

The Eggplant sighed and shook his head.

"He does have the clout to make us dance, FitzGerald."

"When I saw you come through that door, I made that assumption."

"I take him at his word. He's going to make a parallel investigation
through his own sources. And he's going to try and get you and Prentiss
off the case."

"If you want, we'll go quietly," Fiona said.

"You've never done anything quietly, FitzGerald. You think I want a
gender discrimination case in my face?"

"Hell, you said in front of witnesses that we were the best. We'd win
hands down."

He chuckled as he pushed open the door.

What struck her immediately was the way in which Herbert and Gail
were positioned. They were still sitting in their respective chairs, but they
had moved closer to each other, their knees almost touching. As a good
judge of body language, Fiona speculated that Gail was in the process of
charming the man, winning his confidence, doing the good-cop waltz.

"I was explaining to Mr. Herbert the theory behind the Captain's pairing
us, the motivation behind the arrangement."

"Officer Prentiss has, at least, put it in perspective," Herbert said grudg-
ingly. He gave Gail a benign kindly nod. He turned to look at Fiona. "She
gave me a little background on you as well, Sergeant. I knew your father
when I was a young Assistant U.S. Attorney."

So that was it, Fiona thought. Gail had used the time for a bit of name-
dropping to a man to whom clout, big names and connections meant
everything. Fiona shot an unseen wink in Gail's direction. She was slowly
putting the pin back in his grenade.

"We were out there arranging for you to have a copy of the autopsy
report, Mr. Herbert," the Eggplant said. He, too, was apparently relieved
by the environmental change.

"I still intend to enhance this investigation."

"And don't think we aren't appreciative," the Eggplant said. "We need all the help we can get. Believe me, Mr. Herbert, we're determined to find this monster."

"We'll keep you totally informed," Gail said, determining that she had gotten permission to embellish the point. "And we'll cooperate with you and anyone of your choice."

Herbert seemed afflicted with a sudden attack of exhaustion. He was done in, spent. Fiona suspected that he was the kind of man who would devote himself body and soul to bring his daughter's assailant to justice. It was easy to see that his daughter was everything to him. Her death had kicked the props of his life out from under him. Finding the person who had done this to his daughter would now take over his life. It was, Fiona suspected, his way of coping with grief.

For the moment, the fight was out of him. He was facing the reality of what must be done in the next few days, the trip back home, the arrangements, the funeral, the reality of loss. They set up a time and place to meet three days hence.

"I'm sure by then we'll have something to sink our teeth into, Mr. Herbert," the Eggplant said.

Herbert grunted acknowledgment. But it was to Gail, just as he left the office, that he directed his most cogent remark.

"You cannot believe how much she meant to me," he said. His eyes moistened. Grief took charge of him. He left the room and closed the door quietly behind him.

—7—

Phelps Barker was preppy down to his socks, which were yellow with a pattern that struck Fiona as something she had seen on fraternity theme ties. He also wore red suspenders and a striped tie on a buttoned-down oxford blue shirt of the kind purveyed by Brooks Brothers for wannabe men seeking power and influence. He was as transparent as unpolluted air.

With jet black hair, perfectly parted, a straight nose and strong clefted chin, he wore his assured future with an arrogant smirk.

A perennial fraternity boy, Fiona decided, an eager participant at chug-a-lug and a heavy advertiser of his sexual exploits, mostly exaggerated. Her own memories of fraternity boys were of beer-smelling breath and premature ejaculations.

They were sitting in the leather-and-walnut atmosphere of the Federal Club, which had been Barker's choice for their meeting. Perhaps the buttoned-down golden boy wanted to lavish a bit of intimidation on the blue-collar wage earners. This was the attitude Fiona brought into the club. She was not in a good mood.

After waving them to their seats, Barker snapped his fingers at a liveried waiter, who reacted swiftly to the signal.

"They make lovely whiskey sours here, don't they, Walter?"

"For the ladies?" Walter asked.

"Coffee would be fine," Fiona said.

"Same for me," Gail said.

"And one whiskey sour for Mr. Barker."

"You got it Walter."

Walter scurried off.

They had spent the day retracing Phyla's steps in the hours before her death, interviewing the people noted in her date book.

71

Both the female lawyers at Energy and Interior had similar reactions to the young woman. Phyla was bright, charming and self-confident and both woman had, independently, come to the conclusion that Phyla was interviewing them, not the other way around.

"Everything came down from the top," Chelsea Adams said. In her mid-thirties, blonde and freckled, with green eyes and acne covered by makeup, she was with the enforcement division of the Energy Department. Fiona pegged her as a once wide-eyed do-gooder who had come to this place to clean up the planet only to find little interest in serving that cause among the bureaucrats who ran the agency.

"I'm not saying she wasn't qualified. She had it all, great marks, personality, all the right credentials. Above all, she had juice. We had the impression we had to receive her like royalty."

Of course, Chelsea Adams was resentful. She was Brooklyn Law School. She needed the job. Once she had cared. Now she was a cynic, although there was a visible reservoir of decency and compassion.

"Did I like her? Yes, I liked her. Was she qualified? Yes, she was qualified. In the end, I think she spotted both the futility of trying to make a name in this place and the fact that this is not the best career stepping-stone in town, which is what she was after."

The woman's knowledge about what had happened to Phyla came from stories in the Washington *Post*, which, thankfully, were hardly as complete or as graphic as the real truth. The paper had said that Phyla had been trussed and stabbed numberous times by a sadistic pervert. It did not mention the trauma of the dildo.

"Since I read the story, I haven't been able to sleep. Wasn't it awful? I hope you get him."

They heard substantially the same story from Jane Braker at Interior. The clout from the top, the feeling of being interviewed, the sense that Phyla did not think that Interior, like Energy, was upwardly mobile enough.

"What exactly do you mean by 'clout from the top'?" Fiona asked.

"I presume the Secretary. That's what my boss got from his boss."

Fiona let it pass. What she was really hoping for was a credible link with Farley Lipscomb, a doubtful possibility at best. The clout from the top obviously came from Phyla's father.

"What kind of a job do you think she was interested in?"

"Not here. That's for sure."

"Then where?" Fiona had pressed.

The woman shrugged.

"Probably Justice. Maybe tax work. That's where the big money is, once you serve your time."

"U.S. Attorney's office, maybe?" Gail coaxed.

"Only if she could stay in Washington. She wasn't interested in the boonies."

"How about the U.S. Supreme Court, clerking for one of the justices?" Fiona asked, hoping the inquiry was taken as casual.

"Does Famous Amos make chocolate chip cookies? Now there's a stepping-stone."

Neither of the women lawyers knew Phyla Herbert before meeting her that day. Both expressed similar views and both would have recommended her for hiring if she was interested.

Phelps Barker provided a more personal vantage point. He knew Phyla, as he put it, "forever." They grew up together in Winnetka. Barker's father was a prominent physician who served the wealthy clientele of Winnetka, the Herberts included. It was Dr. Barker who attended Phyla's mother during her terminal illness. Throat cancer, he averred, with a shrug.

"Too much booze and 'backy," he said, lifting the whiskey sour that Walter had served and sipping it with delight.

"You don't know what you're missing," he said, winking.

He was cocky, full of himself, with the kind of flashy, white-toothed smile most people call "winning." He could not take his eyes off Gail Prentiss, a not uncommon reaction.

"Would you characterize your meeting with her as business or social?" Fiona asked. Barker tore his gaze from Gail and, with obvious reluctance, shifted his eyes toward her.

"A little of both. She was a buddy." He shook his head. "God, I can't believe it. Multiple stab wounds. Was she raped?"

"Why do you ask?"

"It seems a logical question. I mean that's the obvious conclusion, isn't it?"

He showed some discomfort when Fiona deliberately didn't answer his question, studying his face.

"Was she interested in a job at Justice?" Gail asked. Showing relief, he eagerly turned toward her, flashing a smile.

"I can't say for sure. With Mr. Herbert's connections she could get any job without sweat. Her principal concern was where it could lead. Smart girl."

"And where does it lead?" Gail asked.

"Why do you think we come here, or haven't you heard? This is an obligatory hitch for a lawyer on his way up. We're here for contacts, connections. Government service is strictly a resume enhancement."

"Did Phyla need that?" Fiona asked.

"Hell no. There was an open door in her father's firm. Do you happen to know how powerful that firm is? You know how many lawyers they have?"

"I've heard," Fiona said.

"You think the government is run by the people?" Barker sneered. "It's run by the big law firms. Wake up, America."

"You sound contemptuous," Fiona said.

"Contemptuous? That's the problem with you people. No insight. I lust for success, meaning money, maybe power. For that, I'll do almost anything. The game plan calls for three years max at Justice, then into the trough."

"Is this what she was after?" Gail asked.

"Who knows? Maybe. She had things to prove to Daddy."

"And herself," Gail snapped.

"That, too," he acknowledged.

Fiona felt herself deliberately holding back, waiting for that particular moment when her own questions would have their greatest impact.

"Did she say anything to indicate she wanted a job at Justice?" Gail asked.

"Actually no," Barker said. "Now that you mention it."

"Did she give you any idea where she would prefer to work?" Fiona interjected, seeing her opening.

"Not really."

"She didn't say that she wanted to work in Washington?" Fiona pressed, looking for the link.

"I don't think she said," Barker said, showing some surprise at Fiona's pursuit. "Hell, that's why she was here. Wasn't it? I suppose she had other meetings arranged."

"Did she say with whom?"

"No. But then Phyla is . . . was . . . very tightly strung. There was no way inside."

"Did she offer the slightest hint of where she wanted to work?"

"I can't recall."

Peripherally, Fiona could see Gail register a restless flash of impatience. She had to be confused by Fiona's oddly meandering and oblique questions. Nevertheless, she pressed on.

"Any other agency?"

"I told you. She didn't say."

"What about . . ." Fiona hesitated a moment, an action she regretted since it gave what she had in mind more importance than she wished. "What about the Supreme Court?"

"What about it?" Barker said, confused but curious.

"You know . . . a clerkship to one of the justices?"

Again, she sensed Gail's restlessness.

"You're really pushing, Sarge," Barker said, exchanging a glance with Gail and taking another sip of his sour.

"Just routine inquiries, Mr. Barker," Fiona said. "By the way, how do you rate that as an upwardly mobile situation for a young lawyer fresh out of law school?"

"A clerkship to a justice?"

Fiona nodded and Barker grew thoughtful.

"On a scale of one to ten, I'd give it an eleven."

"You think she had a chance for that?" Fiona asked.

"With Daddy's help, probably a damned good chance."

"Was he close to any of the justices?"

"I don't know, but I wouldn't be surprised."

"She never said?"

Barker shook his head.

"Phyla wouldn't have said. It was a given. Daddy knows everybody. I'd say she wanted to make it on her own."

"That would be difficult . . . I mean, getting a job working for a justice without Daddy's help?" Fiona pressed, sensing she was going too far down that path, but unable to stop.

"Oh, she had the stuff. But for a job like that you need a direct connection."

"Like being buddy-buddy with a justice?"

"Do I have to tell you how the system works?"

He snickered and winked at Gail, who seemed a confused spectator, watching a game she didn't understand.

"And she herself never mentioned any direct connection with the Court, with a justice?"

"No. I'd remember." He paused and studied Fiona's face. "You seem to be working on a single track."

Fiona sensed the need to retreat.

"One track of many, Mr. Barker," Fiona said, looking at Gail. "Have you any questions?"

Gail grew thoughtful.

"Were they close? Father and daughter?"

"I'll tell you this, I think her old man would blow up this whole town if it would have helped his daughter. She was everything to him. He must be shattered."

"He is," Gail said.

"Was he everything to her?" Gail asked. Fiona caught the personal connotation.

"Who am I to say? He had juice. She had ambition. If it was my old man, I'd take the juice."

"But it would be a feather in her cap to get a job on her own, without his help?" Fiona interjected.

"Listen, ladies. Phyla was the kind of person who could make it on her own, anywhere, anytime. But she knew the value of connections and was willing to use them."

"Did she tell you that?" Fiona asked.

"Not in words. Hell, the woman stank of ambition. Sure, she'd like to make it without Daddy. But she knew that Daddy held some pretty good chips and she was willing to play them."

"Something she said?" Fiona asked.

"Something she showed. She was not a teller. She held her cards very close to the vest."

Fiona herself was uncertain where all this was leading. She was trying to bushwhack a path to Farley Lipscomb's door, but no one seemed to be cooperating. Either that or she was bushwhacking in the wrong direction. Inadvertently, Gail came to her rescue.

"Was she a sexually active woman?" Gail asked. Phelps Barker seemed somewhat taken aback. He reached for his drink and upended the glass. So far he had been more than cooperative, but Fiona could see he did not take kindly to Gail's question. He became instantly belligerent.

"Are you asking whether or not I balled her?" he smirked. "Phyla? We were buddies. It would take a leap of faith for me to see her any other way."

"Are you saying she had no interest in you other than as a friend?"

"Phyla was Madame Purie," Barker said, taking a deep sip on his sour. "She did not seem amenable to . . . let us say . . . sexual congress."

"Meaning she rebuffed you?" Gail pushed.

" 'Rebuff' suggests that I might have made some moves on her. No way. She sent no messages. I might have entertained something when I was twelve or thirteen, but any urges, none of which come to mind, would have been self-squelched. In that department, she was not my type."

"What is your type, Barker?" Gail asked.

He studied her for a moment, then winked.

"I'd say that you present enormous possibilities, lady."

"So you were buddies," Gail said, ignoring his remark. Fiona sensed that this was beginning to look like a pointless interrogation.

"I told you. I grew up with her. We both went our separate ways after high school. I went to Harvard and Georgetown Law. She went to the University of Chicago, undergraduate and law school."

"Did she have any boyfriends?" Gail asked.

"You mean the plural?" Barker asked with what Fiona interpreted as superior, preppy sarcasm.

"What is that supposed to mean?" Fiona snapped, giving in to a sudden urge to lower the boom on his self-satisfied smugness.

"It means . . . ." He looked Fiona over as if she was sitting in a hole beneath him. "What was your rank again?"

"Does it matter?" Fiona snapped.

"No," Barker said, after a long deliberate pause as he stared into her eyes, hoping she would flinch first. She didn't. "No, it doesn't matter."

"We were asking about her personal life," Gail said, ignoring the interruption. She was now relentlessly on the man's case. No doubt she was following her own hunch. Intuition was a homicide detective's stock in trade, a kind of art form, and Fiona knew better than to inhibit such vibrations.

"Her sex life, you mean?"

"Have it your way."

"Look, she was, for all us studs, outside the line of fire. By her choice. She was more brain than body. She sent out no signals. Not to anyone I know."

He snapped his fingers. Walter rushed over.

"I'll have another sour, Walter," Barker said, pointing to the coffee cups on the table in front of them. "More java, girls?"

Gail ignored the question. Fiona shook her head for both of them and the waiter disappeared.

"So you compared notes about her . . . her charms?" Gail asked.

"In my adolescent world, all girls were under discussion, including Phyla. There was general agreement that, although attractive, she did not stir the gonads."

The waiter brought Barker's sour.

"Thank you, Walter," Barker nodded with the same superior look he had given Fiona earlier. He lifted his glass in a mock toast and drank off a sip. "You're missing a great drink."

"And where were you Saturday evening, Barker?" Gail snapped suddenly. Did Gail seriously believe he was involved?

"Me?" He tossed his head back and laughed. "Am I under suspicion?"

"Yes," Gail shot back with a deliberately intimidating glare. Barker reached for his sour. Despite his air of disconcern, he seemed to be searching for an appropriate response.

"You can't be serious," he said.

"But I am," Gail pressed, with a sidelong glance at Fiona, who wondered what she was thinking.

"Actually, if memory serves, I was at a party in Bethesda," he said. "One of those singles events for the upwardly mobile. Lots of quiche and white wine." He giggled nervously.

"Why didn't you invite your old buddy?" Gail asked.

"But I did."

He finished the last of his second sour and snapped for Walter to bring another one. Walter responded with servile alacrity. It struck Fiona as a sensible ploy on Walter's part to hustle tips from this pompous ass.

"These are really wonderful," he said. "Are you sure you won't try one?" His eyes roamed from one face to the other and he shrugged. "Your sobriety gives me a real sense of security, ladies. All murderers beware."

"Why did she turn down your invitation?" Gail asked, her eyes narrowing. She apparently knew all the dramatic tics that were useful in embellishing the questions.

"Actually, she didn't turn me down," Barker said after an unexpectedly long pause, as if his answer had to be thought out. It was the kind of gesture that could send up rings of suspicious smoke signals. Fiona could see that Gail had responded to the signals, which encouraged her to press on relentlessly.

Even Fiona could acknowledge that Barker invited suspicion, but suspicion of what? If there was guilt present, it seemed disconnected and irrelevant to the girl's death. Gail apparently thought otherwise.

For a moment Barker dropped his mask of devil-may-care sophistication. "Shit. She should have come. Probably have had a lousy time, but at least she'd be alive in the morning." He sucked in a deep breath and shook his head.

"So you gave her directions?" Gail pressed. "To where the party was being held?"

"Yes, I did. Wrote them down in case she wanted to attend the festivities."

He was obviously trying to find his way back to his original persona. Fiona speculated that he might be offering the explanation to cover himself in case the directions had been found among her effects.

"And she never showed up?"

He shook his head, but there was something tentative in the gesture.

"Was there a big crowd?"

"Yes," he said. "It was a mob scene. A friend's house in Bethesda, jammed to the rafters. Shared by four guys who all had their own circles."

"Would she have known anyone there?"

"Maybe. School chums. Youth-on-the-march types."

"Like you," Gail suggested.

"Rungs behind, darling. Rungs behind."

His old arrogance was being restored, although the contrived casualness seemed less sure.

"How can you be so certain that she would have had a lousy time?" Gail asked.

"I've been trying to tell you that she was basically a loner. Very serious and focused. She did not, in all the years I knew her, show any signs of a light heart." Walter brought another sour and Barker immediately took a deep sip.

"How long did you stay at the party?" Gail asked.

"Still on that kick." He grew thoughtful. "I think I left around eleven. Some of the guests were already getting speechless and a bit too raucus for my tastes."

"What are your tastes, Phelps?" Gail asked, using his first name for purposes of sarcasm. Why was she pushing so hard, Fiona wondered. Did she know more than she had let on?

"Well, well, aren't we getting a bit personal here?"

"I hope so."

Gail fired away, obviously enjoying herself, although Fiona was at a loss to explain her motive. It seemed more like a fencing match between them. Was he really hiding something? Fiona wondered.

"Is it possible you might have missed her?" Gail asked. ". . . in the mob scene."

"I'm a trained observer, Madame Detective," Barker sneered.

"Booze dulls the senses, Phelps," Gail said, looking pointedly at the half-empty whiskey sour on the little table beside him. He followed her gaze.

"I was perfectly sober that evening," he smirked, turning to Fiona in search of an ally.

"Hardly likely," Fiona said, looking at the whiskey sour. As if in defiance, he picked it up and finished it off.

"As you can see, I appreciate good booze. Cheap wine and a couple of kegs are the fare at these events, accompanied by a wheel of cheese melting under the lamp. This is what passes for hoity-toity in that crowd."

"Did you leave alone?"

He forced a chuckle, but again he hesitated enough to sow doubt.

"No one worth cutting from the pack," he sneered. "It was my weekend for self-love."

"You went straight home?"

"Normally that's where the art is practiced."

He leaned over the table, picked up the whiskey sour glass, noted it was empty, then clicked his fingers again. His cheeks had flushed and the alcohol seemed to accelerate his inherent nastiness, although his tongue maintained its clarity. He did not strike Fiona as a happy drunk.

"Then you went to sleep?" Gail prompted, giving no ground to his sarcasm.

"Yes. The boredom of the evening left me somnolent and aching for oblivion."

"Did anyone see you go into your place? Is it an apartment?"

"A townhouse on Capitol Hill. I don't think I was seen. All the muggers had apparently taken the night off."

"So you have no corroboration," Gail said, her remark deliberately accusatory. Her eyes seemed to bore in on his. Her tenacity was awesome.

He shook his head and studied Gail's face for a long moment, then he turned to Fiona. "Is she serious?"

"I'm afraid so," Fiona replied.

"Alright then," Barker said, stretching out his arms, wrists together. "Cuff me and take me downtown for questioning. Better yet put me in a lineup. It'll be a gas."

"I like that idea," Gail said, exchanging glances with Fiona. She wasn't fooling. She was onto something, pursuing it with highly focused energy.

"I don't believe this. Are you hounding me for attitude or genuine suspicion?"

"Look, Barker," Gail said. "If you can account for your time Saturday evening, it will make matters simpler for all of us. We have a horrifying, ugly crime on our hands. It can't be cavalierly dismissed with wisecracks. You knew Phyla Herbert. You admittedly invited her to a party."

"So you're harassing me because I told you the truth," Barker said, serious now, all flippancy gone. "Not very skillful interrogation, I'm afraid. I can understand your frustration about your inability to find the real perpetrator. Phyla Herbert was a long-time friend. Your implications that

I somehow did her in are absurd. Besides, bondage is not my sexual preference."

Gail shot a glance toward Fiona, who raised her eyebrows and shrugged. Bondage?

"We haven't used that term," Gail said.

"Do you think I'm an idiot?" Barker said. He was lashing out now. "A woman trussed, mutilated, probably sexually violated? I can read between the lines. And I do understand this little game. Well, let me tell you something, girls. I don't need an alibi for Saturday night. I came home and went to bed." His cheeks grew redder. He was angry now, an anger accelerated by the alcohol he had imbibed.

His voice rose for a moment, attracting some nearby club members who looked up with annoyance. Sensing this, he lowered his voice and, eyes steady, stared into Gail's.

"I did not, could not, would not abuse Phyla Herbert in any way, sexually or otherwise, and I resent any inference that I might be capable of such an act."

Walter, who might have momentarily retreated until the fracas had died down, now emerged with another whiskey sour, which he placed on the table next to Barker. He nodded his gratitude, then reached for the drink, putting it quickly down when he noted that his hands shook.

Gail had certainly rattled Barker. But why? Fiona wondered, content to be on the sidelines as Gail pursued her as yet inarticulated theory. It surprised Fiona that she held no resentment for Gail going off on what seemed like a tangent. Hadn't she done the same? Without consultation?

"When you invited her to the party, did Phyla indicate that she had a previous engagement?" Gail asked, her voice modulated into softness, as if she had changed the style and direction of her interrogation.

"Not in words," Barker replied with equal control, greatly relieved that Gail had set aside the matter of his alibi. "The fact is that Phyla always seemed to have a previous engagement."

"Or maybe she simply did not want to party with your upwardly mobile friends," Gail said without sarcasm.

"Actually you have a point," Barker answered, reaching for his drink. His hand was steadier now and his attitude less belligerent. In fact, he was almost docile.

"Phyla would rather be with people who had arrived than with a bunch of full-of-themselves wannabes," Barker said, sipping his sour, then neatly, with enough ceremony to call attention to his steadier hand, returning the glass to the table beside him. "Fact is, her father could set her up with almost anyone to look after his little girl and dispense an evening of dinner and advice."

"Like who?"

"Any number of big shots."

"Be specific."

"Congressmen, senators, even members of the Cabinet."

Fiona suddenly found herself afforded another opening.

"Supreme Court justices?"

"I wouldn't be surprised."

"Any justice in particular?" Fiona asked casually.

"You're really hung up on that aspect, Sergeant," Barker said, looking at her with eyes that gleamed, showing the effect of the sours.

It was apparent by then that the interview had lost focus, although Gail made no move to go. Fiona was the first to stand up.

"We'll be needing you at some point again," Fiona said. Gail, with some reluctance, also stood up. As a mark of politeness, Barker also stood.

"I didn't kill Phyla," he whispered.

"We never said you did," Gail said. But it was clear from her face that she had not completely dismissed the thought. "But I do believe you should reassess your position with regard to your whereabouts Saturday night."

"That again," he sighed.

"It's not going to go away, Barker," Gail said.

"Look," Barker said. "Like me or not, in this town careers are busted by perception. You could bomb my future with your implications, especially if the media gets to play with it."

"Phyla Herbert's future was bombed," Gail murmured as they moved away.

Before they left, they saw him resume his seat, reach for his sour and snap his fingers for Walter.

"You were really pushing him, Gail," Fiona said. They were in the car heading back to headquarters. Fiona was driving.

"He had an attitude problem that needed some work."

"True. But do you really believe he could be part of it?" Fiona asked.

Gail pondered the question for a long time.

"He's hiding something, Fiona."

"Maybe so. But there is no evidence. No fingers pointing." She looked toward Gail. "Except your intuition."

"Unconscious reasoning," Gail said. "It has its place. There's more there. I know it."

"He's an obnoxious little frat boy twit," Fiona said. "But I don't see him involved in this one."

She did not want it to sound like a total rejection.

"Notice when he broke stride," Gail said, "when I asked him if he had left the party alone."

"But he said that Phyla never showed," Fiona retorted.

"That's exactly what he said. Another signpost of his edginess."

"Alright, maybe he did go home with someone. Surely he would not want her involved."

"Or him."

"Then let's be broadminded. Say 'him.' None of which has anything to do with Phyla Herbert. His sexual orientation has no relevance in this situation."

"Sexual conduct is always relevant," Gail said. "And sexual deviation and perversion invariably lead to ugly consequences."

"Invariably? That's a pretty blanket indictment of people with different strokes."

Fiona was clearly offering a rebuke. And she could tell from Gail's stoic reaction the underlying motive. A certain rigidity on matters sexual, an extreme, unyielding moral posture, without any leavening or tolerance. She had seen such attitudes before in black women of education and achievement.

It was more than simply a heightened sense of morality. It was an aggressive conviction, a commitment to the idea that sex was between loving married partners only. Perhaps, too, it was motivated by a need to distance oneself from a bigot's perception that all blacks were moral cripples.

The idea gave Fiona a deeper insight into Gail Prentiss's motivation for joining the police, namely a firm sense of moral certitude and self-righteousness that brooked no deviation.

"How many times have we seen it in our trade, Fiona?" Gail said. She was not backing down. "Sexual violation of the innocent and unprotected, with murder a frequent companion. Rape. Child abuse. Sodomy. Sadism. Masochism. The statistics are appalling and those are merely reported figures."

Fiona could see that she was winding up for a debate, something she wished to avoid at all costs. Her respect for Gail Prentiss was not diminished, but the possibility of greater candor between them was. Fiona and her lifestyle would definitely not meet with her approval. It crossed her mind that Gail might still be a virgin.

"We both know that intuition is important, Gail," Fiona said. She saw the unfairness of her position, keeping from her partner the true nature of her suspicions about the identity of the perpetrator. It was against every caveat in police work, especially in homicide.

She was aware, too, that the moment would come when Gail would begin questioning her about her fixation with the Supreme Court and her constant allusions to the justices. Fiona was certain that it had not escaped her notice and was bound to surface. She hoped it would be later rather than sooner, when she had gotten further along in her quest, but the possibility of revelation filled her with dread.

"I need to follow this line, Fiona," Gail said. It was obviously eating at her.

"That's pretty obvious," Fiona replied. Where was the harm in that, she asked herself, searching for some rational way to soothe her guilt.

"Look, Fiona. We're partners and I'm new here. And I really want to make it with you. I know you're good and, with all modesty, I know I am as well . . ."

"It's okay, Gail. I don't need the speech. You've made your point and I won't stand in your way."

"Stand in my way? I want you to join me. Phelps Barker knows a lot more than he's saying."

"I just don't believe he was the one," Fiona said with obvious conviction. "In the absence of any evidence."

"I'm not accusing him. I'm only saying he seems to be hiding something that could be relevant."

Round and round it went. Fiona drove steadily through the traffic. The discussion seemed pointless.

"You're probably right," Fiona sighed, swallowing her deception and offering complete surrender. No matter how hard she searched her mind, she could not find an acceptable way to enlist Gail Prentiss in her pursuit of Farley Lipscomb.

"So I have your permission to follow-up?" Prentiss said.

"You don't need my blessing, Gail" Fiona said.

"How about your help?"

"You're my partner," Fiona said, reiterating the point, but dreading an arrangement that meant hours of nonproductive make-work in what Fiona believed was the futile pursuit of Phelps Barker. She was more inclined to spend her time trying to find a link between Phyla Herbert's murder and Farley Lipscomb.

"Problem is," Fiona said, mulling a way to disguise the deception, "we'll have to divide the labor, work different sides of the street. Clearly, this case needs more personnel. Only there's not enough to go 'round. While you work the Phelps Barker angle, I'll fish around elsewhere. It won't do to get hung up on a single track."

The mixed metaphors were troubling, and Fiona knew they needed elaboration.

"For example, I'd like to touch base with that assistant manager again and go over the hotel guest list."

They had, of course, requested the guest list, which would require painstaking scrutiny and, perhaps, another dead end. But it did have an acceptable logic. Peripherally, she could see Gail's consenting nod.

"We'll stay in close touch," Fiona promised. "The Eggplant will want daily verbals."

Fiona could not find the courage to turn from her driving and look at Gail. It hurt her to know that she was being disengenuous. After a long silence, pregnant with smoldering cogitation, Gail said:

"I am confused about something, Fiona," she said.

"About what?"

Fiona braced herself. She knew what was coming.

"This business about Phyla wanting to work for a justice of the Supreme Court. It seems well . . . disconnected."

"Disconnected?" Fiona replied, searching for an appropriate answer. It was too premature for a valid answer. "Popped into my mind. It just seemed to fit. People who have clerked for Supreme Court justices have had hot careers. Phyla seemed a logical candidate."

"It's just . . . well, you seem to have something in mind."

"Nothing specific," Fiona lied, trying her best to remain casual and vague. She forced herself to keep her eyes on the road, hoping that her answers would put the matter to rest, at least for the moment.

"It just seems to keep coming up," Gail pressed. Did she sense that Fiona was hiding something?

"Comes from growing up in what used to be called the power structure," Fiona said. "There's lots of reflected glory in working at the Court. And since there are only nine justices, a young lawyer gets to enjoy a certain exclusivity that sets him or her apart in any future endeavors."

Fiona caught herself trying too hard, rambling, a dead giveaway. She wondered if Gail would notice.

Of course she would, Fiona decided. Gail was too smart not to notice.

—8—

The worst part of the case was the obsessive way it had intruded on Fiona's life. Re-intruded, she corrected. It was like a disease long in remission that had emerged again, more destructive, virulent and unforgiving, packing a greater fury than on its first unwelcome visit.

Tossing in her bed like a cork on a white-capped ocean, she slept in gasps of exhaustion. Periodically she awoke in a cold, syrupy sweat as images of that day, returning in oblique but unmistakable configurations, swirled in her mind. Even the terrible physical pain that had been inflicted came back to plague her body. It seemed worse in recall.

She hated being alone in her bed, yet feared that a call to Harrison Greenwald would strike him as a summons to a sexual event in which she simply could not participate. Even the idea of such a coupling of the flesh was appalling. Harrison, she knew, would not take kindly to rejection, especially without explanation.

What she needed, she told herself, was to concentrate on ways to reach across the clueless void to find the truth. Was Farley the perpetrator or not? It did not take much insight on her part to understand that, in her heart, she wanted him to be the guilty party. Vengeance, she speculated, would be sweet. Justice would be done. And she would, at last, be released from the prison of her own guilt.

Yet she detested these feelings. They were unprofessional and inhibiting. Besides, there was a code of ethics to uphold. Even the perpetrator of the most beastly crimes was innocent until proven guilty.

An official confrontation with Farley Lipscomb, a man in a position of such prestige and veneration, was out of the question. Even the barest hint of suspicion, without good reason and foolproof back-up evidence, would call down the wrath of the department on her head. But did this rule out an unofficial confrontation?

She went downstairs and made herself a strong cup of tea, hoping it might soothe her mind and stimulate those portions of the brain involved with imagination and gamesmanship. By morning, after a couple of hours sleep, she came up with a logical course of action.

She would have to meet Farley in a casual, nonthreatening manner, which meant a social context, where she could observe his reactions and attitude first hand. Any objective conclusions, she knew, would be based more on the subtleties of silent communication than on hard information. The idea begged comparison with Gail's gut reaction to Phelps Barker and those mysterious messages she was picking up. Except that Fiona had the considerable advantage of painful personal experience.

Not long after dawn, as she watched the lightening sky against the large oaks that rimmed her scrupulously maintained property, she got the first faint glimmer of how to accomplish her objective.

With the Supreme Court in session and the Washington social whirl in full swing, she could, with little effort, find out at what events Farley Lipscomb and his very social wife were scheduled to spend their evenings. A Supreme Court justice was always a trophy guest, a fact that had surely enhanced Letitia Lipscomb's already awesome social reputation.

At the first respectable moment of the morning, Fiona called her friend Daisy Hodges, a former inmate, along with Fiona, of Mount Vernon School for Girls, still a bastion for the young daughters of the power elite. Daisy had married a real estate developer who had sold out at the top of the breaking wave of recession and was now pursuing her own social agenda in a huge house in Spring Valley.

Daisy had acquired clout and social cachet from her father, a member of the Kennedy Cabinet. She had embellished it by marrying well enough to spread her bucks like manure around the Washington social scene. Now an accomplished hostess, Daisy's home was the scene of constant action, a must-attend for the currently important on the Washington merry-go-round.

Fiona still maintained a place on the social circuit. Between "relationships" she was often invited as the "extra" girl to even up a dinner table and she received a good share of invitations to the best houses and embassies. She entertained occasionally as well, in the large elegant house she had inherited from her parents.

Wise in the ways of Washington, she pursued a minimum of the social niceties just to keep her image afloat in that world and her presence welcomed in her own right. Those that knew her profession accepted her as a socially acceptable eccentric and let it go at that.

Many of the present Washington elite, like Daisy, were childhood friends of Fiona. Those in her age group were rising rapidly as the Washington cadre, meaning those who were the mainstays of social power and who had the wherewithal to entertain the top rung of the invading armies of eager power seekers who arrived in town with each succeeding administration.

Bonded by girlhood confidences of a most personal nature, Fiona knew that, despite their life choices, Daisy and she would always consider each other "best girlfriends," having pledged to each other a fealty that would carry them through to their graves. From time to time, although they could drift for months without contact, Daisy would avail herself of Fiona's sympathetic ear and, once or twice, at low points, Fiona, too, had sought out her friend for hugs and sympathy. The passage of time diminished nothing between them.

"Daisy!" It was ten minutes before eight. "Did I wake you?"

"Wake me? Donald already did that. He's a glutton for a morning poke."

Knowing it was Fiona, she could let her hair down and did. They had, back in their teenage days, confided everything to each other. With maturity had come private secrets, which was natural. But their trust in each other was implicit. Daisy knew about the long-ago teenage affair with Farley, although not about the incident that ended it.

In those days, before AIDS, a sexual scalp, particularly belonging to someone high in the power pecking order, was an honored trophy. Daisy, who was sexually active at fifteen, a prodigious Lolita, had accumulated an exhibit hall full of scalps. Marriage, three children and skyrocketing social status had tamed her considerably, although there were complicated circumstances early in her marriage.

In recent years it was Fiona, with her checkered love life and inability to form lasting liaisons, who provided the spice to their confidences.

"How's the flatfoot?" Daisy asked. She was one of the few of her childhood friends who actually approved of her choice of profession, on the grounds of it being both dangerous and adventuresome.

"Still running after the bad guys."

"Lucky you." Daisy's voice indicated that she was stretching langorously. "I could use a bad guy right this minute."

"I could talk dirty, Daisy."

"Wouldn't be the same, Fi."

They exchanged a series of inquiries. Fiona inquired after the health and status of Daisy's offspring and husband and Daisy pumped Fiona on the hard facts of her love life.

"You and Harrison Greenwald still in thrall?" Daisy asked.

"Sort of," Fiona admitted.

"Meaning declining interest?"

"I'm into a celibacy phase."

"Poor thing."

Because of her errant flippancy, the real purpose of her call generated a twisted and inaccurate impression.

"I'm interested in seeing the Lipscombs in a social context, Daisy."

"You little devil. I thought that was over . . ." There was a short silence. "Was it fifteen years? No more."

"You're a filthy minded slut," Fiona said, reverting to the words and intonation of their school days.

"Always was. Always will be. Who was it that introduced you to the joys of masturbation?"

"God, Daisy."

"And the proper way to fake an orgasm."

"It's entirely unrelated to the big 'S', Fiona said, falling into the rhythm and idiom of their teenage speech. "I'm working on a case that could use free judicial advice, given casually, a kind of pre-opinion that I don't want to have in an official capacity. You get my drift."

"Ah, the joys of the traveling Washington crap game. If the great un-washed only knew how things worked in this town. All those cute little competing agendas. I love it."

"You're the chess player, Daisy. Move my piece into position."

"Dear Farley. He's became very self-important and scholarly. Still attrac-tive. Remember how he used to flirt. He was quite a bon vivant. I can understand how you could drop your bloomers with a guy like that. Even today. He can turn it on, I'll say that for him."

"You ever see him do that?"

"Do what?"

"Turn it on to impress some sweet young thing."

"Are you contracting me to observe, Fi?" Daisy giggled.

"Just curious."

"At least, Fi, you have indulged yourself with all three branches of government, a true constitutionalist." Daisy giggled. "But pre-Supreme Court doesn't really count, does it? I mean you didn't exactly crawl under that black robe."

"What is it with you this morning, Daisy?" Fi asked, noting that Daisy was into one of her wiseacre fits.

"I'm suffering from an orgasm deficit, dahling. My man has left me bereft. He's becoming the bing-bang man," Daisy roared into a laughing spell, obviously enjoying the lack of control and decorum normally required of her present status and position.

"Let me know . . . dahling . . . when you can work me in."

"Gotcha."

Fiona hung up, her spirits lifted. Daisy could do that for her with her wonderfully irreverent wisegal talk. Jumping into the shower, Fiona got ready for what she sensed might be a another dead-end day, while looking forward to the results of Daisy's research.

The phone rang while she still dripped moisture on the bathroom tiles. She picked up the portable that lay beside the sink. It was Gail Prentiss.

"I'll be seeing the guy that hosted the Saturday night party, Fiona. He's a congressional AA. We're meeting on the Hill."

"Great," Fiona said with mock enthusiasm.

"I'm heading to the Mayflower," Fiona said. It seemed the only logical destination. She would go through the motions at her own pace without Gail's second guessing. Perhaps, too, there might be a hidden lead that, she hoped, could point her in Farley Lipscomb's direction.

They made arrangements to compare notes at headquarters later in the day. Then Fiona called the Eggplant and filled him in on what they were doing, which, while not satisfying him, led him to believe that they were making the right moves.

"We need this one, FitzGerald," he said.

She reassured him, hating herself for dissembling. The irony was that she had dissembled before, mostly in the interest of keeping him momentarily placated. But this situation seemed more a betrayal, a step down from what would ordinarily be considered a simple white lie.

As she was leaving the house, the phone rang again. It was Daisy.

"A six-to-eighter at the State Department open rooms tonight. I've put you and Harrison on the list."

"Harrison?"

"I just assumed . . ."

"Of course," Fiona said. Yes, she decided, it would seem less official if she brought a date. "You do have clout, Daisy."

"I've contributed enough antiques to those rooms to furnish a palace," Daisy said. Her official day begun, she was less playful than earlier.

"You think Farley will be a sure show?"

Names were a commodity in Washington, often used as a lure for others to attend this or that event. On most occasions the owner of the famous name did not show up for the affair.

"He's both a sponsor and a presenter. Some award. I forget which."

"Will you be there, Daisy?"

"Three things on the schedule. It'll be dash in, dash out. I'll probably miss you."

Fiona was about to say her good-byes, when another thought intruded.

"Daisy. Have you ever heard of a Tom Herbert?"

"Herbert. Herbert," Daisy pondered aloud. "Oh yes," she said. "That poor man. The one who's daughter. My God was that awful."

"Yes, it was."

"What a ghoulish business you're in, Fiona. But yes, I've met Herbert. Chicago. Very well connected. In town frequently. On the social circuit. He's single and straight, a rare commodity. As a matter of fact, I think I fixed him up once or twice. Fran Thompson, it was. The widow of Senator Thompson. I think they were an item for a time, then it terminated for whatever reason. I forget. I'm sure the fellow is a mess, considering what's happened. She seemed like such a nice girl."

"You met her?" Fiona asked, startled by the assertion.

"Oh, yes. Herbert brought her around from time to time. Are you on this case, Fi?"

"As a matter of act . . ." Fiona replied.

"From what I've read, it was real kinky."

"Yes, Daisy. It was."

"I'm not pressing. You probably can't talk about it."

"Not at the moment. But as soon as we catch the man, I'll give you the blow-by-blow."

"Goody, goody," Daisy said. "You never know about people. Herbert has to be devastated."

"He is," Fiona said, considering a follow-up, but restraining herself.

Fiona heard another phone ringing in the background. Daisy excused herself and hung up.

But the conversation had confirmed that Tom Herbert was indeed plugged into the Washington social scene. In this arena it did not take a leap of faith to find a connection between the Herberts and Farley Lipscomb.

—9—

Throughout the day Fiona went through the professional motions of an experienced homicide detective. What she needed was authenticity that would pass muster with the Eggplant and especially with Gail Prentiss, who would undoubtedly arrive back at headquarters with a hatful of suspicious clues designed to justify her theory about Phelps Barker's perfidy.

In a room behind the Mayflower registration desk she interrogated the assistant manager and a steady stream of hotel employees who had worked on the days that Phyla Herbert had been a guest at the hotel. On the drive in, she had come up with yet another idea. Perhaps one of the employees might have seen a man fitting the description of Farley Lipscomb sometime Saturday night.

To this end, she had gone to the main branch of the public library and obtained a book that had some informal pictures of the various current justices of the Supreme Court. Then she went to a one-hour photo shop and had three of the pictures of individual justices, including Farley's, blown up and carefully cropped to eliminate any sign of their judicial raiments.

She knew the process was dangerous, rife with hidden minefields. Someone might recognize the man as a member of the Court, which could light the fuse that would snake its way into the various Washington media offices. The resultant explosion would rock the town. Any hint that Farley Lipscomb was under suspicion of such a bestial act, without anything more than the flimsy evidence of a picture recognized by a casual eyewitness, would have all the earmarks of a frame-up.

She knew she was playing with fire. The Court was a powerful instrument of American democracy, a sensitive tuning fork, which set both the limits of freedom and the ideological agenda for the entire country. It was the holy citadel of the great American experiment and with only nine people to carry such a burden, the slightest ripple of impropriety, no less one of such staggering proportions as that involved in death and sexual perversion, would have the impact of a poisoned dagger stuck into the heart of the system.

Fiona, a child of the system, was aware of the dangers. Indeed, even if she had hard proof, such a revelation could have personal implications of monumental impact to herself, a fallout that could injure her forever.

She could tell herself that moral purpose had its own reward, that retribution could be both cleansing and satisfying and, perhaps, she might escape the fate of exposure. But was the risk worth the victory? Would it trouble her to see Farley, if he was the perpetrator, be free to try again?

This was very much in her mind as she began her interviews at the Mayflower, pictures in hand. A few of those whom she had paraded through the office had only the vaguest recollections of Phyla Herbert. The bellman who had taken up her bags and explained the workings of the air-conditioning and the pay bar had remembered her as aristocratically polite, a woman who said little and produced a two-dollar tip with the aplomb of someone used to receiving good service.

"She was cool, polite and indifferent," the bellman, a middle-aged, experienced sizer-upper explained. Had he seen her after she had checked in? No recollection. It was the very essence of this kind of grunt work where tipping was the only real mode of communication.

"I have a daughter," he explained, as if to provide himself with a shred of dignity and compassion. He studied the pictures with great concentration.

"In this business middle-aged men are like Chinese waiters. They all look alike." He shook his head. "Sorry."

The chambermaid on duty during the days of Phyla Herbert's stay was a San Salvadoran who barely spoke English. She needed an interpreter, a sallow-faced young man hastily recruited from the room service department, whose English resembled pig latin. The woman was frightened, had turned ashen and her lips trembled.

"She no see," the young man said, after a spirited exchange in Spanish. "Says she do room in afternoon after lady gone."

Fiona set the pictures on the desk in front of the woman. The woman studied them with glazed, indifferent eyes.

"No, notheeng," the young man said.

Earlier she had shown the pictures to the assistant manager, neatly turned out in a morning coat and dark pants with a razor-sharp crease. His features were delicate, and he wore a tiny Band-Aid where he had cut himself shaving.

"They look vaguely familiar," he said, tapping his teeth with a manicured forefinger. "But I can't say they ring a bell."

He had arranged for other hotel employees that were on duty to be present. One was the bartender, a handsome black man with graying hair, who had been on duty in the cocktail lounge. When shown the pictures, he shook his head, but only after an inordinate time of study. Fiona had the impression that he secretly might have recognized one or two of the three, but it was highly unlikely that an old hand like him would court the kind of hassle that went with the identification.

"Are you sure?" Fiona pressed.

He shook his head.

"And the young woman?" Fiona asked, after providing a brief description.

"Sorry."

She interviewed a number of the waitresses, security people and other employees on duty at the time. Long shots, she knew. There was no payoff. Phyla hadn't ordered any room service. Only the security people had vague recollections of seeing Phyla, but their comments seemed more for self-protection than informational.

Again she reviewed the guest list of the hotel, which had been partially filled with a convention of pediatricians, most of whom had left town on Sunday evening. The hotel had provided a computerized list and the names were being run through a central data system for any MO matches, which so far had revealed nothing of any consequence.

Using the phone in the hotel office, she spent a couple of hours calling people who were checked in on the same floor. It was the evening of the major convention social event and most of the people had spent a long evening at the event. None of them acknowledged hearing any strange sounds.

The assistant manager, his name was Harold Barton, provided her with a tray of coffee and a sandwich from room service and sat with her as she ate.

"May I see those pictures again?" he asked.

She handed him the envelope and he slid out the pictures and studied them carefully, tapping his teeth as he had done before.

"Who are these men?" he asked.

"Are they familiar?"

"I'm not sure. Are they sex criminals, suspects?"

"Is there one more vaguely familiar than the others?" Fiona asked.

"I wish I could say."

"We need to place one of them at the scene," Fiona said, hoping to jog his memory. It was the one hopeful sign of the day.

"I realize that, Sergeant," Barton said. "May I keep them for a while?"

"Sorry. Can't do that," Fiona said. She was taking enough risk by flashing the pictures for even this quick glimpse. Of all the people she had shown them to, Barton, who had more opportunity to mix with the upper crust public, was the most likely to have recognized them.

As she drove to headquarters, she did not allow the fruitless day to upset her. It was a longshot idea. Farley would have worked out a clever way to avoid being seen. She recalled how he had disguised himself for their long-ago trysts and had instructed her to register and pay the bill. If Farley had been the perpetrator, she concluded, he would have figured out a way to evade recall. The fact that no physical evidence of consequence had been found buttressed her theory that the man who did this deed could be Farley, or someone equally as knowledgeable in the area of evidence.

The master stroke of his earlier cleverness was his calculation that Fiona would out of embarassment remain silent. A revelation of his propensity, even then, would have ruined him. He could not be accused of lacking insight into his victims. Even in the office, he had been scrupulous about how their affair had been handled, always behind locked doors, after hours.

A private bathroom in his office was also available when danger beck-oned, a footfall, a voice. This was a man who knew how to cheat, how to evade scrutiny, although he had on occasion taken a risk if it meant to serve an overwhelming and immediate need. Fiona had no doubt that she was merely one of a long line of women who had been his prey. After that awful day, this was the way she always saw him in her imagination, a vicious predator without a conscience.

As she neared headquarters, she directed her thoughts to the planned encounter with Farley at the State Department event. She had no clear plan, except to attempt to engage him. That could be the most difficult part of it. He could ignore her, palm her off, withdraw. She would have to improvise.

In the squad room, she called Harrison at his office and tendered the invitation.

"Well, well," he said, his tone pregnant with defensive sarcasm.

She was still in her mode of sexual disengagement, made even more so by her recent recollections. It would pass. Hadn't it passed once before?

"Stick with me, Harrison. I'm going through a stage," she told him.

"No kidding. I've spent the last two nights analyzing it. Another guy, perhaps?"

"Nada."

"Disease?"

"Double nada."

She tried to keep it light, understanding his confusion. It crossed her mind that she might conquer her frigidity, fake it. Daisy had reminded her of that ancient instruction. No way, she decided. Revulsion would consume her. Her previous recovery had happened naturally, healed by time and nature. It could only happen that way again.

"Call it a sabbatical in a nunnery," she told him, reaching for humor.

"I don't know, Fi," he waffled.

"It'll pass, Harrison."

"I'd feel a lot better with an explanation," he said. "Put me at my ease. You know how I feel about you, Fi."

"There's a mutuality here, Harrison," she said. "But I have an impediment."

"I'll understand, Fi. Only tell me."

"Not yet," she told him, hating the byplay, wanting him to say nay or yea to the State Department event. She could always find another escort. He might have sensed her thoughts.

"I'll meet you at the entrance," he sighed.

She hung up and started to insert a record of her day into the computer. It was full of holes, little white lies. No mention of the pictures she had produced. Thankfully, the Eggplant was not present. Most of her colleagues were out on cases. As usual, the murder count was grim, six new ones overnight. The epidemic continued. There was no end in sight.

Late in the afternoon, Gale Prentiss strode into the squad room, breathless and intent, reminding Fiona that she hadn't been in touch all day. She slumped exhausted into a chair behind an adjoining desk and dropped her pocketbook on the floor beside her. But her face was redolent with satisfaction and she quickly showed signs of recovery.

"Lots to report," Gail said, swiftly shuffling through her telephone messages. Then she punched in a number on the phone.

"Goose eggs all around," Fiona said, as they exchanged glances. Gail nodded acknowledgment, then spoke into the phone.

"Daddy, you okay?"

Gail listened with deep concentration, her lips pursed, her nostrils widening in frustration.

"It'll pass, Daddy. I know it will."

There was a long pause as Gail listened. A gloom seemed to engulf her.

"Daddy, you can't diagnose yourself. What do you mean a couple of weeks at the outside . . . alright, Daddy, I'll be by later."

She hung up and sucked in a deep breath, her eyes moistening.

"Courage and dignity. Sometimes I hate it," Gail said, wiping her eyes with a Kleenex. "The man's dying and he's giving me timetables." She shook her head. "He has to analyze every damned thing. Cold logic. That's him. He's infuriating."

Fiona let her calm down, not knowing what to say. She turned away, affording Gail a long private moment.

"I was right, Fiona," Gail said after a long pause. There was no boasting in the assertion.

"Right about what?"

"Phelps Barker."

Fiona made no comment, waiting for the explanation.

"Bottom line. He was with her Saturday night."

"No way," Fiona blurted, then realizing her error, she quickly backtracked. "I mean I'm surprised."

"I'm not," Gail said, her yellow-flecked eyes now sparkling with a sense of victory. "I mean, I'm not psychic. I'm just surprised that my intuition was so on target and so easily confirmed."

"Barker told you this?" Fiona asked. Gail's information was beginning to sink in, badly shaking her Farley Lipscomb theory. An errant thought intruded to chill her. Had they begun a journey where an innocent man would be mangled by the criminal justice system? It was every homicide detective's nightmare.

"Not yet," Gail said. "But he will. We have a witness. A young woman who was at the party, probably had her eye on Phelps. Barker wasn't exactly lying about the time he left the party. But as he left, he met Phyla Herbert coming in. Probably said the party was a bore, persuading her to leave. They left together."

"You sure it was Phyla."

"She described her minutely. Phyla, as we both know, was a genuine redhead. Only then did I show her Phyla's picture. In color. She did not have to ponder the answer."

"How did you find her?"

Fiona cautioned herself. A negative stance would put unwelcome questions in Gail's mind and shake her feeling of alliance and comradeship.

"Grunt work, Fi. The host gave me names. I found her myself. She was a writer at the Voice of America. Sixth try. Beginner's luck, I guess."

"Let's not be humble, Gail," Fiona said. "You followed your hunch."

"She had followed Barker," Gail explained, growing expansive. "Then she stood by the window, and saw Phyla. She wasn't aware of anyone else watching. They were otherwise engaged in the festivities."

A number of questions crowded into Fiona's mind, questions she would have to ration out cautiously.

"She apparently didn't know about Phyla's fate and I didn't tell her. In fact, I said I was looking for the woman as a witness in another case. I wanted to leave her with the impression that Barker was peripheral. I did, however, caution her not to call him."

"So Barker is still in the dark?"

"I wanted to consult with you first. It's a confrontation that we should do together," Gail said. She looked at her watch, as if signaling that they should be interviewing Barker as soon as possible.

"In the morning when we're both fresh would be fine," Fiona said.

"He'll be fresh as well, Fiona," Gail said with some disappointment.

"I do want to be there and I can't make it now."

"You don't think it's a priority issue?"

"He's not going anywhere, Gail."

But Fiona was, her mind on tonight's confrontation with Farley. She needed to make that connection before meeting with Phelps Barker.

"I really think we should hit him when he least expects it."

"I'm sorry, Gail. Besides, I don't think the Chief will authorize the overtime."

It was yet another statement that could be categorized as a little white lie. It was true that the Eggplant was being very stingy with overtime, in fact, penurious. To grant it required paperwork and justification. Yet in high-profile cases like this one, he would be open for persuasion.

"I take full responsibility. Tomorrow morning first thing."

Gail pondered the idea for a moment, then shrugged with resignation.

"Whatever you say," Gail said.

Fiona began to gather up some of the papers on her desk prior to leaving. She had to go home to dress. It would not do for her to approach Farley wearing clothes that looked as if she were on duty. The meeting had to be casual, coincidental. She had to look the part.

But there was a question that could not wait.

"Do you think he did it?" Fiona asked.

Gail's long graceful fingers stroked her chin as she considered the question through a long pause.

"Can't say, Fiona. No record. No bad stuff. Not officially. But who knows? The thing is, we've put him where the action is and that's something."

"We can't deny that," Fiona agreed.

"Neither can he," Gail snapped.

Fiona nodded and their eyes met. Gail could not hide her annoyance.

"People carry dark secrets inside themselves," Gail said, as if she were addressing someone unseen. Fiona felt suddenly vulnerable, the cliche hitting home, as if she were transparent to the probing intuition of Gale Prentiss.

"Tomorrow then," Fiona said, forcing a smile, starting to leave the office.

"I'll set it up," Gail said, reaching for the phone.

"Do that," Fiona sighed. But before she moved out of the squad room into the corridor, she looked back briefly. Gail Prentiss was hunched over her desk speaking into the phone. If body language was accurate, it revealed a woman determined, obsessed with an idea, single-minded, perhaps fanatic. She had seen that kind of tenacity before. Sometimes in herself.

Gail Prentiss was going after Phelps Barker's jugular.

—10—

The public rooms at the State Department consisted of a large ballroom and a number of exquisitely appointed salons created from donated antiques.

Fiona entered with Harrison Greenwald, whom she had met in front of the building. Wearing a short cocktail dress, she was appropriately decked out for the event, totally transformed from the suited blandness of her police work clothing. Harrison looked distinguished, his graying curly hair blending nicely with his white shirt and striped blue tie.

She allowed herself to be cheek-kissed, the accepted Washington form of social greeting between men and women. It was irritating to discover that even this harmless touching of flesh on flesh made her cringe. She hoped Harrison had not noticed, but he was an astute man and she could tell from the suddenly saddened look in his large brown eyes that he had picked up her signal.

"Just bear with me, darling," she said in a comment meant not to be specific to the kiss, but a general assessment of her condition. "It will pass. I promise you."

He nodded without conviction and they proceeded to the elevator, his usual ebullience muted. Upstairs, the rooms were crowded. The event was apparently in honor of a number of prominent judges from Russia's highest courts, who were currently touring the States and had alighted in Washington to be lavishly entertained by their American peers.

They entered through a reception room where a receiving line consisting of honored guests and the hosts of the evening, Farley Lipscomb and his wife, were suitably placed. They greeted the steady stream of guests with practiced ease. The Lipscombs were the last on the line of seven, busily attentive to each guest who paused briefly to shake hands and utter the appropriate greeting and small-talk niceties.

As she moved along the line, a fist seemed to close on her chest, her knees shook and the remembered pain of that awful afternoon palpitated her sphincter muscle. She felt beads of sweat roll icily down her back and, oddly, moisture sprouted on her scalp, dampening her hair.

She must have changed color as well. Harrison, moving behind her in the line, asked: "Are you okay, Fiona?"

"Of course," she snapped back at him, then turning, forced a smile. "I'm fine."

"Good," he said, not entirely convinced as he inspected her face. It hurt her to be unduly cruel to him, a man she adored, and who had been a kind and considerate friend and lover. Please, she begged him silently, endure this.

They moved first from Russian to Russian, the majority of whom smiled politely, although two attempted a brief conversation in badly broken English. She felt herself growing faint as she approached the Lipscombs, mightily fighting with herself to remain upright, to stay cool.

She passed through the line like a robot, forcing a smile, watching Farley peripherally. She was already feeling the spell of his flashing azure eyes. Actually, she had forgotten their power. They seemed to magnetize their images, as they watched, intense and focused, mysterious and predatory behind his high cheekbones. Once, they had the power to arouse her to an erotic heat seldom experienced since.

Although his hair had become steel gray and the lines had deepened around his mouth, his Prussian posture had remained ramrod straight and she was certain that his vanity had prodded him to maintain an exercise program that kept his muscles hard. As she moved closer, she imagined she could still ingest his distinctive aura. Her knees weakened as she moved forward.

Yet, for a brief moment, she sensed the faint prod of forgiveness, as if she was willing to accept blame for what had happened to her. Hadn't she consented, perhaps wishing for the pain, as if his infliction of it was as necessary as her surrender? And suddenly he was there, tall and straight, his glance like blue searchlights boring into her, heating her brain, rendering her mute.

Her throat constricted. She literally found her vocal chords paralyzed.

"So good to see you again, Fiona," he said smoothly, betraying not the slightest hint of anything resembling heat or discomfort or, especially, guilt. It was the rooting of her feet into the ground that saved her from toppling. But it was the touch of his flesh, the hated touch, as if it were maggot-ridden, with running pustules that recalled the old abuse, the humiliating agony, the whirring sound of that terrible spear of pain that recalled the moment.

"Been a while, Farley," she said, recovering her sense of place. "Farley", not "Judge," spoken through tight lips, was, she hoped, the message that carried the still festering depth of the old anger.

"Has it?" he replied with polite indifference, still smiling, exhibiting not the slightest tinge of discomfort as he kept his eyes focused on hers, his smile thick with practiced ingratiation. His expression showed no recall, no history, a blank slate of memory, as if she had been just another slab of flesh on his sexual cutting block.

"It's really wonderful seeing you again," he said, trying to pass her off with the slightest nudge toward Letitia Lipscomb, who was just winding up the greeting of a portly man she recognized as a Cabinet member.

Only then, panicked by the briefness of their meeting, did she find the words that she hoped might make some impact on him. Deliberately, she resisted his attempt to move her toward Letitia.

"I'm actually a cop now, Farley. Homicide division here in DC," she said, trying to arrange her features in a way that might suggest suspicion. He reacted as if he hadn't heard, his eyes already drifting to Harrison, who stood behind her.

"How nice," Letitia Lipscomb said, as Fiona reluctantly moved in front of her. Lips met cheeks in a perfunctory greeting.

"You're looking wonderful, Fiona."

"Thank you, Mrs. Lipscomb."

Letitia Lipscomb was the controlled social expert that she always had been, at the very top of her calling as the wife of a Supreme Court justice.

As she stood before her, Fiona's mind crowded with possible questions. Did he practice these abominations on you? Did you know about him and me? Have you any idea that the man you share your life with is a perverse monster? Or, more specifically, was he with you Saturday night?

What ironies lay just beneath the surface of these mental meanderings. The persona her husband showed the world, which was reflected in his well-reasoned articulate decisions, was of a man tuned in to compassion, the leading liberal thinker on the Court, great and devoted friend of her gender, more giving on the issue of human rights for women than any other. The right to choose, the right to equal compensation, toppler of barriers. A sadist? A sexual deviate? A murderer? Who could possibly believe that?

"It is so nice seeing you again," Letitia Lipscomb said, nudging her forward, turning to engage Harrison, coming up behind her. Letitia did not break her stride, concentrating her attention on Harrison. When he had been run through the line, they moved to the ballroom and into the milling crowd.

A groaning buffet graced one wall of the ballroom. At a spot directly across from the buffet was a lectern on which was a microphone for the use of the speakers.

"Why are we here?" Harrison asked.

"I thought it would be fun," Fiona began, unsuccessfully avoiding Harrison's skeptical glance. "Scratch that."

"A case?"

Fiona nodded, feeling uncomfortable. For a brief moment, dismissing the idea almost as soon as it surfaced, she contemplated a modified form of confession to Harrison Greenwald. On rare occasions, mostly in moments of post-coital serenity, she had offered confidences about her life, always edited with tact and caution.

Harrison was one of the those philosophizing Jewish men, an over-analyzer of psyches, especially his own. His wife and he had separated because of career displacements. She had been a doctor involved in research at UCLA. Childless, they had apparently simply drifted apart. Separate agendas had created separate lives, which indicated to Fiona that their affection and love for each other was not enough to hold them together.

"She has a fine mind," Harrison had concluded, meaning his wife. Fiona guessed that they had probably talked their way out of loving, intellectualized their relationship, leaving passion bereft. What Harrison needed and Fiona provided was an attentive ear, a good sense of humor and the experience of a strongly sexed woman, which he seemed to have missed completely. To be deprived of the sexual feature of their relationship was undoubtedly cruel and inhuman punishment as far as he was concerned.

What he gave her, aside from the complete cooperation of his body, which she acknowledged was beautiful, with a level of remarkable endurance that suited her perfectly, was a kind of soothing, fatherly wisdom and, ironically, the fruits of a fine mind. He did not have Dr. Benson's natural compassion, but he was able to articulate ways to face fate and its vicissitudes.

This was something that her father had once provided, the sense of moral protection, the understanding of life's foibles and how to meet the challenges of one's own vulnerability. Fiona had adored her father, and all the men in her life since his passing years ago were a replication of him in some form or other. If there were sexual implications, she did not acknowledge them as such. In this, perhaps, was the root of her tight bonding with Gail Prentiss.

The most admirable thing about Fiona, as articulated to her by Harrison, was her honesty, her forthrightness and the logical way in which she expressed herself. Unlike many of Fiona's suitors, who hated the fact that she was a police detective, Harrison reveled in it and showed a deep interest in those cases whose details she shared with him. He was far enough removed from the process so that her revelations would not be considered a violation of police procedures.

"Do we have a suspect here?" Harrison said, putting a hand up as if to shade his eyes, while rotating his head in a mock search.

"I'll explain," she said. "I promise."

"Everything?"

"That, too."

She took it, as she knew he would, as a commitment. What it required was a build-up of courage. They grazed at the buffet table and picked up glasses of white wine, standing around while they ate and observing the surroundings, speaking little. Harrison must have known she was concentrating deeply. She needed, more than ever, to instigate a confrontation with Farley Lipscomb.

It would be a chore to engage him, she realized. Undoubtedly, he was playing the game of indifference. She allowed herself to believe that it was a conscious pose of shrewd evasion.

There had to be a way to draw him out, create some litmus test of his guilt . . . or innocence. Seeing him, after recovering from this brush with her own vulnerability, had forced her to clear her mind of all extraneous hubris. She must concentrate on jarring him out of the clever facade he had erected, rattle his cage, cause him to react.

She watched him walk to the microphone, smooth and confident, in full possession of himself, the wise prince to be fawned over and lionized. He knew how to handle that role well. His persona seemed created especially for the purpose.

Fiona recognized the under secretary of state, who had come in late by a side entrance, a man of lesser presence than Farley, bringing with him the laudatory words of introduction while Farley Lipscomb stood modestly to one side. After a burst of applause the associate justice made the customary self-effacing remarks and bade welcome to his Russian friends, lifting his glass, his voice smooth, its timbre silken.

He was so good at it that Fiona found it difficult to superimpose this other image, the one that she carried with her, the laughing, sneering monstrosity, delighting in her defilement, urging her on to a disgusting refrain as he plunged the hard, vibrating object inside of her, ordering her to relish the pain, to love the pain, to feel the pleasure of the pain.

A film seemed to descend on her vision, which she found difficult to blink away, and Farley finished in a misty cloud. She had lost the content of the windup of his speech, but by then she had begun to take command of herself again. I am a cop on the trail of a killer. Nothing less than that. Alright, there was a lot more, and she would use that anger to prod her action. Hatred, she had learned, was a great motivator, especially when it was personal, the target clearly defined.

After a reciprocal toast by one of the Russian judges, the formalities were declared over and the socializing began in earnest. Fiona watched Farley move through the crowd, working the room with practiced efficiency. Harrison had met a colleague and was deep in conversation, although his eyes followed her protectively.

She insinuated herself into the wave of people sliding like a pulling tide toward the associate justice as he moved against it, dividing his attention appropriately to each person in turn. His wife moved in her own orbit, a master of brief small talk, as she passed from person to person.

Although Fiona fixed her stare on the oncoming Farley, he made no sign of recognition until he was directly in front of her. Lifting his eyes, he smiled generously, showing no sign of anxiety, an unruffled presence soaking up the plaudits of the crowd.

She had calmed down by then, steeling herself for what she knew would be a battle of wills. Tenacity, she realized with heroic intensity, would be her only real advantage. She would surely be outgunned by his deviousness, his intimidating cleverness, and, of course, the power of his reputation and mesmerizing persona.

But nothing, nothing was going to impede her confrontation. In a split second she had decided to go directly to the heart of the matter. Risk everything. Under the spell of that compulsion, she felt helpless.

"It was so nice seeing you again," he said with old-fashioned, chivalric politeness. She was conscious of the sea of people behind her waiting to touch the hem of the great man. But she stood her ground, determined to make her presence indelible.

"I know what you did to Phyla Herbert," she said, her gaze concentrated on his face. Farley looked at her blankly, showing no sign of any emotion, not an iota of fear or hint of anxiety.

"Phyla Herbert?" he responded, shaking his head briefly, offering a genuine look of puzzlement.

"The Mayflower Hotel, Saturday night," she said, which instantly struck her as redundant. Did she have to remind him of the scene of the attack?

"I'm at a loss . . ."

"What you did to me years ago."

It was, she knew, a bold, perhaps foolish, gambit. There seemed no point in subtlety. She needed to pound into his solar plexus, astound him with surprise and direct accusation. He looked at her with a strange mixture of confusion and rebuke, his smile broadening as if in mock exasperation for some childish infraction on her part.

Her voice was just above a whisper, the words for his ears only. It wasn't that he was deaf to them. He simply did not register the expected reaction. The message of his expression was tolerance for the irrationality of an unbalanced mind, a judicial posture as if he were listening to the ravings of a hallucinator.

"Are you saying that you have no recollection of what you did?"

"I must confess to total ignorance," Farley said calmly, shaking his head with what seemed like genuine perplexity.

"Really, Farley. Phyla Herbert as well," Fiona replied quickly, unwavering, lashing out, showing him he was in danger.

"I'm sorry . . . I'm at a loss to understand."

His expression remained unmoved, except for pleasant confusion and benign tolerance. He did not appear to be the least bit frightened by her remarks.

"Seventeen years might dull one's recall, but Saturday night, Mayflower Hotel, Phyla Herbert. Haven't changed your modus operandi, have you, Farley?"

Not the slightest reaction. No fear. No sense of danger. He was acting. Fiona was sure of it. He raised his eyes and looked beyond her, calling to someone behind her.

"Harold. I haven't seen you for an age."

Sidestepping, he left her standing in his wake. She had made her point, she assured herself, and he had shown his own strategy as well. Denial and an attitude of indifference were familiar weapons of evasion for criminals in the face of police action. But the familiarity of the response was tinged with disappointment. Considering the monumental impact his aberration had made on her life, she felt resentful of his denial and insulted by his unwillingness to acknowledge it. In fact, she was furious.

Steady, she told herself. It wouldn't do to lose control of her emotions. She had to assess his reaction, think about it. Did it signify guilt or innocence? Or was she overreacting, fantasizing? Was hate goading her? Was the desire for revenge corrupting her judgment? Would he react? And if so, how?

Treat this as merely the opening gun in a tricky operation, she told herself. But his indifferent reaction touched a raw nerve. She vowed to muster her own arsenal of weapons, stalking, confrontation, harassment. Perhaps some of it would stray over the line, just enough to push him to react. React how? Confession? Perhaps, but unlikely. This was not a man with a conscience. Carelessness? Fear and annoyance might shake loose his tongue.

Would bringing down his vaunted reputation be enough satisfaction for her? Or would nothing less than imprisonment do it? No either/or on her agenda here. She wanted to see him punished to the full extent of the law . . . and beyond. Forever. For eternity.

"What was that all about?" Harrison asked when she had made her way back to his side. She had felt him watching. "You look flushed."

She did feel the heat in her face. But she hoped she had kept the ferocity in her heart well hidden.

"He was a friend of my father years ago," she said, clearing her throat of a sudden hoarseness.

"Was he?"

"He was a lawyer in private practice then. I worked for him briefly."

"Did you?"

She sensed that he knew she was deliberately not filling in the blanks. Thankfully, he didn't pursue it. She felt him sinking into resentment.

They went down the elevator and when they reached the street, he asked: "Want to talk?"

"Not yet, Harrison," she sighed.

"It's all quite mysterious," he said. "You know I really care about you, Fi."

"I'm betting on that to keep you from walking away," she told him.

"Just a phase," he said. "Is that it?"

She nodded, knowing the gesture was inadequate. Actually, she hated people who used that as an excuse for conduct that hurt others.

"And when will it end . . . this phase?"

"Soon."

It was, she knew, a blatant lie. There was no way of knowing. In fact, no way of knowing if it would ever end. Her confrontation with Farley Lipscomb seemed more like an act that would prolong her frigidity than one offering any signs of a thaw.

She said good-bye to him in front of her car with a forced meeting of lips with cheeks. As she drove away, it crossed her mind that this thing with Farley might be pushing her further and further away from reality.

Yet she could not shake her suspicion. Was he guilty or wasn't he? She needed to know. It was driving her over the edge.

— 11 —

Barker had begun to perspire, a dark stain spreading under the arms and along the upper chest of his blue shirt, They were sitting in his office, where he had deliberately arranged them around the conversation area of upholstered chairs. In the corner of his office were a coffee machine and a small refrigerator.

"Black for both of you, right?" Barker said.

Fiona and Gail nodded and Barker filled their order, putting full mugs on the table in front of them. Then he opened the refrigerator and pulled out a can of Diet Pepsi.

Fiona knew it was a ploy to put people at their ease, the personal service, the move away from the awesome officialness of his desk. Only this time he was the one seeking to disarm what was clearly, from his vantage, the enemy. Gail had arrived with guns loaded, her yellow-flecked eyes reflecting a steely determination. Fiona, for her part, brought with her the baggage of skepticism.

"As I mentioned on the phone," Barker said, opening the can and taking a light sip, "I'm really pressed today. I hope this won't take"—he looked at his watch and smiled—"more than a half-hour. A big meeting with the boss."

Fiona had been apprised by Gail of the meeting in Barker's office at Justice by a message on her answering machine when she returned from the State Department.

"I'll meet you there at nine," Gail had said, her voice bursting with enthusiasm. "Lots to fill you in on. I think we've got something here."

Fiona, who had suffered through a bad night wrestling with the fury generated by her confrontation with Farley Lipscomb, had overslept, meeting Gail just as both arrived at Phelps's office.

Actually, she was being assailed by a cloying sense of self-disgust, which was beginning to manifest itself in physical ways. Her appetite, normally robust, had disintegrated into a constant nausea and clot of pain in her stomach. Her heartbeat would accelerate without warning. She had experienced hot flushes last night, worried that it was a harbinger of a change-of-life crisis, supposedly years away. She was also sweating profusely under her dark wool suit.

As they entered Barker's office, Gail, in a chameleonlike miracle of change, presented herself with a benign charm that carefully masked her obvious goal of bashing down Barker's defenses.

The tactic offered a clever new twist to the interrogation, considering the adversarial way in which their earlier interview had ended. Gail now assumed the role of the compassionate, understanding good cop, all smiles and gushing with good cheer. She put out her hand, another contrived gesture of good will. Barker, who must have been confused at first, seemed taken in by this sudden burst of charm.

Fiona decided to maintain a demeanor of strict neutrality, an uncommon role for her. But she was not yet ready to let go of her theory about Farley Lipscomb. She hoped that, no matter how aggressively Gail honed in on Barker, however much his facade was ripped away, whatever layers of perfidy were exposed, none would be relevant to the death of Phyla Herbert. That role she had reserved in her mind for Farley Lipscomb.

"I hope you'll forgive my conduct yesterday," he said. "I was so upset about Phyla . . ." Apparently he, too, had decided on a new tack, reining in his arrogance and showing a humility that seemed oddly ill-suited to him.

"We understand," Gail said, nodding and blinking her eyes in a gesture of acceptance. She reached over and picked up her mug, taking a deep sip. Fiona let hers stand. She had no stomach for coffee at the moment.

"Somebody you grew up with"—he made a sound of sucking air through his teeth—"to die like that."

"Actually we've had somewhat of a break," Gail began blandly, casting a glance at Fiona who nodded, offering what she hoped was a gesture of assent.

"I'm certainly glad of that," Barker said.

"It puts a whole different complexion on the case," Gail said. "We think we know who was the last person to see her alive."

"Fantastic," Barker exclaimed, taking a deeper sip on the Pepsi, his Adam's apple bobbing. "I never meant to disparage your police work."

"We never thought you did," Gail replied. She put her coffee mug back on the table, suggesting that she was stripping down for action.

"So tell me," Barker began. "How can I help you?"

"A couple of fill-in details is all we need," Gail said.

"Shoot."

Gail took out a small pad and opened it slowly. Mostly for effect, Fiona thought. While she did so, Barker finished off the Pepsi and put the can next to the mugs as if, he too, were also stripping down to defend himself.

"You say you left the party Saturday night at about eleven?" Gail asked gently in review, holding back her power, waiting for the right moment to spring.

"About that time, yes," he said alertly. He wasn't a fool, Fiona knew, and their return engagement surely had made him suspect there was more to this than a purely informational interview.

"And you never saw Phyla again?"

He frowned.

"What are you driving at?" he asked, his benign facade starting to crumble.

"Just trying to get some of these details straight," Gail said.

"Didn't I tell you that yesterday?" Barker asked, his eyes shifting to Fiona's face and back to Gail's.

"Yes, you did," Gail said. "That's why we've arranged this interview."

He was getting the message. The perspiration stain on his shirt seemed to spread.

"I don't . . ."

"Just give us a straight answer, Barker," Gail said, snapping her voice like a whip cracking as she finally revealed her intent. Two round balls of hot blush suddenly appeared on Barker's cheeks.

"I don't like your insinuation," Barker said.

"What exactly am I insinuating?" Gail asked, all pretense gone.

"Why belabor the obvious?" Barker snarled. "If you have something, spit it out."

"She was seen coming to the party as you were leaving. You were observed chatting, then leaving together."

The revelation was expected to strike him like a hard physical blow. Instead, he seemed relieved. His nostrils flared as he took a deep breath.

"Caught," he whispered, shaking his head, changing the strategy of his defiance as if he had expected the accusation. "Can you blame me for this little white lie? Where was the upside in getting involved? Good police work, ladies. My congratulations. It was a most unsuitable and inconvenient meeting, I'm afraid."

Back was the superior arrogance of the fraternity boy of the day before. Fiona half-expected him to snap his finger to summon the eager Walter for a whiskey sour.

"We appreciate the compliment, Barker, now we would . . ."

He lifted his hand to stop Gail from continuing.

"Fate has been cruel. Yes, she did come to the party at my invitation and I waylaid her at the door to tell her that it wasn't her cup of tea."

"And you left together?"

"Yes, we did. I had my car."

He paused, waiting for Gail to offer questions. An experienced interrogator himself, it was obvious that he was going to let Gail lead the way, responding sparsely.

"Where did you go?"

"For a drink."

"Where?"

"A bar next door to the Mayflower. Bentley's, I think.

"How long did you stay?"

"An hour, no longer."

"What did you drink?"

"Vodka and soda. She had a Diet Coke."

"How many drinks did you have?"

"Two, no, three."

"What did you talk about?"

"Our futures. The government. The past. I told you we were friends. We talked about what had happened to other friends. Stuff like that."

"Who made the first move to leave?"

"She did."

"And you complied without argument?"

"Of course. It was getting late."

"Did she look at her watch and say something like, it's getting late, I have to be going?"

"Yes. Something like that."

"And then?"

"I paid the check and walked her to the hotel entrance."

"Was there any talk about you going to her room?"

There was a barely perceptible pause, which was odd, since he surely had anticipated the question.

"Yes, there was," he said, sucking in a deep breath. His eyes glazed and he turned away.

"But you said she wasn't interested in such things," Gail pressed.

"Not in my experience. She just wasn't interested in me, I guess." He seemed suddenly regretful, revealing an emotional part of himself that he seemed to have preferred to keep hidden.

"But you were interested in her?"

"I could have been, yes," he admitted. "If she had ever given me half a chance."

"She was rich, beautiful and smart."

"All of the above."

"So after she turned you down, you left her in front of the hotel."

"Yes, I did."

"And she made no mention of meeting someone later."

He shook his head. The sweat stain was deepening and creeping down his sides. Gail exchanged glances with Fiona as if it were an offer to participate. Fiona nodded with closed eyes, signaling that Gail was doing fine on her own. But her instincts told her that Barker was holding something back.

"You say you said good-bye at the lobby entrance?"

"Yes."

"And that was the last you saw of her."

"Yes."

"Is that all, Mr. Barker?" Gail asked, her eyes, laserlike now, boring into him. So Gail, too, was not quite comfortable with Barker's answers.

"What do you mean by 'all'?" Barker said, frowning, his head cocked to one side, listening.

"I had a long conversation with Mr. Herbert last night," Gail said.

Fiona sat up stiffly, moving forward in her chair. Gail kept her eyes leveled on Barker. It was troubling to Fiona not to have known about this conversation. Had Gail deliberately kept it from her?

Surely, Fiona thought, Gail would have briefed her if Fiona had been on time. Yet why hadn't she been told beforehand that Gail and Herbert had spoken? When was it set up? Had they spoken before? Did Gail suspect that Fiona, too, was working on her private track, thus giving herself permission to pursue her own?

"How is Mr. Herbert?" Barker answered, a touch of surliness creeping into his voice.

"Not very good," Gail replied. "In fact, mighty vengeful. And with excellent reason."

"I suppose you might say that's his nature," Barker sighed.

"He told me everything," Gail said.

"Yes, he would do that. So what?"

Gail suddenly turned her attention to Fiona.

"At sixteen he was accused by the thirteen-year-old daughter of the Barker family maid of forcing his attentions on the young lady."

"Rape?" Fiona asked, hiding her surprise.

"An accusation only. Dr. Barker, Phelps's daddy, asked Mr. Herbert to talk to the maid, who apparently was prepared to make the charge to the police."

"It was a total lie," Barker said. The rouge marks mantling his cheeks now spread downward to his neck.

"He told me you had said that," Gail agreed.

"It was a shakedown pure and simple. Dad talked to Mr. Herbert, who talked to the woman, and that was that."

"It was more than talk, Barker. Mr. Herbert said money changed hands. Ten thousand dollars, if I'm not mistaken."

"He told you that. The son-of-a-bitch. He had promised that the matter would never be brought up again. I can't believe he did that."

"That man is going to leave no stone unturned. No matter who gets hurt. He will be completely ruthless about finding the man who caused his daughter's death. He told me that the evidence was overwhelming. That the young girl showed marks of violence on her body."

"Did he also tell you that this spic bitch also accused her own father of violating her and that she had actually seduced me, waved it in front of my face, for crying out loud?"

"Yes," Gail said. "He told me about that. He said that was also part of your defense."

"Mr. Herbert said he believed me. My father did, too. It was clearly a case of blackmail to extort ten thousand dollars from my father. It was awful. It could have ruined any hope for my future. How dare you throw this back in my face. Mr. Herbert violated a trust." His anger was accelerating as his fulminations increased. "That lousy fuck. That girl was a lousy little whore. I was a vulnerable sixteen-year-old boy. I really resent this. I really, really do. What is it with you people? Alright, you need an arrest, but dragging me into it will lead nowhere. Nowhere."

"Tell me about your engagement to Ann Lawton."

"Jesus," Barker said, turning suddenly to Fiona. "She's trying to nail me to the cross."

"I spoke to her," Gail said.

Busy little bee, Fiona thought, her resentment rising. They had paired her up with a lone wolf, a glory-seeking cop. She wondered if Gail had informed the Eggplant of these little tidbits. That, she decided, would be beyond the pale.

Fiona felt her accelerating irritation. Was it because Gail was closing in on Barker? Or was it the resultant explosion of her theory about Farley Lipscomb?

"And she does not speak kindly of me, am I right?"

"She was not unkind. I would call her 'guarded.' "

"Did she also cry rape?"

"She put things in a much more generous way. She said you and she were incompatible. She implied that this incompatibility was of a physical nature."

"My God. Are there no secrets? Ann is now a fanatic feminist and a commited lesbian."

"Yes. She told me that. Told me other things as well."

"I don't believe this," Barker said.

"She said you liked to see her make love to another woman."

He shook his head, despairing.

"Alright, I have a strong libido. Many men like to see that. It turns them on. Actually, it turned her on as well, witness her present orientation. What turns you on, Officer Prentiss?"

"Finding the bad guys," Gail said coldly.

That remark made Fiona suddenly reflect on her own logic. An instinct for the truth, she discovered, is an acquired skill. Not all detectives ever reached that level of sensitivity, only those with an interior operating system that is able to program itself out of the hubris of personal experience. It was not infallible and only worked under certain conditions.

Unfortunately, such a skill was only practical if it led to the conviction of the perpetrator of a crime. To nail a criminal required facts that could convince a district attorney to make a presentation to a grand jury. The district attorney did not deal in insincts or suppositions, only the quality of facts and, of course, his or her own powers of persuasion to motivate a grand jury to return an indictment.

But everything began with the detective. The detective was the source. Instinct was the cutting edge that sliced through the rope that held the package together. And once the box was open and the lid taken off, the detective might find the validation for his or her instincts.

Watching Gail hone in on Phelps Barker, Fiona could see that she was pursuing a trail bushwhacked by her instincts. Gail, apparently, truly believed that Phelps Barker was the perpetrator, but so far her instincts had led merely to supposition based on Barker's sexual track record. Was it enough to screen out Farley Lipscomb? It was exactly on this point that her logic and instincts went to war.

Despite Barker's bravado, Fiona could see that Gail was breaking him piece by piece. Perhaps she hoped for a confession. Without it, Fiona was certain that, despite Gail's relentlessness, there was, so far, no hard evidence to support her contention.

"Are you certain, Mr. Barker, that you have nothing more to tell me?" Gail asked sharply.

Barker's eyes shifted from side to side as if his mind wanted to jump out of his face to some other reality.

"Like what? You have no right investigating me, dredging up my so-called checkered past." He leaned over toward Gail. "You know this could be actionable."

"I know the limits of my official capacity, Mr. Barker," Gail shot back.

Barker turned suddenly to Fiona.

"You've been awfully quiet, Sergeant. Or is this a good-cop/bad-cop scenario?"

"I'm a good listener," Fiona said, deliberately displaying her neutrality.

"Suppose I told you that I have a witness to your being inside the lobby that night," Gail said. "Not outside, as you contend."

He seemed to go suddenly white, swallowing hard. Fiona's irritation accelerated. Was Gail putting bait on her hook or had she found a witness? If so, why wasn't Fiona consulted?

"Now really . . ." he began.

"You bought a package of mints at the stand in the lobby. The person was just closing up."

"Jesus," Barker said. "Jesus."

"How could she know it was me?"

"How could you know it was a she?" Gail said, triumphantly cutting a glance at Fiona.

Barker shook his head and pursed his lips. He studied his fingernails. The perspiration continued to pour out of him.

"I just assumed . . ." he said bravely.

"Never assume, Barker. I showed her your picture."

"My picture?"

"Simple. The Georgetown Law School yearbook. You haven't changed much in two years."

He turned to Fiona, his demeanor pleading.

"I don't believe this. She wants to frame me."

"I put you in the lobby and I'll put you in her room," Gail said.

Fiona was beginning to feel insecurity about her neutrality. Gail had, indeed, put him in the lobby.

"Look, I know how this must look. But surely you can't believe that I could do such a thing. Alright, I was in the lobby. I did buy some mints. I was drinking. I hate that kind of taste in my mouth. Is that a crime? I bought the mints and then I went home."

"I don't believe you," Gail snapped.

"Your prerogative. I'm a lawyer, remember. You need a lot more than that to charge me. Put me in the room and I'll concede I'd better get me a good lawyer."

"Don't worry, I will," Gail said.

"She really believes I am the man," Barker said, trying to preserve some fragment of credibility, but he was clearly on the way to defeat. Then, suddenly, any last vestige of machismo disintegrated. "Alright, you probably think I'm an arrogant bastard. But I'm not a killer. No way . . . I hope . . ." He seemed to find it difficult to find words and his eyes moistened. He was no longer able to keep his emotions in check.

Suddenly his throat rasped and he cleared it. "I hope you won't destroy me. I'm an innocent in this. I tried to be of some help to the girl . . . I . . ." He shook his head and held out his hands palms up. "I don't know why I've become a target. I'm . . . I'm not your man."

"We'll see," Gail said, getting up, rising to her full height. Despite her chagrin at being out of the loop on this, Fiona could not dismiss her admiration for Gail's thoroughness and professionalism. The dark side, of course, was her relentlessness in her pursuit of Barker. She admitted to herself that she didn't like him, and Gail, too, probably despised him, but was this enough to mark him as the perpetrator? Fiona left the question open.

"You could have filled me in," Fiona said, as they settled into one of Sherry's much-battered Naugahyde booths. She tried to keep her tone nonjudgmental, but that was difficult under the circumstances.

"I wanted to, but . . ."

"I know," Fiona said, waving away any explanation. "I was late."

"That was part of it."

"And the other part?"

"Sometimes when it comes out fresh, it adds to the impact. Actually, Fiona, I had no intention of doing it this way," Gail said. "And I'm sorry it upset you."

Fiona decided then that it would be counterproductive to show any belligerence. Gail might jump to the conclusion that her nose was out of joint for reasons of ego, which was part of it. But what kept her in check was the other. She still clung to her theory about Farley Lipscomb.

Until there was enough evidence to prove the guilt of Phelps Barker, she was determined not to falter in her pursuit of Lipscomb. Pursuit? It seemed a strong word in the face of her rather awkward confrontation. It hadn't seemed to make a dent in his demeanor, although the obvious posture of denial could be interpreted as a ploy. Of course, that was what she wanted to infer.

What now, she asked herself. How must she proceed? She was worried suddenly that Gail and her ally Thomas Herbert would pump up the pressure on Phelps Barker, twist his mind, confuse him, perhaps extract a confession. She had seen it happen before. A man guilty of one crime confessing to another.

"The point is," Gail said, "I know in my gut that Barker is our man."

"Gut feeling does not a case make," Fiona countered, keeping the rebuke light.

Sherry came up to them in her floppy slippers and took their order. Both ordered tuna-fish sandwiches.

"There's more to this than meets the eye, Fiona," Gail said, sipping the coffee that Sherry had poured into their cups.

"Like what?" Fiona asked, bracing herself for more revelations.

"Those latents we picked up," Gail said. "We couldn't find a match . . ."

"You didn't . . . ." Fiona snapped.

Gail smiled and nodded, took her large pocketbook from the seat beside her, opened it and tipped it toward Fiona. There was the Pepsi can, lying in a bed of scarf.

"Put him in the room, we got something, right?" Gail said.

Gail was lengths ahead of her. Fiona, despite her feelings, offered a nod of admiration. Under ordinary circumstances, it seemed a logical course of action. Now it was, for her, a personal source of shame.

"You're closer, that's for sure," Fiona managed to say. Her obsession with Farley Lipscomb was obviously interfering with judgment.

"We, Fiona, we are closer."

Fiona nodded and sipped her coffee, hoping it would mask her self-disgust.

"And if there is no match?" Fiona asked, further upset by her obvious display of negativity.

"Then we have the tech boys do the room again."

"And then if we find nothing?"

"Back to the drawing board," Gail replied. She paused and Fiona felt the intensity of her gaze as she studied her face. Fiona knew what had to come next.

"You don't seem very enthusiastic, Fiona," Gail said, after a long pause.

"It's a little premature for enthusiasm, Gail. Although I am very impressed with your work."

Gail lowered her eyes, as if trying to avoid commenting on the pallid comment. At that moment, much to Fiona's relief, Sherry brought their tuna-fish sandwiches.

"Oh yes," Gail said suddenly. Having lifted the sandwich, she put it down on her plate again. "Mr. Herbert has launched a private investigation of Barker."

Fiona again tried to tamp down her negative reaction, fearful that it might be possible to build up a good enough circumstantial case, which, whether brought to trial or not, would ruin Barker. The media would fixate on it and provide enough exposure to doom Barker's career dreams. But what Fiona feared most was that, circumstantial or not, a jury could declare the man guilty and destroy him. The law, after all, was not a science.

"Have you told the Chief?" Fiona asked.

"Yes, I did," Gail said, avoiding Fiona's stunned gaze. "I called him first thing this morning."

"Don't you think you should have consulted with your senior partner?"

"Herbert asked me to keep it between us, at least until I had spoken to my superior. I had to keep that confidence, Fiona. And, of course, I'm telling you now and the fact is that the Chief must have interpreted it as if I were speaking for both of us. No harm done, is there? I was careful to make no waves. Herbert is grief-stricken and determined. There seemed no other way to handle it. He is, in fact, making our job easier." She laughed. "I mean it does solve the personnel problem, and if we crack it, it'd be a feather in both our caps. And the Chief would have the glory that comes with the success of his first gender team."

Studying Gail's face, Fiona looked for some sinister intent in this explanation. She couldn't find any, or probably didn't want to. She had her own sense of ethics to contend with, her own violation of the partnership pact between police officers, and she was too vulnerable to protest. What puzzled her most, however, was her absolute unwillingness to characterize Barker as the guilty party. It seemed more like a stubborn, obsessive compulsion.

"You've got a point, I suppose," Fiona sighed. She had been waiting for Gail to question her about the pictures she had presented to the assistant manager and staff of the Mayflower. Surely Gail had gone through the same dance, showing a blown-up picture of Phelps Barker extracted from his Georgetown yearbook. Someone must have mentioned it. But on this matter, Gail was inexplicably silent.

By then, the first bite of the sandwich had turned to stone in her stomach. If Gail noticed her lack of appetite, she said nothing.

After lunch, Gail left for the lab to pursue the processing of Phelps Barker's prints. Fiona went back to the squad room. The Eggplant was just leaving as she came in.

"Looks like we have a break coming on the Herbert case," he said.

"I wouldn't be that optimistic, Chief," Fiona said.

"Prentiss seems to feel otherwise."

"We'll soon find out," Fiona said, feeling foolish. The Eggplant looked at her with some curiosity, then turned and left the room. So her indifference was showing, she thought.

For a long time she sat in the squad room faking work. Her mind felt like a slot machine churning endless, unmatching symbols in their little windows. People came in, talked, made phone calls, joked. When they talked to her she answered in monosyllables with just enough effort to project an idea of alertness.

She felt bottled up, gorged with secrets, unable to find a clear path of action. Her attention drifted to the telephone messages on her desk. One was from Harrison. She called home to get her messages from the answering machine, admitting finally to herself that she had expected Farley to call, to follow up on their confrontation. Despite the vagaries of his reaction, she still believed that her message had been received.

Then she realized the foolishness of her expectation. Farley would never call and leave his own name. She went through her messages again. They were all from people she knew. No unknowns. Could that mean he expected her to call him, was waiting for her call? The more she thought about it, the more powerful became her desire to explore the idea.

Picking up the phone, she called the Supreme Court and asked for the office of Associate Justice Lipscomb. Even as she waited, she felt out of control, possessed. At length she got a receptionist and announced herself.

"He'll know me. I promise you. Fiona FitzGerald," she said.

In a few moments the woman came back on the phone.

"Justice Lipscomb is in a meeting," the woman announced.

"Does he know I'm on the phone?"

"He's in a meeting. I'll be sure he gets the message."

The woman broke the connection. Knowing the consequences, how could he possibly avoid making contact? She called again a half-hour later, making the request to speak to the justice as soon as possible. Was this compulsion a form of madness? she wondered.

"I'll give him the message," the receptionist said icily, hanging up. It was apparent that this was not the method that would get the required response. Of course not, she affirmed. Farley would be far too cautious to accept any contact that could be compromising. A telephone was too vulnerable and, even if he met with her in person, he would most certainly want to be sure she wasn't wired.

A number of alternatives ran through her mind. Finally she settled on an idea whose subtlety he would understand. She would contact Mrs. Lipscomb. Letitia. She called Daisy.

"Me again," she told Daisy. As always, they would slip into their clever banter and wisecracking mode.

"Did I do the trick, Fi?" Daisy said breezily.

"Yes, you did."

"Any return engagement brewing?"

"It's business, Daisy."

"Have you their home number?"

"The chatelaine, is it?"

She paused for a moment, then gave Fiona the number.

"Is this all hush-hush detective work, Fi? Death and intrigue. Sounds so . . ."

"Gory."

"Not before cocktails, dahling. Don't make me queasy."

Daisy's voice helped dispel Fiona's gloom. She dialed the number, then before the ring began, hung up quickly. The fact was, she had no clear idea of her strategy. She was, she realized, playing this like a jazz pianist, moving ahead with the rhythm, improvising as she went along.

She spent the next hour fishing in her mind for a starting point, getting discouraged, fishing again. Then her focus began to wander and she considered Phelps Barker and the forces ranged against him. They would be formidable and, despite her antipathy for the type, she felt sorry for him. He had undoubtedly lied out of panic.

When the phone rang she picked it up quickly, half hoping that it would be Farley Lipscomb. It was Thomas Herbert, asking for Gail Prentiss. Fiona recognized his voice.

"I'll give her your message, Mr. Herbert," Fiona said, identifying herself.

There was a long pause.

"Has she filled you in?"

"Yes, she has."

"Tell her I'm at the Hay-Adams."

"I will."

"We'll need to touch base first thing tomorrow. I'll be expecting some preliminary information by then." He cleared his throat. "I'll expect you both."

There was another long pause. She heard the steady *whoosh* of his breathing as it came through the phone. She debated asking him about the funeral, but thought better of it.

"We'll get him," he said. "We'll get the evil bastard."

She hung up, feeling helpless in the face of what was quickly becoming an inevitablity.

It was growing dark outside, which prompted Fiona to risk the call to Letitia. She could not wait. It seemed important, she told herself, to talk to her alone. A strategy was half formed in her mind. She dialed Letitia's number. Someone, probably the maid, answered and asked her name. She gave it.

Moments later the person returned and said that Madame was busy, whereupon Fiona told the woman that she was a sergeant in the homicide division and needed to talk to Mrs. Lipscomb immediately or, she threatened, she would have to swear out a search warrant.

Her tone probably panicked the poor woman and in a moment Letitia was on the phone.

"Fiona, is that you?"

Fiona had expected her throat to constrict as it had done the other night. It didn't, the words coming out sharp and clear. She felt surprisingly calm.

"Yes, Mrs. Lipscomb. I'm sorry if I frightened the poor woman."

"Why on earth are you calling? And what is so terribly urgent? It's not Farley, Judge Lipscomb?"

"He's fine, Mrs. Lipscomb." There was irony in that.

"Well, then, what is so important that I had to rush to the phone?" Her worry abated, she turned bitchy and imperious. "I don't appreciate this one bit."

"I must talk with your husband, Mrs. Lipscomb."

"Call his office. They might put you through if you get as heavy-handed as you did earlier. But I doubt it." She paused. "Fiona, millions of people want to talk with my husband."

"I know that, Mrs. Lipscomb, that's why I called you at home."

"And where, may I ask, did you get my number?" she asked haughtily. Fiona reached for a cliche.

"We have our methods."

"Well, I, for one, don't like them. May I remind you that we are talking about an associate justice of the Supreme Court."

"Will you please take this number down, Mrs. Lipscomb?"

"You were such a charming teenager, Fiona. How could you lower yourself to become a"—her voice became sneering—"a policeman? Your father is probably turning in his grave."

"Just write the number down please, Mrs. Lipscomb."

"I'm ready, thank you."

Fiona gave Letitia her home number and made her repeat it.

"Are you satisfied now?"

"I won't be until I talk to your husband. Tell him it's urgent."

"I warn you, Fiona. It had better be."

"It is. I promise you."

Fiona hung up, relieved at last that she had found a course of action. Farley lived, above all, in mortal fear of his wife. During their affair, Farley had been paranoid about her finding out and had taken every precaution. She was betting that he still felt the same terrible fear.

Hanging up, Fiona put a note on Gail's desk about meeting Thomas Herbert at the Hay-Adams first thing in the morning, then left to await what she fervently hoped was the call from Farley Lipscomb.

— 12 —

By eleven, she hadn't heard from Farley. It had been a nerve-wracking evening, not only the waiting but a brief and upsetting conversation with Harrison Greenwald.

Harrison had told her that he was "ravaged" by her treatment of him. "Ravaged" was a word he seemed to fix on, since he repeated it numerous times. It had, as he told her, put him off his feed. There was something quaintly literary about his speech, which used to amuse her and which now seemed forced and pompous.

"It's not just the libido, Fiona," he pressed. "I'm mentally ravaged by not knowing what's bothering you. Why bottle it up? I care and I want to help. Besides, it's driving me crazy."

"I can't discuss it. Can't you understand? It has nothing to do with you."

"But it affects me. Whatever it is, I'm in it. I thought we were lovers, soulmates. Relationships mean sharing."

"Please, no lectures, Harrison. I just need some space."

"I hate that phrase," he said. "It implies deep dark secrets and I also hate secrets."

"I know."

"What kind of an answer is that?"

"An incomplete one. I'll explain it soon."

"What does that mean, an hour, a day, a week, a month?"

She was tempted to say "always," remembering a phrase from an old song her mother used to sing.

He was not a man to be kept in the dark. That much she had learned in the eight months they had been together as lovers. Harrison was one of those men who needed to know, which was, in fact, one of the reasons she adored their time together. She, too, was a woman who needed to know.

Yet how could she have told him that, for reasons beyond her control, her life was on hold until . . . until what? The case of Phyla Herbert? The culmination of the Farley Lipscomb trauma? How? What? Perhaps she would remain in this state forever? Whatever the outcome, she sensed that this was something between herself and herself, that she had little choice but to see it through . . . alone.

The conversation with Harrison ended with pauses and monosyllables. How could she tell him that her heart and body were frozen solid? Telling him that would be far more hurtful than leaving him confused.

The anxiety of waiting also took its toll. She couldn't sleep, couldn't concentrate on the various mind-numbing shows that populated the television airwaves at that time of night. She took to roaming the house, moving in and out of rooms. This was her parents' home, her inheritance, and she had cared for it with love and money, planning never to sell it, hoping one day that it might be an inheritance for her offspring, a fading dream. Thinking such thoughts made her gloomier.

In the ground-floor den, she poured herself a straight Scotch and drank it in one gulp, feeling the heat of the liquid sting as it went down. As she started to move out of the den, her attention was diverted by something happening in the front of the house.

A man was walking up the driveway. He was walking slowly, a yet unknown figure, moving almost soundlessly. It was every cop's nightmare, a confrontation with someone they had caught, a psychopath bent on revenge.

In a desk drawer, she kept a piece for emergencies, a police-issue .38, always fully loaded. Lifting it out of the drawer, she gripped it and waited, watching the man move forward. He continued up the driveway, which seemed odd for a stalker bent on murder.

The security system was triggered, but she knew that anyone bent on forced entry would have considered that and taken steps to circumvent it. Short of a bomb thrown into a window, she had the present situation well covered.

The man continued to move forward. He reached the front door. Chime sounds ripped through the silence, startling her. The .38 still in her hand, she moved to the door and looked into the side window normally used for identifying visitors. She flicked on a switch, which showered the visitor in a blaze of light.

Turning off the security system, she unlatched the door. Farley Lipscomb stood in the doorway.

"May I come in?" he asked.

"Of course," she replied, thrusting the pistol in the front pocket of her robe. Her heart was fluttering and she was conscious of her own effort to keep herself under control, as if an eruption was brewing inside of her. Yet she had expected him to react, hadn't she? Now that he had, she wasn't sure she was up for it.

He was wearing a raincoat and an old-fashioned snap-brim hat low over his forehead. Obviously, he had parked elsewhere, probably a good distance from the house, and his costume was designed as a disguise. Same MO, she thought, as he came into the vestibule. He would have taken every conceivable precaution not to be recognized and this nocturnal visit assured him that his conversation would not be recorded.

Knowing the drill, he knew how to avoid the pitfalls. Obviously, he had carefully checked out the house, assured himself that she was alone and made his move.

Fiona led him to the den, where he sat down on one of the leather wing chairs, his raincoat open, his hat on his lap. She was conscious of him watching her as she moved into the room behind him trying to overcome the rubbery feeling in her legs.

"Haven't been here in years," Farley said in his deep voice, the tones measured and cadenced. Even in his odd get-up, he looked elegant and handsome. "Your father and I spent many happy hours in this room going over the momentous events of the times. He was quite a man, quite a man."

"Yes, he was."

"His courage has been a constant source of inspiration to me." He had, Fiona noted, retained, even embellished, his ability to impress. Yes, she remembered, her father and he had been friends. What made it even more ironic was that they were ideological allies as well, and Farley had brought these attitudes to the Supreme Court. He was the quintessential moralist and all his opinions stressed the moral implications of the law above all else. But he was best known for his compassion, which threaded through his decisions and other writings. To Fiona, who had experienced his compassion first hand, it represented the quintessential hypocrisy.

"Would you like a drink, Farley?"

He shook his head. Only a lamp beside the couch was lit, a three-way bulb, at its lowest illumination. She did not make a move to turn it up.

For a few moments, they just stared at each other. Both she and Farley had crossed their legs, but Farley had put his hand on his chin as he contemplated her. Despite the many years since they had been alone together, she still felt diminished in his presence. After awhile her initial shock had dissipated and she felt her nervousness retreat.

"Well, I did get your attention, Farley," she said, offering a thin smile. He did not smile back.

"I rather resented your involving Letitia."

"I was hoping you would," Fiona said.

His face was in the shadows and it was difficult for her to interpret his expression.

"Still playing it safe, aren't you, Farley? You seemed to have really worked it out. Frankly, I expected you to call, not show up in person . . . until I realized that you might think the telephones had been bugged."

"Why are you doing this?" he said, shaking his head. "Considering that our so-called experience happened more than a decade and a half ago."

She supposed the use of the word "decade" was meant to push the event even deeper into the past.

"That's history, Farley. My interest in you is professional and has to do with what happened just a few days ago in the Mayflower Hotel."

"That's the part that confused me," he said. "What the devil are you talking about?"

"Phyla Herbert."

"Phyla Herbert?"

He seemed genuinely puzzled. But Fiona had seen hundreds of suspects portray themselves as genuinely puzzled, many of them without the thespian talents of Farley Lipscomb.

"Thomas Herbert's little girl," Fiona said, not taking her eyes off him, trying to interpet every tiny nuance of his facade.

"Herbert?"

"From Chicago, Farley. Come now, don't be coy."

"Thomas Herbert, the lawyer?"

He said it slowly, his forehead wrinkling. Was it genuine puzzlement or dissembling? Perhaps both.

"He says he knows you," Fiona said, taking a stab in the dark.

"Actually, it could be the Tom Herbert I know. He was three years behind me at Yale Law."

She knew he was being scrupulously cautious, like a man walking on a newly frozen lake. But her play had drawn him out.

"Did you know his daughter Phyla?"

"Phyla? Oh yes. She had an odd name," Farley said with cool aplomb. "Yes, you might say I knew her. Letitia and I have been house guests at their lakefront place in Minnesota."

Bingo, Fiona said to herself. It was a connection she knew in her pores existed and the validation was comforting. She was satisfied that she was on track.

"Have you seen her recently?"

"No. Should I have?" He shrugged and tipped his head in a show of ever-deepening confusion.

"Farley, you've always been a magnificent actor. But I find myself now seeing beyond the performance."

"Are you sure?"

It seemed a challenge. And she took it.

"Phyla Herbert was found dead in the Mayflower Hotel on Saturday night. I'm surprised you didn't see it in the papers."

Deep frown lines knitted his brow and he shook his head.

"How awful. I do have the vaguest recollection, but only in passing. I hadn't noticed the name. I never associated it with Tom Herbert's daughter." He shook his head and clucked his tongue. "Poor Tom."

"Yes, poor Tom."

"I must tell Letitia to pass along our condolences."

"Shall I tell you how she was found?"

"Can I stop you?"

"She was naked, trussed up with ropes on the bed, a blindfold over her eyes, a gag in her mouth, obscene graffiti written in lipstick over her body and her anus ripped apart by a large instrument."

As she spoke, she watched his face, the features unchanging, the eyes leveled on her face. Other than attention, no emotion showed. Not anxiety either and certainly not guilt.

"I assume she was murdered," he said.

"In a manner of speaking."

"What does that mean?"

"Her death was a by-product of the trauma she underwent."

"What was the cause of death?"

She wondered if this was a clue to his culpability. Would it be, she asked herself, a logical question for a perpetrator to ask, knowing that he hadn't caused her death deliberately? She decided to answer his question.

"She was an asthmatic. The episode must have brought on an attack and the fact that she was gagged probably killed her."

He shook his head.

"Poor woman," Farley said. "And you think that I did it?"

"It's your MO, Farley," Fiona said. It was, she realized, a direct accusation. "I was there, remember."

"How can I ever live that one down? I tried for years to erase it from my memory. In fact, I thought I had succeeded until you popped back into my life the other night. I was what the shrinks might call a negative dominant," he said. "I've made my own diagnosis, of course. In this business, one can't be too careful. Such an incident hadn't happened before nor has it since. We were consensual, remember. I went too far. I admit that. It was terrible, clumsy."

"And painful, but then, you enjoyed that part."

"It was meant to be an erotic experience, Fiona. Not traumatic. A game. We were supposed to be playing at harm, not inflicting it. Believe me, I have regretted that day. I was too ashamed to face you at the time. I don't know what came over me." He sucked in a deep breath and looked genuinely contrite.

"A sadistic sickness is what came over you. You should have sought professional help."

"And kiss my future good-bye?"

It was, she knew, a fatuous idea. Of course, he would not risk therapy. The sacrosanct patient-doctor privilege was always in jeopardy from a disgruntled therapist or even his spouse or the offspring who inherits records, particularly tapes, and uses them to fulfill a personal agenda for revenge or profit. No, Farley would be far too cautious for that.

"It might have headed off a repeat performance," Fiona snapped.

"There was no repeat performance," he shot back. "Besides, I found self-therapy much more helpful. I've worked it out through insight and personal control."

A self-cure, he meant, which Fiona believed was highly unreliable. Besides, it also fit in nicely with her theory, which she had not yet rejected.

"You injured me, you know," Fiona said.

"I know. It's taken me years to resolve my guilt. But then, here you are. Safe and sound. None the worse for wear."

Of course, she could not bring herself to tell him of the traumatic after-effects of his little caper and its present manifestation. Seeing him sitting across from her in this room in her own house only added to the intensity of the old memory.

"You did it, Farley. Your fingerprints are all over it."

"Fingerprints?"

She watched his eyes. Did she detect confusion . . . or fear?

"Impossible, Fiona. I wasn't there."

She had meant fingerprints in a symbolic sense, but she made no move to correct his misinterpretation. Let him stew over that one, she decided.

"Come now, Fiona. I was a prosecutor once. That kind of evidence demands action. Besides, if you had my prints, I'd be sweating out an interrogation at police headquarters. The reason you haven't my prints is that I was not present at the scene, despite your wild theorizing."

"Weren't you?"

He shook his head as if he were pitying her.

"I understand, Fiona, where your suspicion is coming from. It's simply not true. The thing I did to you . . ." He paused obviously searching for just the right phrase. ". . . is . . ." He paused and shook his head.

"Is what, Farley?"

"It's part of it . . ."

"Along with the graffiti?"

"Yes," he admitted. "I told you, I went too far."

"With me and her," Fiona snapped.

"With you. It was meant to be theatrics."

"The tie-ups, the blindfold and the gag, the leather, the paddle."

"They're props of the game. You know that, Fiona. Do I assume that it . . . our incident . . . was your only exposure?"

"Yes, it was."

"If I recall correctly, some parts of it were quite stimulating for you."

She felt a flash of heat rise to her face and a familiar sensation surge through her body, which she fought off acknowledging. She cursed her vulnerability.

"I stick by my theory, Farley."

"I understand your strategy, Fiona, and I'm here to tell you it won't work. In the first place, I am innocent. In the second place, I doubt if any evidence has surfaced to remotely connect me with the crime." He paused, waiting for her response. She deliberately kept her silence, not wishing to confirm his statement as truth. She might have said something like "Not yet. You seemed to have done a thorough job of clean-up," but she held her peace.

"It won't work, Fiona," he continued. "I'll admit, from what you tell me, that there was some similarity to . . . our episode. I also understand your wanting to avenge yourself. The fact is that you apparently have no evidence and I won't confess to something I have not done. I must admit your strategy with Letitia worked, but it won't work with me. I wasn't there." Again he shook his head. Then he sighed. "The very nature of my job makes me vulnerable. I was always grateful for your silence, Fiona. Such a revelation would have killed my appointment to the Court dead in it's tracks. You could have stepped forward then, Fiona, and floored me. You didn't, for which I am eternally grateful. You still can harm me, but you could also harm yourself, which brings us to a stalemate of sorts. Although I have more to lose than you."

"Still a snob, aren't you, Farley?"

"I'm just being realistic. Equate a Supreme Court justice with a homicide detective. Where do you come out?"

He was right, of course. To accuse a Supreme Court justice of a crime of this magnitude without evidence would result in certain suspension for her. Not necessarily for him, although he would have to ride out the storm. There were, after all, no witnesses to corroborate her story, which he would deny. He would accuse her of fantasizing, hellbent on destroying him for some yet-to-be-concocted political reason.

"If you did it, I'll find out, Farley. I'll connect you."

Lipscomb shook his head.

"These things can become an obsession, Fiona. Why not leave well

enough alone? What we did is over, over years ago. You're fixated on it.
Let it go. It won't do either of us any good."

For a man accused, even obliquely, he was remarkably calm. In the
lamplit room with its muted shadows, he looked a lot younger than he
was. She knew she was doling out bravado. But how could she admit her
frustration? Worse, she was genuinely concerned that Gail and Thomas
Herbert, in their hyper-zealousness, could cook up a case based on circumstantial evidence and destroy what could be an innocent man.

"Maybe so," she admitted. "But I'm not going to let it go until I'm
sure."

He studied her for a long time.

"I feel very sorry for you, Fiona. Perhaps you haven't yet come to terms
with your own sexuality."

"Are you now practicing psychoanalysis, Farley?"

"If memory serves, your response was . . . fervent." He looked at her
intensely, his expression one of rebuke. "Perhaps you need to learn a new
lesson."

His voice recalled the old memory, troubling now because she reacted
to it, as she had then. It was incredible, the idea of it. Despite his protesta-
tions, she saw, he was still into it.

"I don't need any lessons from you."

"Yes you do, you bitch."

She stood up suddenly.

"What are you trying to do, Farley?"

"You filthy slut," he said, getting up from his chair and moving toward
her. She remained seated as he came toward her, unable to act, mesmerized by his oncoming form.

He stood over her, fists clenched, his face somber, stern. Grabbing her
by the arm, he lifted her roughly from the sofa. She felt her heartbeat
pounding in her ribcage, ribbons of perspiration rolling down her back.
His face was close to hers, their eyes met.

"You're going to get exactly what you deserve for doing this to me."

Then suddenly his arm reached back and he slapped her hard across the
face. Her head swung in the direction of the slap and he slapped her again
in the opposite direction. She felt helpless, paralyzed with humiliation.

"You like that, don't you, you cunt," he shouted, striking her again with
the back of his hand.

She stepped back to avoid his blows, struck suddenly by the grossness of the idea. He was trying to bring her back to the old game and, for a moment, a brief moment, she had been disoriented. Now her head cleared and she reached into the pocket of her robe where she had put the .38. Drawing it out, she pointed it directly at his face.

"I wouldn't, Farley. You cannot imagine how much pleasure it would give me to blow your head away."

He stepped backward. She could see the fear in his eyes.

"Alright," he said, his hands in front of him, palms up. "Just calm down."

"I'm very calm. All I'm looking for is an opportunity to pull this trigger."

"You've got it wrong, Fiona."

"You know I don't."

He kept his hands up and stepped a few steps backward.

"May I leave now?" he said, clearing his throat.

"You mean you're willing to deprive me of the pleasure."

He did not reply, walking slowly past her, watching the barrel of the .38.

"I'm going now," he said, clearing his throat.

"I'll be seeing you. Soon."

He let himself out of the door and closed it quietly, moving soundlessly through the darkness to wherever he had parked his car.

Slowly, she put down the gun and dropped it into the pocket of her robe. The interview with Farley had planted a seed in her mind and, as she moved up the staircase to her room, she felt it begin to germinate.

With her mind churning, she looked at the rumpled bed with distaste. The idea of lying there in the darkness, unable to quiet her thoughts, filled her with anxiety. She paced the room, trying to understand the events of the evening, especially the vulnerability she experienced when Farley suddenly snapped on the ritual language of the bondage-and-discipline theatrical script.

The response it had triggered in her was frightening. She had thought that she had left all that behind years ago. The idea of it sapped her resolve, made her feel further disoriented, raising questions of confidence.

This was definitely not the way a homicide detective was supposed to react. There had to be dispassion, objectivity, an emotional neutrality. Personal involvement could be counterproductive, bias the investigation, skewer judgment. Perhaps, in the final analysis, she was not cut out for this type of work. The intrusion of such a negative thought seemed to shake the foundations of her life. A massive depression seemed on the way.

Then, suddenly, a telephone's signal shuddered into the jumble of her thoughts. As a reflex she noted that the digital clock registered a few minutes after midnight. It was Gail Prentiss.

"I'm sorry Fiona. I had to call."

"It's okay, Gail, comes with the territory."

"I just got home from Dad. It was on my fax."

"What was?"

"We got our match, Fiona. We put Phelps Barker in Phyla's room."

—13—

The pleasantness of the surroundings belied the seriousness of the events. From Thomas Herbert's suite, the sun streamed brightly through the undraped windows, which framed the White House. Beyond could be seen the Jefferson Memorial and the Washington Monument. Picture-postcard Washington, Fiona thought, wedding-cake perfect.

But when her gaze drifted from the view to Thomas Herbert's somber face and Gail Prentiss's dark intense expression, the pleasantness disintegrated.

"It's enough to bring him in for questioning, but not enough to hold him," Fiona said. For the past half-hour she was saying the same thing in different ways and Thomas Herbert was growing increasingly angry.

"He was there. He lied. He's undoubtedly guilty," Thomas Herbert said. He, too, had been saying the same thing repeatedly. "He needs to be sweated, skillfully interrogated."

"He will be," Fiona said.

"I want Officer Prentiss to do the questioning."

Fiona and Gail exchanged glances.

"Sergeant FitzGerald is very experienced, Mr. Herbert," Gail said.

Herbert must have realized he had put Gail in an awkward position and grunted something about commitment.

"We don't presume guilt, Mr. Herbert," Fiona said.

"I know my constitution, Sergeant. But the police have another agenda, to bring forward a convincing case. The man is clearly guilty."

"If he is, we'll make the case, Mr. Herbert," Fiona said, holding back her anger. In the face of this hard evidence, her own private theory was certainly under attack. Nevertheless, last night's confrontation with Farley Lipscomb had given it some additional credibility.

"No 'ifs,' FitzGerald. This man is a menace. He cannot be allowed to walk the streets preying on other young women."

It was the painful cry of every relative whose loved one has been the victim of a terrible crime. In emotional shorthand, it meant vengeance and Thomas Herbert was no shrinking violet in that respect.

"I want him put away forever."

"I can't blame you," Fiona said. "If he's guilty."

"That 'if' again," Herbert said angrily.

"We'll do our best, Mr. Herbert," Gail said. Her tone seemed to mollify him.

Herbert looked at his watch, then picked up the phone and punched in a number.

"This is Herbert." He listened as someone talked at the other end. "As soon as possible, you hear?"

He hung up, then glared at Fiona.

"You bungle this, there'll be hell to pay," he sneered. Fiona could understand his pain and her responses were as gentle as she could make them.

"We won't, Mr. Herbert," Fiona replied, trying to muster enthusiasm, but there must have been still something in her response that troubled him.

He glanced toward Gail, an obviously committed ally. She lowered her eyes. Fiona suspected that they had had extensive conversations on the subject.

The telephone rang suddenly. Herbert answered it.

"Send him up," he growled.

Fiona looked at Gail, who did not return her gaze, which seemed curious until the Eggplant strode into the room.

"Good of you to come, Captain," Herbert said. The Eggplant nodded, looking uncomfortable as he sat down. They were grouped around the table. Herbert had provided coffee and Danish, which the Eggplant refused. Fiona knew him well enough to see that he was fuming underneath. Obviously, Herbert had leaned on him through his superiors. Fiona also knew that the fact that he had answered the summons made him seem subservient, a perception that infuriated him.

"We were discussing Phelps Barker," Herbert said. "His fingerprints prove conclusively that he was in that room the evening of my daughter's murder."

Herbert was, of course, technically incorrect, but the Eggplant held his peace. Fiona could tell it was not easy for him. Herbert's attitude was overbearing, superior, a master and servant thing, which the Eggplant's ego could not abide under any circumstances. She admired his discipline.

"Add to that his sexual history. I had to intervene on a rape accusation, which cost Mr. Barker's family a considerable sum."

"Yes," the Eggplant said. "I've been filled in on that."

"There will be more," Herbert said. "I have a private investigation ongoing in Illinois."

"I'm aware of that as well," the Eggplant said.

"We'll have the bastard dead to rights," Herbert said.

"Circumstantially," Fiona said, more as a reflex. She had not intended any comment. The Eggplant scowled at her, obviously wishing that she would keep her mouth shut.

"It would seem," Herbert said with unveiled sarcasm, "that Sergeant FitzGerald is less than enthusiastic about the course this case has taken." He turned to Fiona. "I think she is more inclined to believe that this man is innocent of the crime committed against my daughter."

"Please, Mr. Herbert, Sergeant FitzGerald is an experienced homicide detective with an outstanding record. Our people are instructed to doubt until they arrive at critical-mass evidence."

The Eggplant's remarks seemed to stoke Herbert's anger. He shot a glance to Gail.

"What do you think, Officer Prentiss? Or are you intimidated by your superior's statement?"

"I do not intimidate my people," the Eggplant snapped. Herbert was getting under his skin. The fact was that the Eggplant could be characterized as a master at intimidation, especially suspects, although occasionally underlings. It was, the staff knew, more bluff and noise than meanness. Mostly, they made excuses for this flaw in his management style.

Herbert's attitude triggered Fiona's police-bonding mechanism and her temper.

"Besides," Fiona said angrily, directing her remarks to Herbert, "we don't intimidate easily, whatever the source."

"I think we're getting offtrack," Gail said in an effort to defuse the situation.

"Way off," the Eggplant mumbled.

"We have Barker in the room, Chief," Gail said. "Under the surface, he's fragile. If he's our man, I feel certain that we can crack him."

"I'm sure we can, Officer Prentiss," the Eggplant said with surprising calm. It amazed Fiona how Gail Prentiss commanded respect from everyone around her. It was a rare gift, a special talent.

"And your view, Sergeant FitzGerald?" Herbert asked. He was back on that.

"It is clear that Barker lied when he denied being in Phyla's room. But . . ."

"There it is," Herbert exploded. "The *but*. He was there, woman. He forced her into this disgusting situation, raped her and killed her."

Fiona started to speak, but the Eggplant silenced her with a glance.

"There is no evidence of rape in the conventional sense," the Eggplant said. "And our pathologist says that she died of natural causes."

"Then the conventional sense is wrong, Captain. I know my daughter. She was exemplary in her conduct."

Herbert hesitated, on the verge of breaking down, trying valiantly to hold himself together.

Dr. Benson had reported in passing that the girl was apparently very experienced sexually, definitely not a virgin. A quick exchange of eye contact with the Eggplant told her to leave that one alone.

"She was penetrated with savage brutality and . . ." Herbert went on, somewhat recovered, although his lips trembled and his eyes had reddened. Pausing, he took deep breaths to get himself under further control. "And it is clear that she wouldn't have died if she had not been subjected to this . . . this degrading infamy."

"I understand," the Eggplant began.

"No, you don't," Herbert interrupted.

"We will do our best to ascertain the truth," the Eggplant began again, keeping his voice modulated to a monotone.

Thankfully, he was interrupted by a telephone call. "Yes, it's on," Herbert said to the voice on the phone. "Good."

He hung up. As soon as he did so, a different kind of ring, indicative of a fax, began in the bedroom.

"I've asked my investigative team to come up with a preliminary report on Barker. It's coming through now. I can tell you that I've spared no expense. I already know some of what is coming. It is not a pretty picture."

He got up and went into the bedroom. As soon as he was gone, the Eggplant spoke.

"We bring him in for questioning as soon as we leave here," he said.

"He's at his office," Gail said. "I've already checked."

"And be careful," the Eggplant warned. "By the book."

"Of course," Fiona said. She hoped that she did not show any negativity. Barker had to be interrogated. There were also questions that had to be asked of Herbert, questions pertaining to his and his daughter's relationship with Farley Lipscomb. Somehow, she had to manage it without causing an explosion.

"Remember," the Eggplant said, lowering his voice, speaking quickly, "this has all the earmarks of a consensual beginning that got out of hand. Herbert wants nothing short of an indictment for murder. He can give us a fit." A nerve began to palpitate in the Eggplant's jaw. "He's already giving me a fit. He has powerful friends."

Herbert came back into the room, looking over a sheaf of faxed papers.

"He's our man. No question about it," Herbert muttered. "Listen to this. At Harvard he was reprimanded for participating in a drunken orgy in his fraternity house in which one woman insisted she was gang-banged by a group of men. Unfortunately, she was drunk herself at the time and later retracted her earlier testimony. Two women who dated him during his college days said he was too aggressive sexually for their tastes, although they did not accuse him of rape. The same is true of a woman he dated at Georgetown. In fact, there is a club of ladies who give him bad marks in that department, although they asked that their names not be used. Oh, and here's something." He paused to read the text. "While at Georgetown, a woman was treated for contusions about the face and breasts. She was living with Barker at the time, although she did not attribute the beating to him, preferring to say it happened at the hands of a burglar. Now, really. What we have here is a picture of a man who equates violence with sex."

"May I see that, Mr. Herbert?" Fiona asked.

Herbert handed over the papers and Fiona began to read. As she was doing so, the Eggplant rose.

"We'll be bringing him in for questioning as soon as Detectives FitzGerald and Prentiss get to him. I'm sure your investigation will be extremely helpful, Mr. Herbert."

"It's continuing, Captain. This is only a preliminary report."

"I want to assure you of our complete cooperation," the Eggplant said. "If Barker is the perpetrator, I promise you, he will be charged."

"No 'ifs,' Captain," Herbert said. "He is our man."

After the Eggplant left, Fiona finished reading the papers and handed them to Gail. Herbert's interpretation was remarkably accurate. According to the report, there was no question that Phelps Barker had an aggression problem when it came to women. Certainly, the evidence of his potential guilt was piling up. More than ever she needed to talk with Herbert privately. Unfortunately, now was not the time.

"This should be very helpful, Mr. Herbert," Fiona said. "Very."

"Are you willing to commit yourself to the idea with a bit more fervor, Sergeant?"

Fiona nodded. There was no sense showing less than full enthusiasm. She needed to reassure him, gain his confidence for what she must ask him.

"I'm very encouraged, Mr. Herbert," Gail said. "He'll never know what hit him."

When Barker was hit, he did, indeed, know it.

At his request, they had picked him up on the corner of Fourteenth and Constitution, a few blocks from the Justice Department. More routine questioning, he had been told, a follow-up to their earlier interviews. They gave him his option as to the site of this additional questioning. He said he preferred that it be held outside of the Justice Department.

Fiona suspected that Thomas Herbert had also put in his oar at Justice. If he had, Fiona considered such an action a travesty. Unlike the first few days of the investigation, where she had, in a sense, abdicated her seniority, she took charge this time. If Gail was miffed, she said nothing.

Fiona had made the call to Barker. She asked if he wanted a lawyer present. He declined, pointing out that he was innocent and did not see the need to escalate the situation.

Although Barker didn't ask, Fiona assured him that everything would be handled in confidence. His principal fear, it seemed, was of the media. This indicated to Fiona that he might be relying on his innocence to protect him, a reassuring reaction in terms of Fiona's hypothesis. He also seemed reassured that it was FitzGerald, not Prentiss, making the call.

They brought him into a private room off the squad room. He wasn't exactly happy about the choice of venue, but he seemed willing to endure it. He had also shed his earlier pose of fraternity-boy arrogance.

Entering the room, he took off his blue blazer and hung it on the back of a chair, then sat down at a battered table, opposite Fiona and Gail. He folded his hands, waiting for their questions.

Fiona found the atmosphere both disturbing and ironic. Gail had acknowledged that she thought he was guilty. Fiona was still unconvinced, her antennae still probing in the direction of Farley Lipscomb. Both were operating at the nether ends of competing agendas.

"We want to give you every opportunity to be straightforward, Mr. Barker," Fiona began. "All we ask is for your complete candor and honesty. On our part, we intend to be scrupulously fair. Do you understand?"

Gail Prentiss sat beside her, saying nothing, deferring to Fiona, who had no illusions about Gail's real role. She was Herbert's monitor.

"First, let me say that we know you were in Phyla Herbert's room on the night in question."

He seemed to have expected the allegation, making a gesture of resignation.

"The Pepsi can, right. I'm not exactly stupid." He turned to Gail. "I'd do the same. Problem is, I'm not the guilty party."

"We haven't made any accusations, Mr. Barker," Fiona said.

"You found them on the wooden arm of one of the chairs. I went over it in my mind for days. Am I right?"

"I believe so."

"Surely, it's obvious," Barker said brightly. "I made no attempt to remove my prints. She let me into the room. I came in. Sat down. We talked for about fifteen minutes. Then I left. The fact is, I had no reason to remove any prints, because I had no reason to cover up anything."

"Then why did you lie to us?"

"As I told you before, I'm not crazy. I had no desire to be implicated in this. Let's face it. Being implicated in something so awful is not exactly a career builder. I read the story in the paper and I wanted to distance myself. What I was hoping was that my fingerprints would have been rendered useless by the person who had obviously come after me."

"Nonsense, Barker," Gail said, unable to remain silent. "It was an oversight. You did a good job elsewhere. No one came in after you."

Fiona turned and gave Gail an unmistakable look of rebuke. This is mine now, was what she hoped her expression conveyed.

"Sorry," Gail shrugged.

"I was there no more than approximately fifteen minutes," Barker said. "I saw that by the clock behind the hotel desk when I passed it on the way out. It was eleven-fifteen. It was not quite eleven when I entered her suite."

"Did she invite you in?" Fiona asked.

"Not exactly. I pressed her. I admit it."

"For what reason?"

Barker sucked in a deep breath.

"I wanted to sleep with her."

"Considering all the history you provided us with, one would think that would be a monumental challenge."

"It was. But I could tell from the moment I was in the room that she was not interested in anything more than a polite brushoff. She made it clear she was not interested."

"You didn't press her?"

"Actually, she was standing in the middle of the room and I attempted to embrace her."

"And what did she do?"

"She pushed me into the chair."

"And you stayed there?"

"Yes. Then she explained that she was not the least bit interested in me, never had been, never would be."

"Did she say why?"

"No. Not directly."

"What does that mean?"

"I had the impression that she had another boyfriend."

"Did she say that?"

"Purely a feeling on my part. Like she had pledged fealty to someone."

"Someone?"

"Like a married man?"

Fiona sensed that Gail was studying her. When she turned she saw a very troubled expression on her face, as if she disapproved of the way Fiona was conducting the interrogation.

"Maybe. Somebody secret. Just a feeling, you understand. It was the way she explained it, that she had no interest in me in that way. Not that she ever had."

"People in my business would characterize that as a red herring," Fiona said, shooting a glance at Gail, knowing she was saying what Gail was thinking. "Shifting the emphasis to a dead end."

"I said it was just a feeling I had," Barker said.

Odd, Fiona thought, how his intuition fit in with her own theory.

"You make her sound very solicitous of your feelings," Fiona said.

"She was. We were childhood friends. Maybe she didn't want me to go home mad. As it turns out, going to her room has proved to be a major disaster for me." He held up his hand. "Of course, I'm a suspect, especially since I lied to you."

"You are and you did," Gail said. Again she had crossed the line. This time Fiona shot her a sharp look of rebuke. Then, from her pocketbook, Fiona took out the faxed sheets they had looked at earlier. She started to outline what the sheets contained. Barker stopped her.

"I admit it. I've not been a good boy. I told you what happened to me when I was sixteen," he said. "Believe me, that was the truth. As for my conduct later, I admit everything. I'm too aggressive sexually and I'm working on a more disciplined approach. In today's world I'm vulnerable. I know it. By today's standards, I'm a female harasser . . ."

"I have a question for you, Barker," Fiona interrupted. "Do you know anything about B and D or S and M?"

She felt Gail stir beside her. Peripherally, she could see that Gail was confused by the question.

"You mean whips and chains. Sadism and Masochism. B and D means what?"

"Bondage and Discipline."

"You mean tying up, spanking . . . things like that?"

"Or variations thereof."

Barker looked puzzled. He shrugged.

"I may be a little aggressive, but when you get to stuff like inflicting pain and enjoying it, I'm way out of it . . . way way out of that."

"May I see you privately for a moment, Fiona?" Gail asked suddenly. Fiona exchanged glances with her and saw by her expression that she was not pleased with the interrogation.

Outside in the deserted squad room, Gail said:

"He's having a joy ride. He's charming you with his openness and I think you're falling for it. I'm sorry, Fiona, but I think you're being much too gentle on him. You'll never break him this way."

"Maybe there's nothing to break," Fiona said.

"Well, I don't agree. You're even putting an alibi in his mouth. This business about a secret married lover."

"I didn't put it there, Gail," Fiona said.

"This is the man, Fiona. Why can't you see it?"

Fiona mulled over an idea, then gave herself permission to proceed.

"Barker could be our man. I won't argue that point at this time. But I'm still convinced this was consensual," she said. "Requiring no aggression . . . at least when the episode was begun."

"I'll never buy that. Trussed up like that, blindfolded, gagged, her body written on, then abused. What woman would consent to that?"

"It's theater, Gail. It wasn't meant to go beyond that," Fiona said, watching Gail's expression of disbelief.

"With respect, Fiona, that's ridiculous," Gail said. "You're saying that the girl was a willing participant in her own humiliation."

"The humiliation part, yes. Not the business of the pain," Fiona replied, pausing. "Not what he did back there."

"That's sick," Gail said with disgust. "She was coerced, forced. Barker might have had a weapon, threatened her."

"I doubt that."

"Doubt that Barker did it?"

"Maybe that, too."

Gail shook her head vigorously.

"Why are you willing to whitewash him without first trying to break him? That's what I don't understand. An attempted rape at sixteen, a record of aggressive action against women. He's got the perfect MO for this, Fiona."

"But no real S and M or B and D background," Fiona said. "You saw the props."

"Props?"

"The ropes, the leather blindfold, the gags, the paddling evidence. Props."

"You seemed to know a great deal about that," Gail said. Fiona ignored the implication.

"The woman was theatrically posed for a B and D session. The knots were carefully tied, the blindfold carefully administered. Even the gag was put on with skill. None of this could be done without her absolute trust and consent."

"I don't believe this."

Fiona wasn't sure whether this was a personal manifestation of repugnance or an official denial. She had already determined that Gail Prentiss was morally rigid in her sexual standards. If she had provided any sexual favors, they had been, Fiona was certain, proferred reluctantly. There was a sense of repression about her, Fiona decided, responding to her own instincts based on a Catholic upbringing.

Gail's attitude about sex reminded her of her mother, whose inhibitions in that regard sent her father off to a string of mistresses to whose existence she cast a blind eye.

"People do it because it makes them feel good, Gail," Fiona explained.

"And the dildo that tore apart her anus. Did that make her feel good?"

"The work of a negative dominant. He got carried away. He harmed her. In this context, that is perversity. The perpetrator of that is guilty and, considering what the pathologist has found about the subject's cause of death, I doubt if we could get the kind of sentence that Herbert wants."

"Are you so sure Barker isn't into this D and B obscenity?" Gail asked, avoiding any follow-up reference to Herbert.

"B and D," Fiona corrected, quickly adding, "I can tell. He may not be ignorant of the practice but I suggest he's not very conversant with the rituals."

Gail looked deeply into Fiona's eyes as if searching for the hidden message.

"You should have let me interrogate him," she said.

"Think I've blown it, Gail?"

"I'm not sure."

"I don't want to see a miscarriage of justice."

The remark, Fiona knew, was open to different interpretations.

They studied each other through a long silence.

"I think you owe it to me to let me try," Gail said.

"Are you appealing to my sense of fairness?" Fiona countered, tamping down her irritation.

"Yes."

Fiona mulled the point. She concluded that, in the light of their diametrically opposing views as to Barker's guilt or innocence, she had better accede to Gail's demand. Gail, Fiona had learned, was a fiercely tenacious hunter who needed a shot at her prey.

"Alright, hotshot, do your thing," Fiona said with obvious reluctance, but without visible rancor. After all, she reasoned, Gail was unaware that she wasn't playing with a full deck.

"I will," Gail said through tight, unsmiling lips.

The conversation seemed ended and Fiona turned to go back into the room. She was recalled by Gail's voice.

"How do you know so much about this, Fiona?"

"This?"

"The bondage stuff."

It was to be expected, of course. It was one of those issues she had wrestled with last night. To tell or not to tell. Not yet, she decided, hopeful that she might find a solution long before such a confession was required, if ever.

"Lots of research," Fiona replied, which was partly true. Indeed, the subject was not as esoteric as it seemed. The sex squad regularly provided information on various sexual practices, but, as Fiona knew from personal experience, it was disbursed as a catalogue from a freak show, with the psychological factors glossed over and related only to the criminal aspects of the practices.

"I thought you forgot me," Phelps Barker said when the women had returned. From his sudden change of expression Fiona could tell he had sensed the changed dynamics in the room. Although they took the same chairs upon their return, Gail moved hers inches closer to Barker.

"I'm afraid you're still on our mind, Barker," Fiona said.

"Am I still a hot suspect?"

His attempt at recapturing his old wisecracking arrogance fell short.

"Yes," Gail said ominously. There was no mistaking her attitude. She paused for a moment, extracted a small notebook from her pocketbook and opened it. "I'd like to go back to your assertion about the young woman who accused you of rape when you were a teenager."

"I've explained that."

"Not to my satisfaction," Gail insisted. His forehead crinkled as he turned toward Fiona, who nodded slightly in what was meant to be a gesture of reassurance. Gail's questions were a gauntlet he had to go through. She hoped he was up to it.

"Why would you have needed a go-between to negotiate a settlement if you were innocent?"

"I've already explained that," Barker said calmly. "It was a conspiracy to get money from my father."

"And you did not rape her?"

"Absolutely not. She consented to the intercourse."

"She claimed you held her down, spraining her wrist, that you stuffed her panties in her mouth to stop her from screaming and that you threatened her with a knife, which you held to her neck after cutting her on the arm to show her you meant business."

The blood drained from his face and his lips began to tremble. Again, Gail had been privy to information that she had withheld from Fiona. Only this time Fiona did not accept it silently.

"Where did that come from?"

"Mr. Herbert."

"Why didn't you tell me this, Gail?"

"There is more to this than meets the eye, Fiona," Gail said firmly. "May I proceed?"

"We'll discuss this later," Fiona said. Experience had taught her that one must never display police dirty laundry in front of a suspect. On a level playing field, Fiona would have promptly taken her aside, chewed her out, threatened charges and put in for a partner change.

"Kiss and make up girls," Barker said, in another abortive effort to get his old élan back. His ashen face belied the attempt. Gail turned to him again.

"Are my facts wrong, Barker?"

"Her facts were wrong," Barker shot back. "She concocted the story. It was all a lie. She consented eagerly. I told you the truth." His voice became shrill, his entire face beet red.

"Truth? You don't know the meaning of that word. I talked to the woman herself."

"Probably on welfare with nine kids."

"She's an accountant, Barker," Gail said triumphantly.

"She signed her name to an agreement . . ."

"Cash for silence," Gail hissed.

"I'll sue her ass." His nostrils flared and flecks of saliva rolled down his chin.

"There was also another part of that original agreement," Gail said. Fiona turned quickly. Gail raised her hand as if to say "Don't interrupt. I know what I'm doing."

"I don't have to sit here and take this," Barker said.

"If you require, we could always make it more official," Gail replied.

"And I could have a lawyer present."

"You have one. Yourself." Gail said.

"Very funny."

"We were talking here of truth, Barker," Gail said. She had quickly changed modes, back to the soft gentle woman, a role she had so efficiently perfected. Who is the real Gail Prentiss, Fiona wondered.

"So far you haven't exactly been a paragon in the truth department, Barker," Gail continued. "Look, here are the facts and Mr. Herbert can easily corroborate them. Part of the deal was that you get yourself a therapist to deal with what was and perhaps still is a problem . . ."

"Now I see where you're headed," Barker said, jumping up. "You're going to use my past to frame me."

He was extremely agitated, but he made every effort to get himself under control.

"I did go to a therapist," Barker said. "And may I remind you that there is a confidentiality in that relationship . . ." He broke off in mid-sentence. Fiona remembered what Farley Lipscomb had implied about his own so-called self-therapy. Medical records, her experience told her, leaked like a sieve.

"Just relax, Barker," Gail said softly. "What we're trying to do is eliminate you as a suspect." She shook her head and shrugged. "Mr. Herbert believes you did his daughter. What we're trying to do here is absolve you from all suspicion. He is a very powerful man. He can hurt you. If you are innocent of this crime, convince us. You can only do that by telling us the truth. So far you've been evasive and, I must say, a bit too theatrical in your attitude. Tell it straight. That's all we ask."

Again she had changed roles. Now she was playing confidante, the good cop, wanting to save him from disaster. Fiona had to hand it to her. She was good.

Barker sucked in a deep breath, then sat down.

"Yes, I kept my part of the deal. But that didn't mean that the woman told the truth. She lied. I didn't rape her. She wanted it the hard way . . ."

He suddenly froze, obviously wishing he hadn't put it that way.

"She begged me to do it that way. It was like a game. I was only sixteen, for crying out loud."

"She was fourteen," Gail sighed.

"Going on forty. She was experienced. I wasn't."

"And the others?" Gail asked.

"What others?"

He seemed suddenly disoriented. Fiona had raised those episodes reported in the fax and he had admitted to them with some changes of emphasis. Was he now denying that? Or had he forgotten that he had offered a general confession to past misdeeds.

"The college women. The woman you once lived with. You admitted harassment, Barker. Remember?"

"Each of those incidents can be explained," he said, but it was obvious that even his own sense of conviction was running out.

"What are we to think, Barker?" Gail said. "You have a history of rough sex." She shot a glance at Fiona. "Or am I exaggerating?"

"Some women like that. Molly . . . that's the lady I lived with when I was going to Georgetown. She was a glutton for it. I hated participating. I hated it."

"But you went along?"

"That's the way she got it off."

"Then one day it got out of hand . . ."

"Yes, it did. Molly pushed me for more. Then more. You can't imagine how horrible it was." His eyes seemed glazed as if he were looking deeply inside of himself, plumbing his memory. It struck Fiona that Gail's instincts about Barker were at least partially valid. He was prime suspect material. She sensed the first signs that her own theory was beginning to disintegrate.

Gail suddenly turned toward her and motioned with her head that they should again leave the room. When they were back in the squad room, Gail spoke:

"Still a nonbeliever?" Gail asked.

"I'm getting there," Fiona admitted.

"Let's lay it out for the Chief. Fiona, it adds up. We've got an MO. We've got prints."

"But no confession. And it's still circumstantial. The Chief will turn us down," Fiona protested lamely.

"Barker is the man," Gail said. "We could push him further."

"He's a lawyer in the Justice Department. We make a mistake on this, we're dead meat." Fiona was surprised at her own assertion of bureaucratic fear.

"We're close, Fiona."

"There's got to be more. Maybe a search of his apartment . . ."

"If we don't book him, Herbert will go through the roof."

"It's not his call. Frankly, Gail, I don't know why you keep deferring to him."

"He's a victim." She hesitated and, watching her, Fiona wondered if she was going to change her pose yet again. "I understand his pain."

For everything there is a reason, Fiona thought. There was something fundamental to this message that Gail was sending, something deeply embedded inside of her, obviously stemming from something ravaging in her past. Fiona allowed a long silence to ensue between them as if waiting for Gail to say something more. She didn't.

"Let's not rush to judgment on this, Gail," Fiona said gently. "Barker's not going anywhere. His apartment might just cough up enough to make the case."

"I don't agree. We have enough to make an arrest," Gail pressed.

"Let's call it insurance."

"How about delay?"

"Where's the harm? It's unlikely he'll skip."

Gail studied Fiona and rubbed her chin. What was she seeing? Fiona wondered, not without a tinge of guilt.

"What is it, Fiona?" Gail said suddenly.

"What is what?" Fiona replied defensively.

Their eyes met until, finally, Gail shook her head.

"I'm your partner, Fiona," Gail said. "Let me in on it."

"On what?" Fiona began, but she knew that Gail was on to her.

"Alright," Gail said gently. "I've deliberately held things back. Not out of malice or ambition. I hope you can see that. Frankly, I was trying to shake you up, force you to tell me what's really going on . . ."

She was having difficulty getting the words out with her usual smooth articulation. "I . . . I know about those pictures, Fiona. The ones you passed around the hotel."

Fiona had, of course, expected that to surface, although she had never worked out the response in her own mind. She felt adrift now, spinning in an eddy of confusion.

"Do you know who they were?" she asked finally.

Gail paused and studied Fiona's face.

"I haven't seen the pictures," Gail replied. "But Harold Barton, the assistant manager, did some research on his own. He thinks they're members of the Supreme Court."

Framing a response was difficult, although Fiona did feel the urge to confide, to unburden herself. Could she trust Gail?

"Can we let it lie for a while, Gail?"

"We have," Gail said. "Maybe too long."

"I need time," Fiona whispered. Even to her own ears, the words sounded like an appeal. Finally, Gail nodded.

"Okay," she said with a shrug of resignation. "We'll put Barker on hold."

"Not for long," Fiona said. "I promise."

When they returned, they found Barker sitting there, abject, his head slightly bowed, all the arrogance wrung out. He lifted his head expectantly.

"If we need you again, Barker, we know where to find you."

He was obviously relieved and managed a thin smile. Inexplicably, he remained seated as if he could not find the energy to pull himself up.

"I've something to ask," he said. "A favor."

"Then ask," Fiona said.

"I . . . I don't want to be destroyed by this. I've got a good record with the Justice Department, a good reputation. I'm a damned good lawyer, real aggressive helping people, fighting discrimination."

He looked toward Gail, playing to her race. To her, Fiona was sure, it was a blatant and rather transparent attempt at ingratiation, probably a turn-off. Fiona saw it as a genuine plea.

"If my superiors get wind of it . . . worse, if it hits the media, it could bury me. Not only my job and future. My parents. My brothers. I mean, this could strike deep. I don't know if I can handle it."

"That's not our intention," Fiona said, exchanging glances with Gail, who remained silent.

"I didn't kill Phyla. I couldn't kill anyone."

Fiona had heard that before, sometimes from the most vicious murderers in the face of overwhelming evidence. She found herself wanting to believe him, wanting to keep her theory about Farley Lipscomb alive.

"As you can see, we're not going to hold you," Fiona said. "But I can't promise that we won't be talking with you again."

He nodded and stood up, looking at his watch.

"They're probably wondering where I am," he said, nodding awkwardly as he moved out of the room. When he was gone, Gail turned to her.

"There goes a guilty man," she said.

Fiona did not respond, although she felt almost ready to agree.

—14—

Fiona, Gail and the Eggplant sat in a darkened corner of Benny's Bar sipping their drinks. The Eggplant was exhausted and depressed, hardly in any shape to hear more disheartening news. But, at least, the ambience of the bar was better than the Eggplant's gloomy office.

Fiona waited until the first shot of Scotch started its mellowing effect on the Eggplant.

No, Fiona told him, they had not extracted a confession from Phelps Barker. Fiona, with a nod toward Gail, carefully explained that they had not yet arrived at a point where they had enough evidence to hold Barker and that they needed a search warrant to go through Barker's apartment.

"You think so?" the Eggplant sighed, probably contemplating what additional pain Thomas Herbert would inflict as a result of the delay in arresting Barker. He motioned the waitress to bring another round. Fiona was drinking white wine. Gail was nursing a Diet Coke.

"What do you think you'll find?" the Eggplant asked.

Gail shrugged, obviously deferring to Fiona.

"Maybe a sign that he was into Bondage. Magazines. Sex toys."

"The thing he used on her?"

"If we find that, he's nailed," Fiona said with a sidelong glance at Gail, who showed no reaction.

"You believe he's the one?" the Eggplant asked, turning to Gail.

Gail nodded.

"And you, FitzGerald?"

Fiona hesitated before answering.

"If we find things at his place," she said cautiously, "no question."

"And if you find nothing?"

"Herbert will fry us," Gail piped. "He expected an arrest today."

"What's another nail in the coffin?" the Eggplant sighed. He seemed more discouraged than ever.

"He is not going to be kind," Gail said.

"It's still not his call," Fiona said.

Gail nodded, as if she understood. Despite her obvious disappointment in not booking Barker, Fiona was grateful for her not registering any protest.

"You got that right, FitzGerald. It's mine."

"You could get off the hook, Chief," Fiona said cautiously.

"You mean, order his arrest."

"You're the man," Fiona said. She wondered if she were deliberately goading him to foreclose on her delaying tactics, wanting it to end here and now.

"Only if you both agree."

Fiona glanced toward Gail.

"Let's get the warrant," Gail said.

"That settles that," the Eggplant said. He turned to Fiona.

"As the Sergeant knows, I always back my troops."

Not always, Fiona thought. Their relationship was sometimes contentious, but always respectful. She had learned a great deal from this egotistical, ambitious, and sometimes insufferable black man. Aside from his professional knowledge, he had, at times, shown extraordinary insight into the motivation of human beings. His hunches were more correct than most, although her record was also formidable.

It was true that race was the prism through which he viewed life. Indeed, it was a condition, sometimes she considered it an affliction, of most of the blacks she knew, especially those among her colleagues. But there had been moments when his mind, and hers, had met in what could be described as neutral space, a kind of vacuum, without the bacteria of gender, race, ego, ambition and fear to influence judgment. Always, this place was where pure reason resided and where they had made the most profound and cogent decisions in their work.

Unfortunately, their visits to this place were rare, too rare, although at times they began their journey away from the squad room, in out-of-the-way places, where straight talk was encouraged between them. Like now.

Certainly, in his present state, he was in no condition to make any wise decisions. A bulldozer of events had flattened his spirit. It took two Scotch-and-sodas to uncork his emotions.

"It's like a funnel directly over my head, with raw sewage being fed into it and slopping all over me. There are well-armed bands of terrorists out there." He looked at Gail. "They have us outgunned. There will come a point, after they realize the futility of turning their guns on their own, when they will turn them on us."

"And then?" Gail asked.

"The reckoning," the Eggplant said, turning to face her. "First must come the reckoning. It will be devastating. Only after that will come the resurrection."

"Pretty heavy symbols, Chief," Fiona said.

"The police department, as we know it, will be obsolete. We will become more of a paramilitary organization, God help us."

"You paint a gloomy picture, Chief," Fiona said.

"How can it be otherwise? Murder, you see, has vast political implications. The leadership, the mayor, Congress, even the President, wants quick solutions. Find the bastards, take them out." He shook his head. "Like our friend, Mr. Herbert. He has power. He can exert pressure. In the end, he equates us with the perpetrator, as if we are deliberately covering up the crime, as if we are allies of the bad guys."

"You got that right, Chief," Fiona said. She, too, was well into her second round of white wine, unusual for her. Gail continued to nurse her original Diet Coke, listening to their conversation, but contributing little.

"He'll probably bitch to everyone that our little experiment with gender is a big flop," the Eggplant said, upending his drink. He looked at his watch. The alcohol seemed to have mellowed him, taken the edge off his depression.

"Do you think so, Chief?" Fiona replied.

"It's my idea, remember," he said, showing a slight smile for the first time since they had arrived.

"Don't write us off yet, Chief," Gail said suddenly. "We're getting there." She looked toward Fiona. "We just need a bit more time."

Fiona could sense something in Gail percolating to the surface. At some point soon, she knew it had to be addressed.

"If we don't close this one soon," the Eggplant said, rubbing his eyes, increasing their bloodshot condition, "they'll find a way to close down the idea." He sighed. "There's already rumbles. Some of the guys are calling it discriminatory. Shit. Everything in life is discriminatory. Hell, I meant well."

He put down a twenty and stood up.

"My share," he said. "Let it not be said that the old Eggplant can be bought for a few drinks." He chuckled again to show that it was a joke. He was already slightly tipsy. Despite his bulk, he was not a good drinker. Then he walked stiffly toward the door.

"Thanks, Gail," Fiona said.

"For what?"

"Not pushing."

Gail stared into Fiona's eyes.

"You owe me for that, Fiona," she said, looking at her with laserlike intensity, her lips tight. "And I'd like to get paid."

—15—

Fiona made some coffee while she recounted the history of her house to Gail, how she had inherited it from her mother, how important it was to her, how much care she lavished on it.

Gail had listened attentively. On her father's death, she had explained, she would inherit their big house on the so-called Gold Coast. Gail, Fiona could tell, knew all about the symbolism of houses.

Like Fiona's house, it, too, was a mansion. It, too, stood for a kind of validation. Fiona's father was the grandson of an impoverished Irish immigrant. Gail's father was the grandson of a slave. The commonality seemed another bond between them.

Gail followed Fiona to the den and, without being directed, took the leather wing chair that Farley Lipscomb had sat in so recently. Fiona poured two cups of coffee and handed one to Gail. Ignoring the irony, she sat on the couch, in the same spot she had occupied when confronted by Farley.

"The worst part of this, Gail," Fiona began, after taking a deep sip of the coffee and putting the cup beside her on an end table, "is worrying too much about managing your reaction."

"Why should that bother you?"

"I'm a bit of a fraud, Gail. I don't have any female friends . . . real friends. All-the-way friends. I've never really confided in people of my own gender. I mean the real confidences, down to the marrow. The fact is that the only female I think I know is myself. Do you understand what I'm saying?" Before Gail could reply, Fiona continued. "Oh, I've had so-called women friends. We've confided, of course. Maybe I'm asking too much, expecting too much. Can we ever truly know enough about each other to even qualify as true friends? The fact is that I don't think I know very much about women in general. For example, everything I know about real intimacy, even sex, especially sex, I've learned from men. And men have dominated my life. Not me, understand. But my life."

"Except for my father, I must say that I never learned much from men," Gail said, drawing in a deep breath. "I'm not very experienced in that regard." She forced a laugh. "It might comfort you to know that I don't have any female friends either. Oh, I have acquaintances, family, aunts, cousins. No female siblings, though." A shadow descended over her face.

Fiona noted how Gail avoided any reference to the issue of sex. Once again, it confirmed her suspicion that Gail was tremendously inhibited on the subject, both in talk and action. But Fiona felt it was important to broach the subject, especially if she was going to tell Gail about her experience with Farley.

"Are you a virgin, Gail?"

She bucked immediately.

"I don't think that's any of your business," Gail shot back.

Was it possible? How old was she? Thirty? A virgin at thirty? If so, it seemed incredible, especially for a cop in the homicide division, where matters of sex were part of the landscape. Yet, when the subject was depersonalized, as in police business, Gail seemed to have no problem discussing the subject.

"You're right, Gail. It is none of my business."

"I didn't mean to sound harsh," Gail said.

"I know you didn't. It's my risk," Fiona sighed.

"Risk? I don't understand."

"You will."

Fiona felt her throat constrict.

"You don't have to, Fiona," Gail said.

"I do now," Fiona replied. She paused through a long moment. "I . . . I was almost convinced that I knew who was responsible for the death of Phyla Herbert," Fiona began, watching Gail Prentiss's face. She would have to endure that, Fiona decided. No hiding allowed. "My theory . . . I believed that the man who did that to her was Farley Lipscomb."

Gail seemed stunned.

"The Supreme Court justice?"

Fiona nodded.

"Not all political scandals in Washington are based on sex. Only most of them," she said.

"Are you serious?" Gail asked.

"Absolutely," she replied, clearing her throat. "It was a replication of what he did to me seventeen years ago, down to the tiniest detail."

"My God!"

"I mean *everything*, Gail. The same injury."

"How terrible," Gail exclaimed.

"I told no one about this. Not ever."

"I'm so sorry, Fiona. I had no idea."

"I thought it was a dead issue. Long forgotten. Then this. It brought it all back." Fiona could not contain a tremor in her voice.

"That explains a great deal, Fiona."

"I wonder. I just can't get the idea out of my mind. It was me I saw in Phyla's place. Me. I felt certain he was there. That he did this thing . . ."

"Are you sure that the . . . the situations are identical? They might have seemed identical."

"Believe me, as near as I can remember the details of my encounter with him, they are identical." Fiona paused. "Certainly close enough."

"The memory plays tricks, Fiona," Gail said.

"I know. I also know that any basis of comparison is in my mind. But the trauma came back."

"Trauma?" Gail's brows knitted with curiosity.

"Something clicked inside of me," Fiona said. She told her about what had happened after the episode, the bout with sexual revulsion, the long road back. And how it was replicating itself now and wreaking havoc in her relationship with Harrison Greenwald and what it was doing to him as well.

"Is it possible that you're over-reacting on this, Fiona?"

"Possible? Worse. I am . . . absolutely."

"And you firmly believe it was him, Justice Lipscomb?" Gail asked. "Even in the face of what we know about Barker? About him being in the room? About his lies? About his past?"

Fiona felt the strain of wrestling with this dilemma.

"To be brutally honest. Not beyond a shadow of a doubt."

"You see, your experience has colored your judgment. I'd say it was only natural."

"But not professional," Fiona said with resignation.

"It does confuse one's ability to reason," Gail said gently. "In Barker's case, there was a clue. Clues. In the case of your Justice Lipscomb, there is nothing, not a sign, not a trace."

"He is very clever," Fiona said. "He would have probably worn a disguise of some sort to prevent people remembering him. He was always extremely cautious. And he knows a lot about evidence and police procedures. He was a prosecutor once and knows what we had to look for. Knowing his methods, I'd say he could pull it off."

"And Barker?"

"On the face of it, very compelling."

"But you're still not one hundred percent convinced?"

"It' driving me bonkers."

"A Supreme Court justice?"

"A man," Fiona sighed.

"And Phyla would have just opened the door and let him in, then allowed him to do with her as he wanted?"

"I'm afraid so. I did."

Gail's disbelief was tangible. Nor could she hide her confusion.

"You let him?"

"The truth is that I consented gladly."

"To be abused like that? It's not normal, Fiona."

Gail's eyes widened as if she were a child confronted by a movie monster.

"I thought I loved him. When it comes to love, normal sex has little meaning," Fiona explained. Gail seemed totally perplexed.

"To allow yourself to be tied like that, like an animal? And beaten? Gagged? A dildo inserted in your anus?" She made a face of disgust and shook her head rapidly from side to side to emphasize the horror of it.

"It was meant to be a game," Fiona said. "And it got out of hand."

"Some game. It can kill."

"Killing is not part of the scenario," Fiona sighed. "I gave myself to him because I trusted him. I thought I loved him. I was willing to do anything for him. Earlier we had reversed roles and he was the one to be disciplined."

"You did that to him?"

"Not the dildo business, but I tied him up, whipped and paddled him. He was tremendously stimulated. He loved it."

"And you?"

"I . . . I think I loved it, too. I mean . . . when it was a game."

"I can't understand that," Gail said. "Sex is supposed to be beautiful. This practice is perverted."

As expected, Gail was repelled by the idea of it and no amount of explanation to a person that repressed would convince her otherwise. Nevertheless, Fiona owed it to herself to try to offer some rationale based on her own research.

"I know it's difficult for you to understand, Gail. I really had to delve into this, to find out why I might have enjoyed it at the beginning. There are various scientific explanations. Like people who have been painfully ill or repressed as children finding a way to process this pain into pleasure. Or people who are control freaks needing the punishment game to keep them sane. It's supposed to be comforting. When it comes to sex, to the things that excite people to pleasure and relief, we're all somewhat confused. Just as I was. I thought I was proving my love, showing my trust, laying myself bare. The experience left me jolted, filled me with self-disgust. At times, I felt it was all my fault. The man deliberately ripped me apart. What he did to me was definitely not part of the scenario and I could never ever give my unconditional trust to anyone again. I gave myself to him. I gave him my will and my body and he betrayed me. It has haunted me to this day and telling it to you now is the hardest thing I can remember doing in my whole life."

Despite Fiona's determination to maintain control, she felt herself losing it. Her tongue felt heavy and her body began to tremble.

"I never told anyone about this, Gail. First there was pain, then self-loathing, then shame. Finally came revulsion, although I tried to find out as much as I could about it. As I told you, it took a long time before I could get back my appetite for sex."

"It's very hard for me to relate to it, Fiona."

"I know. And seeing this happen to someone else with such terrible consequences has had a terrible effect on me. It's all come back. Just the thought of making love to Harrison induces nausea. I can't even fake it . . ."

She stopped, abruptly burying her face in her hands. The breakdown had come with no real warning. The process of peeling away the years of containment and silence took its toll. A wave of hysteria rolled over her and she could not stop the eruption that wracked her body.

Then Gail was beside her on the couch, enveloping her in her warm, strong arms, and Fiona was sobbing uncontrollably into her ample bosoms. It seemed to take forever to get herself under control again.

"There's a lot I don't understand about this, but that kind of hurt I can understand, Fiona," Gail said.

After a while, Gail opened her arms and Fiona sat up. Gail reached for her pocketbook and handed Fiona some tissues, waiting patiently until she was composed again.

"I guess this reaction was inevitable. It has been inside so long," Fiona said, forcing a smile. Their eyes met.

"I'm not a virgin," Gail said suddenly. She stood up and began to pace the floor.

"You don't have to do this, Gail," Fiona cried.

"Yes, I do. Your confession gives me permission," Gail said. "It sticks in my gut, makes me feel like ice inside. I haven't been a virgin since I was nine years old."

Fiona was stunned at the revelation, watching her as one might watch a tennis match, as she strode across the room and back like a caged animal.

"We were playing in the playground in Memphis, where my father was in practice. My sister . . . yes, I did have a sibling once . . . and we were simply little girls playing. He came up behind us, grabbed us, threw us in his car. Then drove us to a wooded area."

"Please, Gail. It's not required."

Gail didn't seem to hear, going on with her story.

"First he raped me, then he raped my sister and, in the process . . . he . . . strangled her to death. I saw it. Then, when she was dead, he started to do it again to her. That was when I ran away. Nothing was ever the same after that."

Fiona saw no tears, only cold fury. Beneath the surface, she could detect tangible icy rage.

"No. Nothing can ever be the same," Fiona sighed. For herself as well.

Fiona reached out and took Gail's hand. They were silent for a long time until Gail spoke again.

"You might say I've been a virgin since then."

"No relationships?"

She shook her head.

"It's . . . it's so hard to believe. You're so . . . beautiful . . . a bigger-than-life female."

"Bigger than life," Gail squeezed Fiona's hand. "Just nature's protective coat."

With her free arm, Fiona put it around Gail's shoulders and felt the weight of Gail's body press against her. They were silent for a long time.

"He was here last night, Gail," Fiona said.

There seemed no need to explain whom she meant.

"In this house?"

"In this room."

Gail shifted her body suddenly and sat upright, turning to face Fiona.

"I did a stalking number." Fiona recounted her visit to the State Department, her call to Letitia Lipscomb. "I know all his buttons and I pressed them."

Fiona felt Gail studying her face, waiting for her to continue.

"He denied it," Fiona said.

"Then why can't you accept Barker as the perpetrator?"

"I can't believe Farley, Gail."

"Can't or won't?"

"Both."

"I just don't understand . . ."

"He's still into it, Gail. The B and D. Heavy."

"How . . ."

Fiona explained.

"Unbelievable," Gail said, letting go of Fiona's hand. She stood up and walked the length of the den and back. She stopped at the couch and looked down at Fiona.

"Barker is guilty, Fiona. Your judgment is distorted by your personal experience. Just as mine would be . . ."

At that moment, the sound of the phone's ring jangled into the room. Fiona, with an odd sense of relief, picked up the phone. It was the Eggplant.

"We got a shitload of trouble, FitzGerald."

She covered the mouthpiece and looked up at Gail.

"The Eggplant!"

"You there, FitzGerald?"

"I'm here, Chief."

"It's all over the bulldog edition of the Washington *Post*. Herbert's work. I'm sure of it. Says we have a suspect in his daughter's murder and we're planning to pull him in."

"Does he mention him by name?"

"Yup."

"Jesus."

She looked toward Gail and shook her head in despair.

"Barker will go up the wall," Fiona said.

"He already has. Blew his brains out nearly a half-hour ago. A neighbor called us. He left a note to you and Gail and one to his parents." There was a long pause. "We opened the note addressed to you. You want to hear it?"

"Of course."

"Six words," the Eggplant said. " 'Sorry. It's too much to bear.' "

—16—

"There could be any number of explanations," Tom Herbert said. "Mine is that he was trapped in his own guilt, too ashamed to admit what he had done. He couldn't face the music."

They were sitting in Herbert's suite in the Hay-Adams. Herbert sat in one of the upholstered chairs, legs crossed, looking imperious. He seemed smugly convinced of his lack of culpability in Barker's death. Gail, her long legs crossed in front of her, sat on the couch.

The revelation last night about Barker's death had had a strange effect on Gail. She had been stunned by the news and had left Fiona's house in what could only be described as shocked silence. She had said little in the car coming over to the Hay-Adams. During the ride, Fiona had reported on her own search of Barker's apartment.

Before picking up Gail, she had stopped by Barker's apartment alone. Since it was the scene of a death and under the jurisdiction of the police, she had no problem getting inside. The resident manager was very cooperative.

The body, of course, had been removed, although there were still blood spatterings on the floor and walls of his bathroom, where he had done the deed.

It was a small efficiency apartment, rather messy, but typical of that occupied by a single man. It had the feel of a hotel room that had rarely, if ever, been cleaned by a maid. Fiona rifled through drawers and closets. She found books, magazines and newspapers scattered all over the place, but nothing that could remotely be associated with the subculture of Bondage and Discipline. Nothing. No props. No magazines. Not even run-of-the-mill porno magazines, which seemed a staple in the living quarters of single males.

The results of the search, while not conclusive, buttressed Fiona's original theory about Farley Lipscomb.

*   *   *

"There's a certain flawed logic in your interpretation, Mr. Herbert," Fiona said. She had not sat down and was gripping the back of a chair. "The man feared media exposure most of all. He was panicked by it."

"Of course. Because he was guilty," Herbert said.

"We never proved it," Fiona snapped. "Nor did he confess to the crime in his note."

"His own action proved it," Herbert replied, turning toward Gail, who continued to observe a stoic silence.

"You could have prevented it. Pulled him in. Put a twenty-four-hour guard on him. He'd be alive to pay the piper."

"Mr. Herbert, by going to the Washington *Post* you precipitated his action. Don't you realize that?"

"When all else fails, the media is there. I took advantage of that when it was obvious you, the police, were not doing your job. What other recourse did I have?"

"How about the criminal justice system?" Fiona said.

"I'm a lawyer. You can't be serious."

"Did you think we were trying to deliberately cover up this terrible act?" Fiona asked.

"You were overly cautious, fearful, afraid to make a mistake," Herbert said. "The homicide situation is a mess in this city. Your department is a target. You were more interested in covering your ass."

"Why are you so certain that he was the man?" Fiona asked.

"He was in her room. He had lied about what he had done the night Phyla was murdered. And he had a history of violent treatment of women. What more proof do you need?"

"Somebody could have come after he left your daughter's room," Fiona said cautiously. She detested Herbert for what he had done, a feeling that more than overshadowed her initial sympathy for him.

"Don't be ridiculous," he sneered. He looked toward Gail.

"She agreed with me. Isn't that correct, Officer Prentiss?"

Gail seemed to be struggling to find an answer.

"At first, yes," she said finally.

"And now?" Herbert asked.

"His note is not conclusive," Gail muttered. "He was paranoid about media exposure, worried that it would ruin his career."

"I can't believe this," Herbert shot back.

"He was a young and ambitious man," Fiona said. "To be shown in the media as a suspect in a terrible crime like that could be devastating to his career chances."

"My daughter is dead," Herbert said, sputtering with anger. "That is devastation."

"So is Phelps Barker," Fiona said.

"That's different," Herbert said. He was adamant. "He executed himself for his own crime."

"But can we be absolutely, one hundred percent certain?" Gail said, her voice trailing off.

"You can't. But I can. That's because neither of you truly understand the character of a man . . . let me reiterate . . . a man . . . What do you women know of what goes through the mind of a man who would do a thing like that . . . force a woman into that kind of horrible perversion, then do what he did? He couldn't take the shame of it. If he was innocent, he wouldn't have taken such a drastic step."

Fiona resented his resort to using gender to justify his conviction. She also knew it would be impossible to shake his opinion.

"Whatever your conclusion, Mr. Herbert," Fiona said, "the man is dead. He cannot defend himself."

"That was his choice," Herbert said smugly. "If you had any insight, you would face the fact of his guilt. Get real, ladies. This case is closed."

Gail looked at Fiona, shrugged, then reverted to silence. The events of last night had made a profound impression on Fiona. For the first time in her life she felt that she had found an unconditional friend. We are sisters, she told herself.

Long ago, Fiona was certain, before the connotation of true and loving friendship had been skewed by sexual innuendo, there were relationships like this. To find it in a partner, brought together by random selection, was almost a miracle. She was grateful to the Eggplant for his idea and now she was determined to work her damndest to make the idea viable. Gail's support gave her the courage to press on.

"Unfortunately, Mr. Herbert," Fiona said. "We can't accept the case as closed." Fiona had no illusions as to how the Eggplant would react to such a suggestion.

"We? Come on, girls. This is bullshit."

"Maybe so," Fiona said, determined to be patient, "But wouldn't you at least concede that you could be wrong? I mean as a lawyer, in the face of no real proof . . ."

"As a lawyer," he said, "I will always leave room for a big fat maybe. As a father of a victim, I reiterate my comment. Bullshit! Barker did it. No question about it. I hope he is rotting in hell at this very moment."

Fiona had seen relatives of loved ones who had been murdered deliberately defy logic to accept the concept of vengence. Revenge, despite moralizing opinions to the contrary, was therapeutic, cleansing, a catharsis. She could understand why Herbert clung to the idea.

"We need to continue this investigation, Mr. Herbert. And, unfortunately, we may need your help."

"I gave you my help. I spent money on my own investigation, which proved my theory. What more can I give?"

Again, she could detect the tiniest concession to the idea that he could be wrong, although it was unlikely that he would ever admit it, even to himself.

"I need to know who else she might have known well enough in this town to contact."

"This is really stupid. Hell, she knew lots of people here. We've entertained many of them in our Minnesota place."

"Such as?"

"You're really serious about this, aren't you?"

"Very." Fiona paused. "How would you like it if—this is purely hypothetical, mind you—a man was still at large who could do this again?"

She studied Herbert's face, saw the briefest twitch of doubt.

"There is no downside for you on this, Mr. Herbert," Gail said. "We'd be less than thorough if we just declared Barker guilty, even if he was, without . . ."

"You people," Herbert shrugged with contempt. "Alright, what the hell." He turned toward Fiona. "Yes, we entertained important people. Let's see . . . Both our Illinois senators. The now Vice-President. Two sitting members of the Supreme Court." Gail shot Fiona a quick glance, apparently unnoticed by Herbert. "We're plugged in. I am very involved politically."

"Did Phyla set up any appointments with these people?" Fiona asked.

"She knew them. She could have. Frankly, she preferred to do this on her own. I could have gotten her a job anywhere, but she wanted to find one on her own. Eventually she would have gone into the firm."

"Was she close to any of them? Like, who among them did she respect the most?"

Herbert stood up and looked out of the window, which offered a clear view of the White House shining in the morning sun.

"I know she corresponded with a number of them and they were enormously solicitous of a young girl with a very bright future."

He had turned around, then as his eyes began to well with tears, he spun around again. They waited until he got himself under control. When he turned again, he showed more belligerence.

"Are you pointing an accusing finger at these people? Really, how can you possibly think that any of them could be responsible for such a base act? Just the idea of it is repulsive. This is crazy. How do you people justify your jobs?"

Fiona watched him calmly, proud of her own restraint. He apparently needed this little tantrum to preserve his equilibrium.

"By doing it, Mr. Herbert," Fiona said. He did not respond, turning around once again to face the view.

"Okay," he mumbled.

"I was asking if there was anyone special that she was particularly fond of, respected deeply. Someone she might have called or seen when she came here for wise advice. We've interviewed three people who she met with formally. What we are looking for is someone she might have talked with who could have referred her to others."

"She was very fond of the Vice-President. We knew him when he was a senator. The man had a daughter her age and they were friends. She might have called him."

Gail took out her notebook and began to make notes.

"Anyone else?"

"She corresponded regularly with Justice Farley Lipscomb."

Peripherally, Fiona saw Gail freeze. She needed all the self-discipline she could muster to maintain a calm demeanor. But her heart was pounding in her chest.

"Did you ever see any of that correspondence?" Fiona asked, without missing a beat.

"Of course not. Occasionally, she would read me some passages. Usually they referred to some points of constitutional law about which she was seeking clarification. He was remarkably cooperative. She could inspire that kind of relationship."

Fiona masked her excitement with a cough.

"And was he . . . and Mrs. Lipscomb . . . one of your regular visitors at the lake?"

"Yes, they were. He loves fishing. When Margo was alive they came up every summer. It's been more sporadic since she's gone." He had turned to face her, then turned again, to hide his emotions.

"Any other long-term visitors?"

"Our two senators came up regularly with their wives. The governor." He reeled off a list of titles. This was a man who knew how to ingratiate himself with powerful people, especially those with official titles.

"Were you always present when your guests came up to visit?"

"I tried to be," he said, clearing his throat and turning to face her again. "What are the implications of these questions, Sergeant? They make little sense to me. Besides, my patience is being strained."

"Sometimes they came to stay with your wife while you were away?"

"I have a very busy practice."

"But Phyla and your wife were around to host your guests?"

"Yes. When Phyla was in from school."

"And you don't know if she called or saw any of those people who you entertained?"

"If you were thorough investigators, you would have checked the telephone log of the Mayflower."

"We did," Gail said, reading from her notebook. We considered the calls routine. No, she did not call any of your powerful friends, Mr. Herbert. She confirmed her appointments. She checked on her airline reservations. She called some old friends who lived out of town." Gail paused. "There's also no record of her calling Justice Lipscomb. Not from the Mayflower," she said pointedly, again exchanging a quick glance with Fiona.

"Phyla was headstrong," Herbert said. "Maybe she wanted to show me she could do it on her own."

"But her relationship with Justice Lipscomb was . . ." Fiona paused. "More fatherly. Wouldn't she have made it a point to call him?" Fiona asked blandly.

"Her prerogative," Herbert shrugged. "I don't understand where you're going."

"All I'm trying to do is explore all the possibilities. She might have actually gone to see him. There might have been a referral. You know, Justice Lipscomb might have passed her along to someone who might have helped."

"I got a long condolence letter from him in Chicago, handwritten, telling me how much he admired Phyla."

Fiona felt heat rush to her face. She hoped the flush would not catch Herbert's eye. It didn't.

"Did the letter say he met with Phyla while she was in town?" Fiona asked casually.

"No. It made no mention of that."

"Did she ever inquire about a clerkship with him?" Fiona asked.

"If she did, he'd have given it to her without question," Herbert said.

"It might be helpful to know," Fiona asked.

"Know what?"

"If they were in touch. Phyla and Justice Lipscomb."

"Why?"

"She might have said something to him, told him what her plans were, who she was seeing in town . . ."

Fiona knew she was taking a chance. She hoped that Herbert's overbearing vanity, his political star-fucking, would goad him to call Lipscomb, the object being to apply pressure, unnerve him, force him to deal with Fiona.

She shot a glance at Gail, hoping she might get some further encouragement from her reaction. Wisely, Gail, too, showed no emotion.

As Fiona had expected, the idea of proving his closeness to Lipscomb seemed to challenge him. Without commenting, he looked up a number in a leather notebook, then picked up the phone and dialed.

"In session. Terribly sorry. I forgot," he said, instructing the person at the other end of the phone to give Justice Lipscomb the message to return his call.

When he hung up he glared at Fiona.

"Anything else to satisfy your claim to intrepid police work?"

"I appreciate your cooperation," Fiona said.

"I don't," Herbert replied.

In the car going back to headquarters, Gail admitted the possibility that she had been wrong.

"You don't have to, Gail," Fiona said.

"I feel awful about that boy," Gail said.

"It wasn't your fault."

"I could have sworn . . ."

"Even I was getting there," Fiona said, "despite what I felt in my gut."

"I was there. Now I'm not so sure," Gail said, still on the edge of belief, but tottering fast. "But this relationship with Lipscomb. It does make one think."

"It's impossible for me to be objective," Fiona said. "Subconsciously, I was convinced from the beginning. Herbert connected them. I feel a lot better about the logic of my gut."

"But there's not a shred of evidence. Not even circumstantial."

"I told you the bastard was clever. The only chance we have is to get him to react and hope he'll make a fatal mistake."

"Sounds like a long shot to me," Gail sighed.

"I got him to react once before. He needs to feel threatened."

"Alright, Fiona. Herbert's call pushes him . . . but to do what?"

"To come calling, Gail. He needs to come calling."

Gail shook her head.

"Then what?"

"We get to his weak spot," Fiona said, a plan forming in her mind.

Herbert connected them. I feel a lot better about the logic of my gut."

—17—

As they headed to police headquarters, Prentiss called her father on the car phone.

"Is it any better, Dad?" she said, silent as he replied. "I'll be with you tonight. Sorry about last night." She looked at Fiona. "Something came up. I know, Dad. Just do your best. Of course. See you later."

She hung up.

"Fathers and daughters," she sighed. "Why can't all men be like our fathers?"

"Good question," Fiona said. She, too, had adored her father. "Perhaps they just can't measure up."

"No way," Gail said, patting Fiona on the shoulder. The gesture presaged what they would be sharing as friends and how much they had in common.

When they got back to the squad room the Eggplant was fuming, apoplectic. With a crook-of-the-finger sign, a very bad omen, he summoned them both into his office. His ashtray was piled high with unsmoked, chewed-up panatelas and there was a half-filled bottle of liquid Maalox on his desk. When he was in that state, Fiona knew, there was nothing to be done but ride out the storm.

"I have spent the morning being pilloried by the mayor, abused by the police commissioner and reviled by Tom Herbert. In a very real sense, you have both fucked me over."

He stretched out his hands palms upward in an exaggerated pose of supplication. "I have sympathized and empathized with the special problems of your gender. Have I not understood this? Have I not been fair to a fault? Have I not been decent, open, honest, supportive?" He turned to Gail. "You, Prentiss. Have I not sponsored you, been your rabbi? Just to get you into this division required special dispensation."

Gail nodded, her yellow-flecked eyes alert but troubled. "Do you know what it means to have to justify the actions of your troops, to be second-guessed by others? Who was it that insititued this experiment in the first place? Well, my little foray into social engineering has been a fuck-up."

He shook his head, unwrapped another panatela and jammed it, unlit, into his mouth.

"Now," he said, his nostrils quivering. "Whose bright idea was it to get an associate justice of the Supreme Court involved in this case?"

Fiona was about to answer, but Gail spoke first.

"Ours, Chief," she said. "It was merely an inquiry, not an involvement."

"When is an inquiry not an involvement?" the Eggplant shot back.

"It was purely routine," Gail argued. "We simply wanted to be certain that we had touched all the bases before we closed the case." She looked toward Fiona.

"I take full responsibility," Fiona interrupted. "I thought we should take out a little insurance."

The Eggplant held up his hand.

"Let's back up here. We have a man who admitted being in the room with the lady very close to the time of her death. He has a string of accusations against him about violent sexual conduct. He admits lying to us. He commits suicide with an apology . . ."

"Not an apology for the crime," Fiona said. "That's the missing link. 'Sorry' could have meant that he was sorry for creating any problems for those left behind."

"Clairvoyance, FitzGerald, is a dangerous indulgence for a homicide detective."

"It's not that," Fiona protested, unable to bring herself to the point of personal revelation. It was something she simply could not share with the Eggplant.

"I happen to agree with her," Gail said, illustrating to Fiona the strength of their bonding.

"Do you? What spilled between the cup and the lip, Prentiss?" He cut a look at Fiona.

"I no longer believe that Phelps Barker was the man."

"I searched his place, Chief," Fiona interjected.

He appeared to be winding up for an angry reply.

"I doubt if we needed a warrant. All part of procedures, Chief. I found nothing to indicate that he was into . . ."

"I don't want to hear this, Sergeant," the Eggplant fumed. "I don't want anything to suggest that we can't close on this one."

"Even if we're wrong?" Fiona asked, her tone ominous.

The Eggplant's eyes roamed their faces as his anger abated. Despite his constant battle to maintain credible closing statistics, an almost impossible task, and his many other foibles, he had a moral commitment to fidelity. He could not abide even the slightest hint that an innocent man had been railroaded to make a statistical impression. As Fiona knew it would, her question had calmed him.

"So we keep this case open forever and I take the poker up the kazoo from the powers that be . . ." He stopped abruptly and shook his head in disgust, perhaps realizing that this was the wrong image to project at this moment. "All that aside, it does not excuse putting the name of a respected Supreme Court justice into the hopper. Herbert, it seems, under pressure from both of you, called the man to inquire whether his daughter had spoken to him or visited him while on her ill-fated mission to the murder capital of the U.S. of A."

"Yes. We were there," Fiona said. "He left a message."

"And the message he got back from the justice was a scathing indictment of the methodology. If the girl had called him, he certainly would have come forward on his own. It would have been his solemn duty. He was, according to Herbert, quite put out. Who could blame him? A Supreme Court justice is the ultimate untarnished icon."

He smashed out his unsmoked panatela, stabbing it into the pile in the ashtray. Fiona's eyes shifted toward Gail. Obviously, Farley's response indicated that he was reacting. Outrage was exactly the response Fiona had wanted.

"So I am standing here with my pants down, girls," the Eggplant said, "The mayor and Herbert want us to declare the case closed, Herbert because he believes Barker was the guilty party, and the mayor because he doesn't want the hassle. And to buttress their position, our vaunted arbiter, the media, will surely interpret the suicide as an admission of guilt."

"So it's the media that makes our decisions now," Fiona said, shaking her head to deliberately exaggerate the point. "That's not like you, Chief."

She was unloading her entire arsenal of guilt-inducing weaponry. In the Eggplant's paranoid world, the media was the archenemy.

"Know when to hold. Know when to fold. On this one we fold," he said with an air of finality.

"And you believe, beyond a shadow of a doubt, that Phelps Barker is the perpetrator?" Fiona asked.

His hesitation was testimony enough. He was doing the bureaucratically correct thing. In the absence of Fiona's revelation of her past experience with Farley Lipscomb, what was he to conclude?

"All parties will be satisfied," the Eggplant sighed. "And we get to add another millimeter to our miserably short bar graph showing closed cases. Perhaps, too, the harassing armies that surround me will retreat for a day or so. Give me time to polish my protective armor."

"But we can't," Fiona began.

"Can't? Can't? Is that the response I can expect from my lady detective team?" Fiona caught the double meaning of his sarcasm. Although he had decreed an end to the Herbert case, he had not closed them down as a team.

She wanted to explain to him that this was a miscarraige of justice, but then she would have to tell him the truth behind her assertion. Looking toward Gail, she saw a mirror image of her own disappointment.

"But you are in luck, ladies. We have another one that fits your agenda. Female, black, young, raped, apparently tortured. Body is with the medical examiner."

"You won't reconsider on the Herbert case, Chief?" Fiona asked.

"The fat lady has sung," he said, jamming another panatela in his mouth. Then he swiveled around in his battered chair and showed them the back of his head. Fiona knew his method of dismissal well and left him to contemplate the view of the historical landmarks he could barely see through the grime of his window.

After the disappointing meeting with the Eggplant, Fiona and Gail huddled in a corner of the deserted squad room.

"Don't blame yourself," Gail said. "In your place I wouldn't have told him either."

"I'm not too happy with myself, Gail, but I know that if I did tell him, things could change between us and probably hurt my relationships in the department. Bad enough to be female and white. Add kinky to that and it goes downhill from there."

"And, even if he kept the case open, there would be no guarantees that we could nail Lipscomb," Gail said.

"Nobody said life was fair," Fiona sighed. "It just bugs me to see Farley get away with it." She realized that she had circled the wagons around her conviction and was protecting it against attack. "The worst part is that I can't shake my absolute certainty. In the face of no evidence, no real proof, I still feel it's him."

"I hope your instincts are better than mine," Gail said sadly.

"Now who's shouldering blame?"

"I should have seen Barker slipping over the edge."

"In this business, every move you make has consequences. Not to mention all the moves you don't make."

"Damned if you do, damned if you don't," Gail muttered in frustration.

Fiona knew that abandoning her pursuit of Farley would be a long-term, perhaps ultimately debilitating, irritant for her. If it were an ordinary case, she might have gone along with the Eggplant, preferring to accept what looked to be a unanimous verdict by everyone, including the media. But her personal involvement severely complicated the issue, which made the case for those who believed that only the most dispassionate view of people and circumstances was the hallmark of a great homicide detective. Under the circumstances, she definitely did not qualify.

She'd just have to live with it, she decided. Like having to bear unrequited love. About the only satisfaction she could derive from this episode was that on a strictly legal basis the death of Phyla Herbert could be characterized as a case of involuntary manslaughter. More like an accident than a planned murder.

At least she hoped so. It wouldn't do, wouldn't do at all, if the perpetrator had set out to murder Phyla Herbert, knowing that the physical shock that he had engineered would trigger a fatal asthma attack.

She allowed such a thought to dissipate. She would not have folded her cards so quickly if this was a case of premeditated murder. Not that Farley could, in her mind, ever be absolved of guilt. Worse, he would now be free to do this to other women. It was galling to think he was going to get away with it.

"Well, we did rattle the bastard's cage," Fiona said.

Fiona punched in the computer to look at the new case the Eggplant had served up. She read the details.

"Like shoveling shit against the tide," she said. She pushed the print button and got the specs, putting the paper on Gail's desk. Then she looked at her watch. Their shift was over.

"My daddy told me there would be days like this," Fiona said, suddenly feeling spent, tired. She looked at Gail Prentiss and smiled. "New adventures await."

They left headquarters and walked together to the official parking lot where their private cars were parked. They kissed each other on the cheek before they got into their respective cars and sped off into the night.

— 18 —

Back home, Fiona checked her messages. As she expected, there was one from Harrison Greenwald. With trepidation and some reluctance, she called him back.

"You're driving me crazy, Fiona. Is there a future in this? If so, when? If not, why?"

She noted his agitation, but what could she do? Give me time, she begged him in her heart. At the same time she searched for a response that might defuse his irritation.

"As Scarlett said, 'I'll think about it in the morning.' "

"Which morning? Tomorrow morning?"

"I'm not sure," she answered.

"Are we over, Fiona?" he asked after a pause.

"No, darling. Far from it."

"Keeping me on the hook, eh, Fiona?"

"I hope so, darling," she paused, knowing she was courting the danger of losing him. "I can see the light at the end of the tunnel," she said, feeling foolish.

"What tunnel?" he asked. "It's not like you, Fiona. Let me in on it, please."

"Not now, darling."

"If not now, when?"

"Trust me," she sighed, feeling hollow, defeated. He mumbled a response that she could not make out and hung up.

She was exhausted and, once again, put this crisis with Harrison on hold. Soaking in the tub, she tried to empty her mind, squeeze all tension out of her thoughts, hoping that the heat of the water would chase it out of her mind and body. Rubbing herself down with a towel, she flopped naked into bed and was asleep the moment she hit the pillow.

Unfortunately, a dead sleep was not in the cards. The door chimes were persistent. Whoever it was had no intention of going away. She looked at the digital clock. It was a little after eleven and she calculated that she had been asleep for four hours. It was hardly enough.

Still fatigued and slightly disoriented, she moved down the stairs cursing people who would have the temerity to visit at that hour. It was not unusual for a uniform to show up unannounced on orders from the Eggplant and drag her to a murder scene, which was what she expected as she carelessly and without thinking flung open the door.

It was Farley Lipscomb. One look and she was instantly awake.

"You."

"Me," Farley said. She backed up as he came in, discovering that she had left her piece upstairs. He was, she noted, dressed without any thought of disguise, a topcoat and no hat. When he opened his coat, she noted that he was wearing a tuxedo. Obviously, he had just come from a formal event.

"This is an appeal, Fiona. Please don't feel threatened."

"I don't," she lied, heading into the den. She heard him following behind her. In the den, she turned to face him.

"Drink?" she asked.

He shook his head and remained standing. She went to the wet bar and poured herself two fingers of Scotch, taking a deep sip. She sat down on the couch. As she did so, her dressing gown had split showing her thighs. Noting his eyes, she quickly pulled the edges together.

"Does Letitia know about these nocturnal visits, Farley?"

"I'd appreciate if you leave Letitia out of this."

"Still frightened that she'll find you out?"

"She's not part of this."

"No. She never was. I remember to what lengths you went to hide your little . . . peccadillos."

"I would never embarrass her. You know that, Fiona."

"I've always been curious, Farley. Does she know . . . about your . . . preferences?"

"She's an innocent in this, Fiona. Leave her out of it. She's been my wife and helpmate for more than thirty years."

"Helpmate? Now there's an old-fashioned word. Yes she has, Farley. She certainly has blazed a trail for you."

"For which I am grateful. I also still love her."

"That's another hard one to swallow, Farley."

And yet, studying his face, he seemed to radiate sincerity. Despite his age, he was still enormously handsome. He looked exactly like what anyone would want a Supreme Court Justice to look like.

Fiona had always characterized Farley's marriage as one of convenience, so prevalent in Washington. An ambitious woman devotes her entire life to promoting the career of her husband, thereby reaping the social rewards of status. Letitia Lipscomb certainly qualified in that department.

"I promised myself years ago that I would never embarrass her. Never. That has always been my principal fear, Fiona."

"And, of course, nothing to do with your career."

"It's all the same thing. I am her life. Anything that happens to me, careerwise, happens to her."

Was he trying to make Letitia the issue in this? She was hardly worthy of sympathy. Was he really attempting to portray himself as a good family man, a devoted husband? Did he seriously believe that she would buy that?

"I don't appreciate what you did today, Fiona. Getting me involved in this . . . this spectacle. I told you the other night. I was not with this woman. I am not a liar. Why do you persist in trying to implicate me? It is a very destructive tendency on your part and I resent it. You are out to destroy Letitia and me."

"I am out to prevent a miscarriage of justice. And I think we can dispense with this Letitia business. It's you . . . ." She stopped herself, hoping he would see her as coldly logical rather than obsessive. By his very presence, she had already determined that she was on target.

"After all these years . . ." He sighed, taking a deep breath. "As I understand it, the guilty party committed suicide."

"I'd say the guilty party is standing here in front of me."

He shook his head in resignation, as if he pitied her.

"Poor Fiona," he whispered. "Corroded by a desire for revenge. What can I say to you that will convince you that you are wrong?"

"Nothing. My memories preclude ever believing you. I saw that woman. I remember myself."

"I've admitted that what I did to you was . . . beastly. I went over the line. I betrayed your trust. I was out of control."

She studied him.

"You were a very bad boy, Farley," she said, crossing her legs, the edges of the dressing gown opening slightly.

"I admit that," he said. She watched the shift in his eyes.

"And you're still a very bad boy, aren't you, Farley?"

He seemed to hesitate, showing a brief tremor of confusion.

"I . . . I . . ." He groped for a response and cleared his throat. She tapped one of her slippered feet impatiently.

"I don't believe you, Farley. Nothing you can say will ever make me believe you."

He shook his head and looked at his hands.

"I know myself, Fiona. I'm not a fool. And we both know my . . . my interest. I am an associate justice of the Supreme Court."

She continued to tap her foot. Finishing her drink, she put the glass on the table and stood up.

"You're filth, Farley. Trash."

She hoped her tone showed just the right level of contempt. As she moved forward toward him, he took a step backward.

"You'd love me to, wouldn't you, Farley?"

"I don't know what you're talking about," he mumbled.

"Oh, yes, you do, Farley. You'd love me to punish you, wouldn't you?"

"I swear it's the truth about that girl. I swear."

"But you deserve to be punished, right, Farley?"

"I might, yes. But not about her. Not her."

"But you have been bad from time to time?"

As she advanced toward him, he kept moving backward until he was against the wall. Was he fighting it or faking it? She wasn't certain. She was trying to pick up the rhythm of the remembered theatrics. His response did not surprise her. For her part, she knew she felt no emotional or sexual excitement. But was she fooling him? Apparently.

"It's awful. Having to hide my identity, appearing in disguises in strange cities. Not often, Fiona. I swear. And never, never to hurt someone. Indeed, most of the time, I am a bottom, needing the discipline, the punishment." He looked at Fiona imploringly. "My God, Fiona, it is the only way I can keep my sanity."

Fiona paused and studied him. He looked genuinely involved.

"That part I understand, Farley," she told him gently. "But the other . . ."

"What can I say that will convince you?"

"I'm not sure if you can, Farley."

From his expression, he seemed to be traversing a galaxy of emotions. On the surface, he was falling into the pattern of a bondage and discipline addict. He was responding to that. But she sensed that another part of him was fighting it, resisting, but not successfully.

No one would believe this, she thought. An associate justice of the Supreme Court. Yet, remembering what he had done to her and what she believed he had done to Phyla Herbert, she drove herself forward.

"It's not fair. I mean . . . you must know my record on the Court. I am considered the linchpin, the balance, neither too liberal nor too conservative. My decisions concerning women are the most enlightened in the history of America. I am refocusing agendas, creating new ways to look at the modern world. I'm good, Fiona, articulate, compassionate, magnanimous. My interpretations are a model of clarity. Don't you understand? I'm important. If my health holds, I could be good for another twenty years. What point would there be in bringing me down?"

He was whining, begging as if she were someone all-powerful. He was appealing to what he perceived was her power. Then she felt her effort at dominance begin to dissipate.

Was she wavering? Perhaps Phelps Barker was the perpetrator. Perhaps she was being motivated by a false premise, a disorted mindset, based on her own unique experience. But Phyla Herbert's corpse told her it wasn't unique. Phyla's experience was a mirror image of her own. Except that she had not died. Phyla Herbert had been unhealthy, was an explosion waiting to happen. Anything could have triggered it.

Fiona's mind became a jumble of possibilities. Was her attitude softening? She searched her heart for the slightest hint of forgiveness, forgiveness for what he did to her, forgiveness for what he did to Phyla.

Was it for herself or Phyla that she was expending such energy? She felt unfocused, her certainty shaken.

"Please, Fiona. Any connection with this would be a calamity for me. Letitia will be devastated. I will be hung in the media, the butt of ridicule, my reputation destroyed. The Court, judging, is now my life's work. For what I did to you, I am genuinely sorry. But I can't take back what I did. All I ask is that you believe me now. I am contrite. I deserve your punishment. I prostrate myself before you."

Seeing him in this state restored her resolve. She would make him confess.

"You are scum," Fiona roared, her voice snapping into a dominating mode.

He looked at her. He seemed to be making up his mind.

"Down, boy," she snapped. She wished she was wearing leather and was equipped with the other accoutrements of his aberration.

"What?"

"On your knees, dog."

Her voice was commanding as her role defined itself. It seemed to be happening of its own accord as if she were outside herself. He looked at her as a supplicant, then dropped to his knees.

"Crawl over here and kiss my feet, you bastard."

He did so obediently. She did not question her actions or his reaction. Research and her earlier experience had taught her the game plan, the roles and rituals. She felt totally clinical, pushing him.

"Forgive me, mistress," he blurted.

"For what?" Fiona sneered.

"For being arrogant and proud."

"Mistress."

"Mistress," he whined.

Her mind became cluttered with possibilities. She wanted to see him humiliated, groveling, his overbearing, arrogant ego destroyed. Above all, she needed him to confess.

"Into into that corner, you slimy bastard," she commanded, watching him crawl into the corner. When he reached it, he put his head down on the floor like a dog and turned to look at her. Her dressing gown had opened, revealing her nakedness. She made no effort to close it.

"Don't look at me, you filthy monster."

He burrowed his head into the corner. A menu of ideas presented themselves. She realized that she had the power to make him do the most disgusting things that her mind could devise.

"You'll do anything for me, you turd," she cried, testing the power, knowing it was theatrics, yet realizing that she was feeling genuine anger now. Such feelings, she knew, were not supposed to be part of the compact.

"Yes, mistress. Yes, mistress," he whined.

Suddenly, a wave of disgust washed over her. Despite her own experience with him and all she had read subsequently, she felt dehumanized, unclean and, finally, appalled by his reaction.

On an abstract level she could be tolerant and understanding, but as a participant she could not accept either the premise or the psychological explanation for its occurrence. Besides, he had violated the compact, inflicting terrible physical and psychic pain on her, and, she could not be convinced otherwise, causing the death of Phyla Herbert. Nor was there any way of knowing how many others had truly suffered at his hand.

At this point, she could not bear the sight of him.

"Get out of here," she shouted.

"What?" He appeared confused.

"Get out of my sight," she screamed.

"Yes, mistress," he said, crawling out of the room. Who would believe this? she thought. It was beyond most people's experience or understanding. When he reached the entrance to the den, he turned.

"It's over for now. Get up and leave." Her use of the word "now" surprised her. She wasn't quite sure what it meant. What she actually wanted most at that moment was to be rid of him forever.

"Thank you," he said as he rose. "Perhaps next time . . ." His voice trailed off. Fiona could see he was back into his normal mode, wearing his judge's mask. Looking at her, he smiled.

"I knew I could trust the old Fiona," he said. "I hope I have earned your forgiveness."

She did not know how to respond. She felt disoriented and upset with herself. Walking toward the door, he turned again. She had followed him partially, then stood rooted in the hallway.

"On the other matter, Fiona. I am totally innocent," he said, holding the knob of the opened door.

"I doubt that, Farley," she said. "Unfortunately, the case is closed."

He nodded without offering any verbal response, then let himself out of the house. She rushed forward and locked the door behind him, hoping he would never return.

— 19—

A dozen times after he had left, Fiona wanted to call Gail. But revulsion was too strong and she did wish to relive the events of the evening. She felt herself on the razor's edge between compassion and hatred. It was time, she decided, to step back, leave it alone. Farley's infestation of demons was punishment enough. Wasn't it?

What she could not deny, however, was that Farley had, using his powers of manipulation, made her vacillate in her certainty that it was he who had brought about Phyla Herbert's death. Had this certainty become an obsession, crowding out all logic, all reality? Must she be doomed to forever rehash it her mind, looking for clues of doubt to explode the obsession?

By morning she was physically and emotionally exhausted, although in the light of day, a sparkling sunny morning, she was able to push the matter aside and pull herself together. She had every intention of throwing herself into this new case. It was time, she decided, to put the matter of Farley Lipscomb away.

Meeting Gail in the squad room, they began to go over the paperwork involving the young black woman. Dr. Benson's report indicated that large traces of cocaine had been found in her body.

"Drug-related," Fiona groaned. These were the toughest cases, largely because they involved drug lords and gangs. This was their method of advertising the fate in store for nonpayment or territorial usurpation. She and Gail could look forward to long, fruitless interviews leading nowwhere. The chances of closing a case like this were small.

"Just another body count in the murder capital of the U.S. of A.," Fiona sighed, mimicking the Eggplant.

As they studied the various reports involving the girl, the sound of shouting exploded in the Eggplant's office. The door was closed, but it did not deter them from hearing what was going on.

"This is defamation pure and simple," a man's voice said. Fiona had not heard the voice before. "I intend to press for your resignation. And I fully intend to pursue the matter in the courts."

"That is your right," the Eggplant said, not as loudly as the other man, but loud enough to be heard.

"It's more than my right. It's my duty to my son's memory. You have no right to make the charge that my son caused that girl's death."

"I didn't," the Eggplant replied. "I simply answered the reporter's question."

"And who put the question in the reporter's head?"

"Not me. I stay as far away from the media as I can, especially the Washington *Post*."

"I don't believe you," the other voice shouted. "You people love to see your names in the paper. But I resent it. You have no right. I'll see you in hell, Captain."

At that moment the telephone rang on Fiona's desk. Without picking it up, she knew who it was.

"You and Prentiss," the Eggplant growled. "Get your asses in here."

Fiona and Prentiss exchanged glances and hurried to the Eggplant's office. They found him in a state of barely repressed anger. Sitting on a chair in front of his desk was a man in a rumpled suit who looked deeply disturbed. There were dark bags under his eyes and he needed a shave.

"This is Dr. Barker, the father of Phelps Barker. This is Sergeant FitzGerald and Officer Prentiss, the detectives in charge of the Herbert case."

"You people ought to be cashiered out of the police force," Dr. Barker said, his flush deepening. Fiona looked toward the Eggplant, who slid a copy of the Washington *Post* across his desk. A small story in the Metro section was outlined in red pencil.

"You see that?" the Eggplant asked Fiona.

"No," she said, picking up the paper, holding it out so that Gail could also read it.

Murder Suspect A Suicide

"Phelps Barker, 23, a lawyer for the Justice Department's Civil Rights Division, who was found shot to death in his apartment Wednesday night, has been officially declared a suicide, according to Homicide Chief, Luther Greene.

Barker had been a suspect in the death of Phyla Herbert, 22, whose body was found in the Mayflower Hotel last week. Miss Herbert had been brutally assaulted, although death was attributed to an asthma attack brought on by the trauma.

Captain Greene announced that no other suspects had been questioned nor has any further evidence been uncovered other than the fact that Barker's fingerprints were found in the woman's room. Barker had been questioned and released pending further police investigation. Captain Greene declared the case closed."

"They called me," the Eggplant said. "I merely responded."

"That's your story," Dr. Barker said, his voice raised again. "The fact is that my son's name is besmirched. My son was never charged." He turned toward Fiona. "Can you say unequivocably that he caused Phyla Herbert's death?"

Fiona looked toward the Eggplant, who nodded, implying that she was to tell the man the truth.

"We did not charge him," Fiona said.

"That wasn't my question," Dr. Barker pressed.

"His fingerprints were found in the room," Fiona said. "We questioned him about that. We also were able to find some unsavory things in his background."

"Does that constitute guilt?"

"I repeat. We didn't charge him."

"No, you didn't. Instead, you convicted him in the media."

"I was not responsible for that," the Eggplant interjected. "I merely stated that no other evidence had surfaced. I didn't write the story. Nor did I initiate it. We never do in this department. The media can never be trusted to accurately report the facts."

"In addition to the suit I am contemplating and the call for your resignation, I fully intend to demand a retraction from the *Post*."

"Look, Dr. Barker," the Eggplant said. "I sympathize with you and I understand your anger. But your accusations are off the mark. Nor can we be responsible for your son's suicide. We regret it. Believe me, we do. Your son was obviously a very fragile young man."

"Fragile? He was an up-and-comer, my boy was. You people probably harassed him to death." He looked toward Fiona and Gail. "Didn't you?"

Fiona went over the events in her mind. Most interrogations of suspects could be classified as harassment. Yet, she could empathize with Dr. Barker's anger. The fact was that he had a right to be upset. Without question, the *Post* story could be interpreted as having declared Phelps Barker guilty.

"We did our job," Gail interjected. "I'm terribly sorry about your son, Doctor. I truly am. But the truth is that we cannot be responsible for how the media reports. It is often distorted."

"I warn you all," Dr. Barker said, standing up. "I will not be deterred."

He looked from one face to other, the pain and agony apparent in his eyes. Fiona's heart went out to him. No, they had not charged him, she thought, because he was innocent. Knowing that, it would be impossible to push this out of her mind, no matter how hard she tried.

When he had gone, the Eggplant slumped in his chair and stuffed a panatela in his mouth.

"Can't win," he sighed.

"He's in a terrible emotional state," Fiona said. "He'll calm down."

"Maybe. But he has a point. The irony is that just before he arrived, the mayor called me about the *Post* story. "Good PR," she said. He shook his head. "PR. What a crock."

Later, in the car, as they drove in silence to interview relatives of the dead black girl, Fiona acknowledged that she could not let the matter rest.

"I don't know if I can live with it, Gail," she said.

"With what?"

"Knowing that we are sweeping it under the rug."

"In the light of morning are you still convinced about Lipscomb?" Gail asked. Fiona's long silence was answer enough. After last night, she was no longer sure and she said so.

"Now there's a turnaround," Gail frowned. Yesterday, she, too, had been convinced of Farley's guilt.

"Not a full turn," Fiona admitted after another long silence. Fiona realized that she could not keep the events of last night inside of herself. Pulling the car to the curb, she shut off the ignition, and, turning to Gail, told her the story of Farley's visit the night before.

"Denied it over and over again," Fiona said. "Then I did this Band D number and he locked right into it. It was weird. Like something clicked in his head. I could have made him do anything, anything at all."

"Why didn't you get him to confess?"

"I'm not sure. Maybe I was afraid that if I got too close to that, he would buck. Then I got disgusted with the whole process. It sickened me and I couldn't wait to get rid of him."

"It's beyond my understanding, Fiona," Gail said.

"Not mine. I wish you were there. It would have been a real eye opener."

"I'm sorry I wasn't."

It was at that moment that a startling new idea flashed into Fiona's mind.

"You can be, Gail."

"I can?"

Fiona explained her idea.

"Are you serious?" Gail asked.

"You'd be perfect," Fiona said, looking at her. "And if it works, it's probably the only way we'll ever know for sure." Their eyes met.

"I don't know if I can handle it, Fiona. To tell you the truth, the idea of it is pretty repulsive."

"Think of it as a game," Fiona said.

"It's sick, Fiona. I have enough problems with sex as it is."

"That's another thing, Gail. It's not just about sex. I know this sounds weird to you, but from what I've read, it's only fantasy, creating another time and space. The point is that in a disciplined state people are the most vulnerable and that's the way they want to feel, like a little kid again being told what to do by their parents."

"Why not you, Fiona?"

"If I thought it would work, Gail, I'd do it in a minute. But we've got history and the bond of trust might break at a crucial moment."

"So why me?" Gail asked.

"In the first place, you're a stranger to him. He could build a fantasy around you . . ." she hesitated.

"And in the second?"

"You're now going to think I've lost it." Fiona shook her head and smiled. "Look at yourself. You'd be the most mesmerizing dominatrix in the history of B and D."

Gail threw her head back and howled with laughter.

"Protect me, Jesus," she cried.

"Your call, Gail," Fiona said, waiting for her to settle down, which she did finally. "But if you do agree, remember this is strictly against the Eggplant's orders and might backfire. We could be in real trouble. Both of us."

"Do you think your judge might respond . . . I mean to me?" Gail asked after a long pause.

"I'd say that would depend on the quality of your performance."

Fiona could see Gail was continuing to wrestle with the idea.

"You said it was all theater." It was a kind of half-question.

"Yes, it is," Fiona replied. "With props."

"Props?" Gail asked. "What kind of props?"

"I'll show you. There's a place in Georgetown, a sex shop."

Fiona had seen it but had never had the courage to go in.

"I don't know if I'm a good enough actress," Gail said. Fiona could see she was waffling.

"You're halfway home, Gail. You've got the look."

Gail smiled thinly and shrugged her consent.

"Who knows . . . I may get to like it," she said, laughing.

Fiona reversed the car, did a U-turn and pointed the car toward George-town. In less than fifteen minutes they were in front of the shop.

"I've never been in any of these places before," Gail said.

"Neither have I."

Fiona's first conscious reaction was that she did not know how to act. There were books and magazines and strange devices, mechanical dildos in every form imaginable, plastic penises, even large dolls with grotesque simulated female parts, and a huge display of condoms, potions and other elixirs designed to, according to the labels on these items, enhance sexual pleasure.

At first glance it seemed like a store selling magic tricks and equipment for the practical joker.

"Kind of demystifies sex," Gail whispered.

"Maybe that's a good thing," Fiona responded. "Could be we take it all too seriously."

Contrary to expectations, the shop did not seem seedy and the wares displayed appeared more like strange toys than items created to aid sex practices. A lady clerk, attractively groomed, approached them with a smile. She could have been selling shoes, perfume or any other common upscale item.

"Anything special I can help you with, ladies?" the woman asked.

"We're not sure," Fiona said.   .

The woman eyed them curiously.

"Dildos? We have a wonderful collection. They've come out with some marvelous devices." She waved a hand in the direction of the dildo display. "All colors, sizes and patterns. Note how lifelike they are."

"Well, actually . . ." Gail hesitated, looking at Fiona.

"Bondage stuff," Fiona said, barely getting out the words.

"You've come to the right place," the woman said. "We have that collection in a special room downstairs. Would your care to follow me?" The woman stopped by the counter and picked up the phone. "Paul. I'm taking a customer down to S and M. Would you cover for me?"

The woman led them to a staircase, talking as she walked. Her voice was chirpy, and her attitude upbeat. There was an air of the absurd about the scene.

"We have items for all the S and M choices here," the woman said cheerily. "For every taste." Then, as they continued to descend the stairs, she offered a verbal preview of what they were about to be shown.

"Everything is categorized. What we don't have, we can order. Actually, we have a catalogue business as well, but we display much of the material here. Whether your pleasure is whipping, piercing, cutting, hanging, electric shocking, rack stretching, imprisonment, altered consciousness, mummification, tickling, stomping, we have it all. You did say B and D . . . We have rope, twine, cotton thread, wire, leather, cloth, chains, nylon stockings, handcuffs, steel shackles, rubber tubing . . . what else . . . oh yes, straitjackets and we have the harness for the pony game. Here we are."

The room was simulated as a castle dungeon with a number of what could be described as infernal torture machines, including the replica of an iron maiden. She led them to a wall of items displayed under the heading "whipping." There were numerous whips and paddles of every variety, canes, switches, leather straps, chains, knouts, belts and riding crops.

"Unbelievable," Fiona whispered under her breath.

"Weird," Gail said in a whispered response.

The woman turned to them.

"May I ask if you're serious practitioners or beginners." Her eyes shifted from face to face.

"A little experience," Fiona acknowledged. The woman nodded her understanding.

"Tops or bottoms?" the woman asked, her eyes studying Gail. "What a magnificent mistress you must make."

Gail shot a glance of skepticism at Fiona.

"There's money in it, you know," the woman said. "A cottage industry, actually. A good dominatrix can make an excellent living. Many people participate as a form of therapy."

Fiona was tempted to ask the woman what her preference was, but she held off. It did occur to her that the company mailing list would offer a valuable cornucopia for the media.

"In fact," the woman said, "everything in this store is therapeutic. A shame we have all these silly taboos. The body is a wonderful pleasure machine."

"Beats smoking," Fiona cracked, unable to resist.

"Exactly," the woman said. "You can't get cancer from B and D."

Fiona looked over the display. Farley had taught her how to put him through his paces. It's only a game, she told herself. People into this practice lived only with the illusion of danger, the excitement of believing they were on the edge. Farley had taken it a step beyond. He had crossed the thin line between virtual and actual reality.

Gail inspected the various items, handling many of them, some of which were demonstrated by the clerk. They both watched as she took a bunched leather strap from its display and cracked it against the wall.

"The quality of the noise is part of it," she said. Then she removed one of the paddles. "Preferences are individual, of course. But we have one of the best selections in America. We are the capital of the nation, after all, why not be the B and D capital as well?" She giggled at her little joke.

"Oh, yes," she said, leading them to a glass-enclosed display. "We have all the costumes. I presume you're interested in leather."

"How could you tell?" Gail said with a touch of sarcasm. "Do they say *me?*"

"Very much so," the woman said seriously.

"I'm assuming that all these items are legal?" Fiona asked. She knew the remark was facetious, but she was already projecting the legal aspect of what they were planning, wondering if there was any precedent for such an action.

"Completely legal," the woman replied, with a touch of indignation. "We have been harassed, of course. Fortunately, the Constitution is on our side. There is an irony in the issue. We do not, for example, sell weapons of destruction, like guns." She looked at Fiona sternly. "And our materials are made for use in private homes by consenting adults. What people do with these items is their own business."

"I hadn't meant to offend," Fiona said, but she could tell that the woman was wound up and she made way for her to continue. "We are talking about human sexuality. Freud, you must know, was one of the first to explain the deeper meaning of these impulses. They are perfectly natural. Many say, comforting. We don't invent these things. And we wouldn't be selling them if there wasn't a market. How do you propose we show our wares? In some sleazy clandestine environment? This is not a sleazy business. We do not dispense evil here. Harm is evil. And our products are not meant to harm. You cannot imagine how many successful people buy our wares and practice B and D. There are lots of powerful men, for example, who love being submissive. It comforts them to suspend all control over others. In the top category, we have quite a few female customers, women who need to exercise the kind of power they do not regularly have over their own lives. I personally happen to be very enthusiastic about the practice. I like it both ways, top and bottom."

It was a long speech, an advocacy. It struck Fiona as eons away from Farley's resort to hurtful and dangerous excess. She had noted a product called an anal vibrator on display. It looked benign in size compared to the one that Farley had used on Phyla and her. There was one item that had them puzzled. Made of leather, it was labeled a cock lock.

"That encloses the erect penis and locks it in place," the clerk said.

"My God," Fiona commented.

"Actually, it's for the most advanced mistresses. It is rather a formidable item."

She moved around the room describing some of the other items, stopping by a glass case displaying silk stockings and leather lingerie that seemed to be constructed to exaggerate the buttocks and push up the breasts. There were also black lace panties and bras and shoes with five-inch heels.

"For stomping," the woman said, pointing to the shoes.

Fiona and Gail exchanged glances and shrugged.

The clerk continued her tour, stopping at a makeup counter with various vials and lipsticks displayed under glass.

"Mistresses' colors are normally cherry red and black," she said, again studying Gail. "I can make you look marvelous."

"How does one learn to be a good . . . mistress?" Gail asked. In the context of the environment, the question seemed logical and matter-of-fact. Fiona was amazed how quickly they had reached a level of "normality." There seemed a kind of "new age" spirit about the shop.

"Oh, we have lots of instructional tapes," the woman replied. "And of course, we can put you in touch with a number of highly qualified dominatrixes who also teach. This is a very delicate and ritualistic practice. It must be done correctly to avoid any danger. A good dominatrix must know when to call it off."

"Are there people who go too far?" Gail asked innocently. Fiona stiffened. The clerk's eyes narrowed as she inspected Gail's face.

"These people are anathema," she said with indignation. "They must be avoided at all costs. They give B and D a bad name. They are very sick people."

Fiona wondered if the woman was serious. But there was nothing in her demeanor to suggest otherwise.

"Do you take credit cards?" Gail asked.

"We do. But most people pay cash for obvious reasons. There is a great deal of prejudice about people who are different."

Fiona and Gail moved from counter to counter, listening to the woman's advice, making their choices. The woman picked out a leather outfit.

"This should do," the woman said. "You could try it on."

Gail declined politely. The process seemed so ordinary, as if they were shopping for gifts for a wedding shower.

Standing in this room, filled with these Gothic contrivances, Fiona felt an odd feeling of deliverance, somehow diluting the old shame of what she had done with Farley. All she did was play a game, his game.

They were selling games here. What had happened to her and Phyla was not part of that game. Farley had transformed each of them into a human prop.

In fact, she could now sense that nothing, no device in this room, with whatever expertise it was used on her, could possibly give her pleasure again. For her the game was over. All the danger and mystery seemed to disappear in these displays. Nor did she find any superiority in her position. Let others enjoy. It was not for her.

They found enough cash between them to pay for their purchases.

"Would you like your name put on our mailing list?" the woman asked.

"No, thank you," Gail replied for both of them.

"Many of our customers use a box number," the woman said as they parted. "I know you'll enjoy your purchases."

They locked the packages in the trunk of the car and set off to interview the murdered girl's relatives.

"A real eye opener," Gail said.

"All in the line of duty," Fiona replied.

They rode in silence for a long time. Finally, Fiona spoke:

"What are you thinking about, Gail?"

"Sex," Gail whispered.

Fiona decided to leave it at that.

—20—

Fiona sat in the ornate chamber of the Supreme Court observing a case in progress. She was alone and listening with only casual interest. It was a complicated case on a narrow issue dealing with trade, each side offering long, boring arguments, studded with statistics and precedents.

But Fiona was not there to listen to the case. Her mission was to catch Farley's eye and try to convey by her presence a nonofficial, nonthreatening motive. Knowing Farley's paranoia about possible discovery, she had eschewed any other form of communication. No telephone calls. Nothing in writing. No attempts to visit his office.

This was her fourth visit to the court. Usually they occurred on her days off or whenever a break in her schedule permitted. Periodically, she and Farley had exchanged eye contact but she had made no attempt to mime any other signals. After each session she would wait in the corridor on the chance that he would appear. So far he had not shown up and she was beginning to fear that her strategy was off the mark.

Each night after her shift was over, she would hurry home on the off chance that he might simply appear as he had done on those two other occasions. Gail, too, had agreed to remain "on call," in case she was "needed" at a moment's notice. So far, nothing.

Three weeks had passed since they had visited the sex shop. Gail had acknowledged to Fiona that she, in the privacy of her own room, tried on the costume.

"Won't you let me see?" Fiona had asked.

"No way."

"There'll be a time, Gail, when you might have to play the role," Fiona warned.

"God help me," Gail muttered.

Fiona noted that Gail had become increasingly agitated about her father's health. Her mind was not on her work and she seemed to be showing less and less interest in Fiona's obsession with Farley Lipscomb.

Except for Dr. Barker's threat of a lawsuit, the case of Phyla Herbert was, to all intents and purposes, a dead issue. After the statement by the Eggplant, the media had lost interest. Other, more newsworthy, events superseded it. Even Dr. Barker's threat would soon lose its edge. Relatives of victims, caught up in the backwash of a case, were often emotional and prone to wild threats that rarely materialized into action.

The march of death continued in the homicide division, with Gail and Fiona working on a growing number of female homicides, some of which, usually domestics, were quickly closed. Those that were drug related or drive-by shootings were, for the most part, a lost cause.

They did their best, worked hard on each homicide, but Fiona's real focus remained on the Phyla Herbert case and her plans for Farley Lipscomb. Fiona had explained to Gail that what she had planned would be a risk to their careers. In fact, they were deliberately disobeying what the Eggplant had decreed. In the homicide division, there was no greater infraction.

Movie versions of heroics, focusing on apprehending a perpetrator by using methods not sanctioned by police protocol, were far off the mark. In today's frenetic, media-haunted world, being caught using unorthodox means could spell career disaster.

There was no telling how Farley would react if he divined what they were planning or found them out in some way. For Fiona, there was guilt in it as well, mostly for having persuaded Gail to go along with an action that could ruin her.

"Are you still with me?" Fiona would ask Gail from time to time, determined to keep her interest alive.

"I'm your partner, aren't I?" An air of irritation seemed to have become part of Gail's responses.

Whenever a more specific reference to her readiness to perform as a dominatrix surfaced, Gail showed a reluctance to discuss it. She was looking increasingly tired and drawn. Her father's illness was taking its toll on her. He had taken a turn for the worse and she was spending more and more time ministering to his psychic needs and worrying about him.

"It's really rocking me, Fiona," Gail told her, a repetitive theme in their working moments together. Aside from the pressing business of the moment, Fiona kept any reference to Gail's potential "role" to a minimum. Indeed, there were moments when Fiona worried that Gail's personal problems would overwhelm her and she would be unable to participate.

For her part, Fiona, undeterred, continued her preparation for the planned encounter with Farley Lipscomb. She purchased video equipment and set it up in the basement recreation room of her house. She had drilled a hole to fit the lens in a wall behind a bookcase and tested the camera and the microphone with a tape.

Fiona realized that in court a judge might rule that the tapes were inadmissible as evidence. Nor was she certain that her plan of luring Farley into the situation she had in mind would ever happen.

"Suppose he doesn't cooperate?" Gail had asked when Fiona had first discussed what she had in mind. Lately, even that question seemed to have faded from Gail's consciousness.

Aside from her worries about Gail's flagging interest, Fiona's own certainty was getting increasingly threadbare and she began to wonder if her obsession was badly distorting her sense of reality.

To complicate her life further, Fiona was being pressed by Harrison Greenwald, who had finally given her what amounted to an ultimatum. She knew, of course, that it would come sooner or later. It amazed her that he had not walked away sooner.

"I can't go on like this, Fiona," he had told her during a conversation in the cocktail lounge of the Willard Hotel.

"I can't blame you."

"I feel shut out," he sighed. "And not just physically."

"You'll get no argument from me, Harrison."

"Don't you care, Fiona?"

"Yes I do," she replied after a long pause.

"Then what is this all about?"

It went round and round, with nothing resolved. Most of all, she feared that, even if they resumed their previous relationship, she might be so put off that it would ruin whatever future they had. What she needed was to somehow work this out of her system.

In her mind, she assured herself, bringing down Farley Lipscomb would put the finish on this episode of sexual revulsion and cure her, once and for all, of the traumatic effects of her experience. It wasn't, she knew, a very scientific approach but it served to buttress her motivation.

"You seem very interested in court procedures, Fiona."

It was Farley Lipscomb's silken voice, coming from behind her as she waited in the corridor outside of the Court. Turning, she looked at him, meeting his eyes directly. He had changed from his robe to street clothes.

"No I'm not," she replied, tamping down her excitement. Her response had been carefully rehearsed. It, too, was pure theater. "I'm interested in other disciplines."

"Oh," he said, waiting for a further response. She hoped that the careful coding of her invitation would communicate her message without triggering his paranoia.

"My friend is tops," Fiona said, watching his face for a reaction.

"Your friend?" he asked. In the briefest flicker of his eyelids, he seemed to be receiving the message.

"She is extremely orderly," Fiona embellished.

There was a moment of hesitation as he studied her. She assumed he was weighing the risk and hoped that the anticipated pleasure would neutralize his suspicion.

"Is she?" Farley said. His sense of engagement jumped out at her. As she had observed at their last meeting, his addiction seemed to have remained undiminished, perhaps even stronger than before.

"And available. Any night at a moment's notice." Fiona held her breath and watched him closely. "She can whip right over to my place." It was a less cryptic statement than the other, but he seemed to be absorbing it. There was no way of knowing for certain.

"I'll take the matter under consideration," he said, his face expressionless. He started to go, then turned again.

"And the other matter?"

She knew exactly what he meant.

"Over," she said. "Closed forever."

He nodded and offered a thin smile, then moved away. She watched his back recede, a handsome man in late middle age, still ramrod straight and dignified. It was, of course, a facade designed to cover a multitude of sins, she thought, feeling the full impact of her remembered pain.

*   *   *

The next day, as they drove to yet another crime scene, a young girl blown apart in a drive-by gang shooting, Fiona waited for the right moment to tell Gail about her meeting with Farley. She could sense more than the usual tension in the air.

There was also the anticipation of what they would find on their present assignment. Nothing was more awful than an innocent child killed at random.

Worse, the prospect of finding a suspect would be a daunting task, with witnesses either not wanting to get involved or offering conflicting stories. Once again, they steeled themselves for the grief and helplessness of relatives, friends and neighbors.

But the subject had to be broached and, as they drove, Fiona told Gail what had transpired in her meeting with Farley.

"Are you sure he'll react?" Gail asked. Fiona caught an undercurrent of hesitation.

"He has reacted, Gail."

"And I'm still in it?"

"Of course." Fiona studied her face. Gail's expression could not hide her reluctance.

"You're having second thoughts, right?"

"Maybe it's this thing with my father," she began. "I'm not myself."

"I certainly don't want to add to your problems, Gail."

"And I'm not sure I can handle it."

Fiona decided to let the matter rest. There was enough pressure on Gail without adding to her burden.

Later, after a day of accelerating horror, wrung out by the tension of the day, they chatted at the police parking lot before leaving. Gail was going home to be with her father. She had checked his condition a number of times during the day. The prognosis did not look good.

"I hope your father improves, Gail," Fiona said as Gail opened her car door.

"It's beyond hope, Fiona. Just a matter of time."

"Is there anything I can do?"

"I just have to get through this, Fiona."

"Of course, Gail. I do understand. I really do."

Fiona wanted to offer more comfort. But she felt too guilty to respond.

Having made Gail the lure, she wondered how Gail would react if Farley did show up and she was called upon to respond. Fiona was not happy with the prospect. She was calling upon her new friend to risk too much at an especially bad time in her life. It was unfair. She felt awful about it.

At the same time, her instincts told her that Farley Lipscomb would take the bait. Then what?

Before driving off, Gail turned down the window of her car.

"Just be careful, Fiona," she said.

"Not to worry," Fiona replied.

They exchanged glances for a long moment. Then Gail turned away and sped off.

That night Fiona was too uptight to eat. He would come. She was dead certain of that. But when? She half-expected him to show up last night. Waiting had been an agony. Would it be tonight? Or tomorrow? Or when? She allowed herself to believe that he had bought into her suggestive invitation. Fearing that she might trigger his paranoia, she had not been specific, allowing him to set the time frame.

She roamed the house, checked and rechecked the video equipment. And if he did come? Then what?

By ten Fiona was beginning to question her assumptions. Was it an exercise in wishful thinking? Perhaps suspicion had intervened and triggered his better judgment. All for the best, she decided, trying unsuccessfully to put it out of her mind. By any measure, he would be a fool to come. But lust and addiction lived by their own rules.

By eleven her confidence went down another notch. At the same time her guilt feelings about Gail accelerated. It was as if she had been involved in a mental duel with a phantom of her own creation and she had lost. She had the urge to phone Farley and call the whole thing off, to let sleeping dogs lie. But would the dogs be silent forever?

Before she could act, the phone rang. She ran to the instrument and picked it up after the third ring.

"Fiona?" It was Harrison Greenwald.

She paused, disappointed. Had she expected Farley Lipscomb?

"Yes, Harrison."

She knew her obvious indifference would be hurtful, but there were other things on her mind.

"Such warmth," Harrison said.

"I'm sorry. My mind was elsewhere. Forgive me."

"I don't understand any of this, Fiona. I need some resolution. What I need to do is talk. Just talk. Can I come over?"

"No. Absolutely not."

"That sounds pretty final."

"It is."

Suddenly she imagined she heard some movement outside.

"Please, Harrison," she cried. "Leave me alone. I can't talk to you now."

She hung up abruptly, knowing that he would interpret it as a terrible act of meanness, a final blow. It would be over between them.

She ran to the front door, opened it, looked around outside. Nothing. Her nerves felt jangled. She felt torn by overwhelming guilt. For the way she treated Harrison. For involving Gail in her mad obsession.

Picking up the phone again, she dialed Gail's number. An unfamiliar woman's voice answered.

"May I speak with Gail?" she asked.

"She's with her father. This is the nurse."

"Never mind then . . ." Fiona started to hang up. Gail's voice intervened.

"Fiona?" Gail was whispering.

"How is he?"

"About the same. He's under morphine."

"I'm so sorry, Gail."

"There's nothing to be sorry for, Fiona. This can't be helped." There was a long moment of dead air on the phone.

"I'm really worried about you, Fiona. He could be dangerous."

"You can stop worrying, Gail. I'm going to call it off."

She heard Gail breathing through a long pause.

"Will that end it, Fiona?"

"I hope so."

She wished she hadn't sounded so tentative.

"Anyway, Harrison is coming over," she lied. She needed to put Gail at her ease about her security. "Maybe it's time I just let it go."

She didn't feel completely convincing.

"Are you sure?"

"Yes," Fiona said. "I'm sure. Now you get back to your father."

Moving into the den, she poured out half a tumbler of Scotch, took a sip, then reached for the phone again. But before she could dial she heard a faint knocking on the door. Her heart leapt.

Through the side window of the door, she saw him. At the same time, he saw her. He was dressed as she had seen him that first night. He wore a raincoat and a hat pulled low over his eyes. His hands were thrust into the pockets of his raincoat.

Her earlier resolution dissipated. She had got him to come. Her instincts had been correct. Seeing him now, she knew there was no turning back. Calming herself, she opened the door.

"I've been waiting for you, Farley," she said.

"Were you?," he replied, inspecting the surroundings with a predator's zeal. "I was intrigued by your invitation."

"I knew you would be," Fiona said, taking a sip from her drink, noting that the pockets of his raincoat bulged with more than the bulk of his hands. Obviously, his props, she decided. "Would you like a drink?" She started toward the den.

"No," he replied, following her. "I've come for other reasons."

"Yes, you did," Fiona agreed.

"You said she was tops," he said.

Unfortunately, her mind could not formulate an alternative plan, one without Gail. She had to stall him, wait for another idea to cross her mind.

"She is," Fiona replied.

"Is she here?" he asked, facing her now.

Fiona hesitated, debating whether to tell him the truth. But then he might think she had been lying all along.

"No. I have to make a call."

"Not yet, Fiona," Farley said.

Fiona was oddly relieved. Their eyes met. But she could not read the intent behind his expression.

"I'm glad we understand each other, Fiona," he said.

In lieu of finding an adequate answer, Fiona nodded.

"Not many people understand," he said. "After our last meeting, I could see that you were battling with yourself over your desires. That time, years ago, I should have exercised more control over myself. It was wrong . . ."

"It's alright, Farley. That part is over."

"And you do believe me about . . . the other?"

"Yes, Farley," she lied. "I believe you." Did he buy it, she wondered?

"Good," he said, pausing, watching her face. "Why do you wish to do this for me, Fiona?"

"The other night . . . why fight it, Farley? It's not just for you. I saw my need as well as yours. I was frightened by it."

"And now?"

"I'm ready."

"And this person you spoke of?"

"She is a true mistress. Much more caring and better at it than I can ever be. I want to learn from her. I'm not fighting this any more, Farley. It's what I want. What I always wanted."

From his reaction, she felt that she was getting it right. The only missing ingredient would be Gail. And Fiona still hadn't come up with an alternative.

"Where . . ." He looked around the room.

"Not here, Farley. I've arranged things on the lower level recreation room."

"You can call now, Fiona," he said.

"Are you sure?" Fiona asked. There seemed no way out. She would have to involve Gail. Again, she thought of calling it off. Again, she demurred.

Fiona turned and started to move toward the phone. She hadn't taken more than a few steps before she felt a sharp blow to the back of her knees. She buckled instantly, the drink falling to the floor, the glass breaking. She sank forward, hitting the floor hard. Before she could recover her presence of mind, she felt her arms thrust behind her and cold metal clasped around her wrists.

He was on top of her, holding her down. He put a leather plug in her mouth and fastened it around her head. Then he tied a leather collar around her neck. He got off her and stood up, then pulled on a kind of leash. The collar tightened.

"Stand up," he commanded, pulling on the leash. There was no choice. Either choke or stand up.

Her legs felt wobbly, but she did manage to rise to her feet. She wasn't dreaming this. She was totally in his control, vanquished, unable to cry out and stunned by the ferocity of his attack. Deprived of speech, she felt weaponless. With an effort of will she tried to get her sense of panic under control, to force alertness.

She noted that he was wearing plastic gloves, which telegraphed his intention and accelerated her fear.

"Now lead me downstairs, bitch," he said, tightening the leash as she moved down the stairs. She couldn't believe she had allowed herself to get into this situation. In the recreation room below, she stood helpless while he inspected the room. He still had not removed his raincoat but she could see that it still bulked out in the pockets.

He inspected the ceiling and walls. To one side of the room was an exposed pipe painted the color of the wallpaper to hide it. Without looking in her direction, he emptied the pockets of his raincoat. Fiona saw chains, some D-rings, a riding crop, a cat-o'-nine-tails and what looked like a large plastic dildo. She had no illusions of what he had in store for her.

He threw a length of chain over the pipe, then pulled her leash and brought her to the area where he had positioned the chains. Keeping a tight, almost choking, grip on the leash, he took off her handcuffs and attached her wrists to the chains using D-clamps, then pulled them taut. She felt her body stretch to the balls of her feet.

Unable to talk, suspended and painfully stretched, with the leather leash available to him to choke and further torment her, she could only observe him helplessly.

"You are a filthy, lying bitch," he cried. "Everything you get, you will deserve. Do you think I'm a fool, Fiona? You think I'm not aware of your filthy tricks? I'm about to show you some punishment that will live in your memory beyond the grave."

She continued to observe him, fearing at any moment that he would place a blindfold around her eyes. She tried to isolate her mind, free herself from fear and concentrate on finding a way out. Suddenly, he came closer to her and lifted his arm. He was holding something in his hand. Suddenly a switchblade sprang to life.

"Are you enjoying this as much as I am, Fiona?" he asked, smiling. He put the knife against her cheek. "Warm it up, you bitch." Resist the pain, she begged herself. Deftly he placed the blade at the neckline of her blouse and sliced downward. Her blouse sprang open.

"Don't you love this, Fiona?"

Again the blade moved, slicing her brassiere in two. Her breasts fell free. Then he moved the flat of the blade against her nipples.

"See how they pop, Fiona. How would you like me to snap off the nips?" He giggled as her head rolled from side to side. "Oh, we'll get to that. There's so much more to do."

Skilled cuts of the blade split her slacks, which fell to her ankles. Then he worked on her panty hose, which slipped away from her body and bunched on the floor. She was completely naked now.

"How does it feel to be naked and powerless, Fiona? Isn't it exhilarating? And you can't even cry out. How very sad, so very sad."

He moved the flat of the knife down her stomach, then to her pubic hairs. He cut one away and rolled it in his fingers.

"Getting hot, Fiona? Do you feel the thrill in your body? Do you feel the ooze of pleasure? Come, my sweet Fiona, my trusting Fiona, my silent goddess. Let me see your pleasure."

Bear it, she begged herself, watching him, wondering how to convey some hint of enjoyment under the circumstances, to forestall him. Still smiling, he moved backward and, putting down the knife, began to take off his clothes. As she watched him undress to his underwear, she wondered if this were theatrics or a prelude to murdering her. What she needed most of all was the organ of speech. She noted, too, that he was, at least partially, tumescent.

From his pocket, he removed what looked like a vial. He held it up for her to see and smiled. Then he removed the cap. It was lipstick. Cherry red lipstick. The kind that had been used to decorate Phyla . . . and Fiona. She noted that it was not a new lipstick, but one that had been worn partially down.

"Now we must label the meat. What shall we say you are, Fiona? How about this?"

He wrote across her breastbone, just under her neck.

"C U N T," he said, calling out the letters as he printed them. She could not see them. Then she felt the lipstick roll down the front of her body to where her pubic hairs began. Without looking, she knew what it was. The arrow, exactly how it had appeared on Phyla's body and hers years ago.

"How about this, Fiona?" he said, laughing as he wrote in longhand on her left thigh. "Slut, right? That about describes what you are. Now what shall we call the other one?" He wrote across her left thigh. "Whore. Isn't that what you are, Fiona? Whore?"

He stepped back to view his handiwork. Then he moved forward and circled her eyes with black eyeliner and then wrote across her forehead.

"You know what I wrote, slut?"

Inexplicably, she nodded her head, an involuntary reaction. He chuckled.

"Of course, you know," he said.

"Scum," he shouted. "Aren't you scum, Fiona?"

When she didn't respond in any way, he pinched her nipples between a thumb and forefinger.

"Right?"

He pinched harder.

It was unbearable and she screamed inwardly, then nodded her head vigorously.

"Good girl."

He removed his fingers from her nipples and giggled.

"And how about the word 'trash'? I could write that on your butt. Would that do it?"

She nodded, a response that seemed to please him.

"Just for that, Fiona," he said, "you get a nice treat."

He moved backward so that she could see him clearly. Removing his shorts, he threw them on the top of his outer clothes which he had placed neatly on a chair. She noted that he was in full erection. He picked up the cat-o'-nine-tails and moved behind her.

"You'll love this, Fiona," he said. She felt the lipstick moving along her buttocks.

"It looks wonderful back here," he said.

Then she heard the crack of the whip.

"Listen to that music, Fiona."

Suddenly her body was suffused with pain as the knotted cords struck her back, then her buttocks. Blow after blow came down on her. She heard him grunt and wheeze with each blow. The pain was unbearable. She could not scream out. Tears rolled down her cheeks.

Finally, he stopped and came around to face her. He seemed crazed. She noted that he was still wearing plastic gloves. It was an ominous detail.

"I think this needs an accompaniment, Fiona. I haven't heard a word out of you."

He unstrapped the leather gag and pulled it out of her mouth. At that moment the telephone rang. Her eyes looked toward the phone. He froze for a moment.

"Who would that be?" he asked.

"I'm a homicide cop, remember," she said hoarsely. He contemplated her answer as the phone continued to ring. Then the ringing stopped and she could hear the click of her answering machine as it took the caller's message.

"Well," he said. "Isn't technology wonderful?"

She managed to croak out a response.

"It could be urgent. Maybe my boss."

"And here you are."

He reached back and struck her savagely across her breasts. She screamed out in pain.

"Will you play that tune again, Fiona?"

Through her pain her mind groped for escape. He is going to kill me, she told herself, searching her mind for some way to survive.

He put the cat-o'-nine-tails down and picked up the riding crop. Then he moved behind her and struck a blow with the crop across her buttocks. Again she screamed as the pain seared through her.

"You should see the pretty stripes," he said. "Look at that," he said, moving backward. "See the pretty stripes."

She braced for another blow. The telephone rang again. As it rang, an idea pulsed in her brain.

"More," she cried, above the sound of the phone. She heard the message machine kick in. "Beat me," she screamed.

He struck again across her buttocks. And again. In her agony, she lost all concept of time.

"I love this," she screeched, at the top of her lungs. All she could think about now was staying alive, forestalling him. The blows rained down on her.

"Again," she screamed.

She could hear his heavy breathing as he paused for a moment.

"Don't stop," she cried.

"I didn't hear you thank me, Fiona."

"Thank you," she whispered, barely able to talk.

"Thank you, what?" he yelled.

"Master. Thank you, master."

He moved in front of her. His body was glistening with sweat. He inspected her face.

"Oh, we forgot something," he said. He reached for the lipstick again and roughly painted her lips.

"Now that's the look I wanted," he said. "Now smile."

She forced herself to smile, then watched in terror as he reached for the large plastic dildo that he had put on a nearby chair. Picking it up, he flicked a switch and it began to hum and vibrate.

"Remember the sound, Fiona. And how good it felt."

He came toward her. The device looked massive. She knew it would tear her apart.

"You want this, don't you, Fiona?"

"I need more of the other," she managed to gasp.

He picked up the riding crop again.

"You mean this?"

She nodded vigorously.

In his other hand, he held the dildo.

"It's the best part," he said, holding the dildo to her lips. "Kiss it, bitch." She obeyed him. Then he flung the riding crop to the floor.

"This is a lot more fun, Fiona. Remember."

She felt the vibrating instrument roll down her body. He moved it slowly, smiling at her as he did so, until he moved it between her legs.

"Don't you just love this, Fiona?"

Her flesh felt numb. Her legs began to shake uncontrollably. Tears rolled down her cheeks. With every ounce of energy she could muster, she screamed.

"Wonderful," Farley shouted, as if in counterpoint. "More?"

She closed her eyes and screamed again and again. She felt the pressure of the dildo between her legs as the hated instrument moved around her genitals.

Suddenly she heard a sharp crack and the instrument was withdrawn from where it was poised to damage her. When she opened her eyes, she saw Gail.

Gail Prentiss in costume, an amazon in leather. Even in her present state of panic, Fiona was mesmerized by her appearance.

Gail was made up as the ultimate mistress, an unbelievably formidable sight with her spiked heels, lace panties, black silk stockings, a leather corset that emphasized her large breasts. Her lips were made up in cherry red lipstick, her eyes in black eye makeup. In her hand, she carried a whip and by the way she wielded it, she apparently had been practicing.

Farley, too, had been mesmerized by the sight. He stood stock still, naked, watching Gail, who looked at him menacingly, then snapped the whip so that its pay end slapped across his stomach.

"On the ground, you stinking bastard," she cried, briefly glancing at Fiona.

"Now show it to me," she hissed. He was on his hands and knees, his buttocks exposed, waiting for the whip. She pulled back her arm and lashed him again and again until his buttocks were raw.

"Now crawl over to that corner, you scummy piece of garbage."

He did as she asked and started to turn around.

"Did I say you could look at me?"

He shook his head.

"Say, no, mistress."

"No, mistress."

He cowered in the corner.

Gail quickly released Fiona. She keeled over on the floor, exhausted and hurt. Every inch of her body ached.

Exchanging glances with Gail, she nodded and managed to stagger to the other side of the wall, where she had placed the video machine. She pressed the button and heard the faint whirring sound of the mechanism.

Suddenly, she saw a shadow move behind her.

Harrison! She fell into his arms.

"Thank God," she whispered. "I . . ."

"Not now," he replied.

He wrapped her in his jacket and held her as they watched the scene through the monitor.

"You can leave the corner," Gail said, cracking the whip over his back. "But don't you dare look at me."

He came toward her face down until he was directly in front of her.

"I want you to kiss my feet," Gail ordered.

He did so.

Fiona noted that the still vibrating dildo was in her hand now. She heard Harrison gasp beside her.

"If you're not good, I'll use this," she said, showing him the device. "And you know where I'll put it."

"Yes, mistress. I'll be good."

"I don't think you will," Gail insisted. She ordered him to turn around. She moved the vibrating dildo against the raw skin of his buttocks.

"Do you feel that?"

He nodded.

"Say, yes, mistress," Gail ordered.

"Yes, mistress."

"Do you want me to use this?"

"No, mistress."

"Did Phyla mind, Farley?"

He hesitated.

"Did she?"

Again he was silent.

She cracked the whip sharply against his buttocks.

"You want me to stop?"

"No, mistress," he said, shaking his head.

"Tell me about Phyla. Did she beg for it?"

"At first, mistress."

Bingo, Fiona thought. At last. She felt grateful. A sob bubbled up from her chest. Tears ran down her cheeks.

"Phyla enjoyed being a bottom, right?"

"Yes, mistress."

"For years she was your slave, right?"

"Yes, mistress."

"And you came to her room at the Mayflower?"

"Yes, mistress."

"And she loved it, didn't she?"

"Yes, mistress."

"And you loved it?"

"Very much, mistress."

"And she wanted more and more, bigger and bigger?"

"Yes, mistress."

"Now put your hands behind you," Gail ordered.

"Yes, mistress."

He did so and she slapped handcuffs around his wrists.

"You bastard," Gail cried. She put the dildo down and raised her arm. The whip was still in her hand.

Fiona reached out and shut off the video machine. Harrison helped her move to the other side of the wall. Gail was laying lash after lash on him. She noted that Farley had a formidable erection.

"Stop, Gail. Please. Enough. We got what we need."

Gail was bathed in perspiration.

"That was for Barker," she said, out of breath.

"He wants that, Gail."

Bending, Gail grasped Farley by the handcuffs and roughly pulled him to a standing position. He seemed dazed, as if he were just emerging from a trance.

"What is this all about?" he mumbled.

"We're booking you, Judge," Gail said.

He was still not fully cognizant of what was happening. Harrison and Gail managed to put on his pants and shirt. He looked a mess. Gail opened one cuff and attached it to the same pipe to which he had attached Fiona.

"I'll get you a robe, darling," Harrison said. He dashed up the basement stairs.

"Harrison called me," Gail said. "Said you were acting strangely. When you didn't answer, I knew immediately."

Fiona looked at her. Moving toward her, she patted one cheek and kissed the other.

"I don't know what to say," Fiona began.

"I did," Gail said. "And I think I might have talked too much. I told Harrison everything."

Conscious suddenly of her costume, Gail shook her head.

"Weird, isn't it?" she said.

"Thank you," Fiona whispered.

"You don't have to . . ."

"For going along. For believing. For being a friend."

Gail did not respond. Fiona looked into her yellow-flecked eyes. Their gaze held for a few moments.

"I did find some excitement in it, Fiona," Gail said. "It does get one in touch with one's darker side."

"We all have that, Gail."

"I don't think I could ever be in it, but I did understand it."

Fiona nodded. They embraced for a moment, then Harrison appeared with her dressing gown and Gail ran up the stairs. Harrison held open the dressing gown and Fiona put her arms through the sleeves, conscious of the lingering pain as she moved.

"The bastard," Harrison muttered.

Fiona looked toward Farley.

"You're in deep shit, Farley," she said.

The dazed look gave way to feral alertness. He seemed fully aware of his situation now.

"You can't do this, Fiona," he muttered. He apparently was still unaware of his confession.

"Yes, we can," Fiona said.

"I'm a Supreme Court justice," he whispered, still believing in his power and credibility.

"It's over, Farley."

What lay ahead for him was reasonably predictable. His lawyers would advise him to plead temporary insanity. It was highly unlikely that he would ever be incarcerated. Undoubtedly, he would have to resign from the Court. A long program of therapy would certainly be recommended.

The media would have a field day. Few people had any real knowledge of the B and D phenomena. Most would call it perversion. Practitioners and a number of psychiatrists would have another opinion. There were, she had learned through her research, many sides to human sexuality.

But she did know that these practices often got out of hand and had dangerous consequences.

After a while, Fiona speculated, Farley's public humiliation would fade from collective memory. And Farley, forever known as Justice Lipscomb, would resume a lucrative private practice.

"It was only a game, Fiona," he said, half believing it himself.

"Not to me, Farley. It was a horrible experience. I'm sure you wanted to kill me."

"Kill? Death? That was the furthest thing from my mind."

"Like Phyla."

"Phyla?"

"Let's not go through that routine again, Farley. You've admitted it."

"Did I?" Was it a ploy or had he really forgotten?

"We have it on videotape."

He seemed confused by the statement.

"You do?"

He looked stunned, but she couldn't be sure.

"If we need it, we'll use it. My advice to you would be to save yourself and Letitia any further embarrassment. Let your lawyers work it out. You need therapy, Farley. You're dangerous. Believe me, you wouldn't want that tape to be shown."

"Must I tell Letitia?" he asked, still vague, almost childlike.

"I'm afraid so. Unfortunately, she's a passenger on your shipwreck."

He shrugged and bowed his head.

Gail came down the stairs in street clothes.

"The Chief has been alerted. He had mixed feelings about it. First he chewed me out."

"Can you blame him?" Fiona said. "Think of all the hassle he's in for. Everybody, except the media, will be wishing for a quick end to the whole affair."

"Especially me," Gail said. "That tape . . ."

"Might open up a whole new career"—Fiona smiled—"as an actress."

Gail smiled thinly. She went over to Farley, detached him from the pipe and cuffed his hands behind his back. He looked forlorn and Fiona had to tamp down a brief shiver of compassion.

"I'll bring him in," Gail said. Her glance moved from Fiona to Harrison.

"Be gentle," Gail said. "She's had a rough time."

She grabbed Farley by the cuffs, moved him across the room and started up the stairs. Halfway up, she turned.

"My father died," she said.

"When?"

"A few minutes ago. I just called."

"How awful," Fiona said. "I'm so sorry you weren't with him."

"So am I." She sucked in a deep breath, her nostrils quivering. "He would have understood."

She moved up the stairs, pushing Farley in front of her.

After they had gone, Harrison led Fiona to the second floor. He ran a warm bath for her. She soaked in it for a long time. Gently, Harrison helped her remove the ugly graffiti Farley had written on her. After a while she felt the pain flee her body.

After the bath, Harrison gently patted her dry and powdered her.

"It's over now, Fiona," he said as he held the covers open for her to get in the bed. She got in and he pulled the covers up to her chin and kissed her deeply.

"Sleep now, darling," he told her.

She nodded and he started toward the door.

"See you in the morning, Harrison," Fiona said.

He turned and looked at her.

"And tell your office you're taking a few days off," she said.

He looked confused.

"I've got a lot of things in mind to keep you busy around here."

She smiled and started to drift off to sleep. Must remind myself to call in tomorrow, she thought.